The Girls of Lighthouse Lane

Katherine's Story

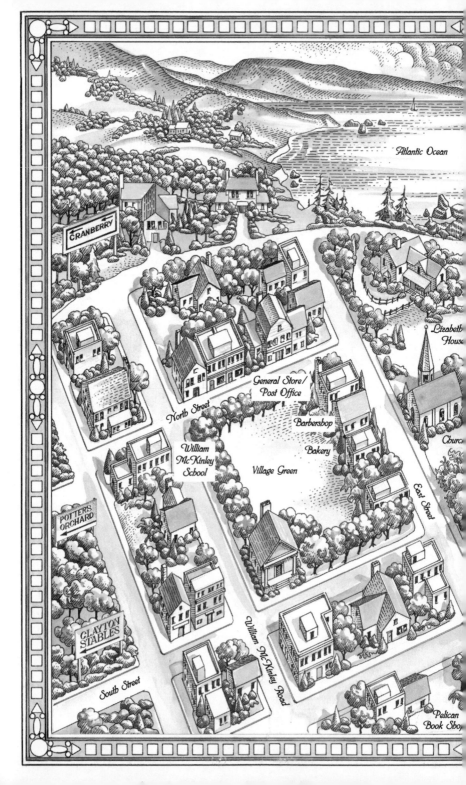

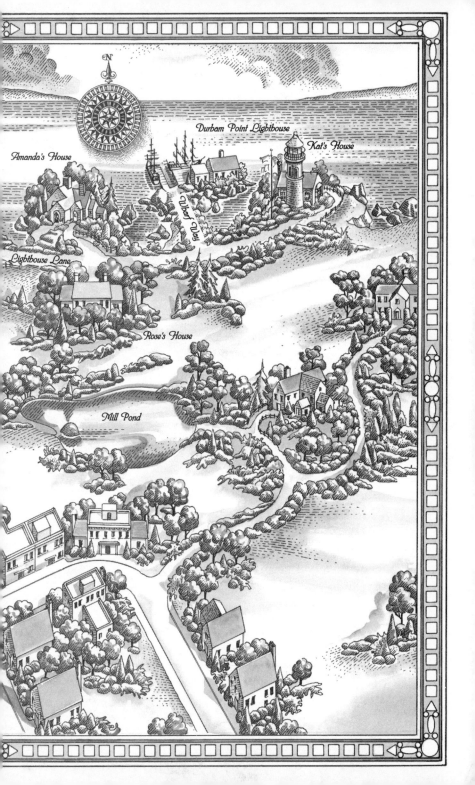

THOMAS KINKADE

The Girls of Lighthouse Lane

Katherine's Story

A CAPE LIGHT NOVEL

By Erika Tamar

HarperCollins*Publishers*

A PARACHUTE PRESS BOOK

Library of Congress Cataloging-in-Publication Data
Katherine's story / by Thomas Kinkade and Erika Tamar. — 1st ed.
    p. cm. — (The girls of Lighthouse Lane ; #1)
    "A Parachute Press Book."
    Summary: In 1905, while pursuing her dreams of becoming an artist, the twelve-
year-old daughter of the Cape Light lighthouse keeper learns the value of family, home,
and friendship.
    ISBN 0-06-054341-8 — ISBN 0-06-054342-6 (lib. bdg.)
    [1. Artists — Fiction. 2. Lighthouses — Fiction. 3. Family life — New England —
Fiction. 4. New England — History — Fiction.] I. Tamar, Erika. II. Title.
PZ7.K6192Kat 2004   2003009555
[Fic] — dc21   CIP
                                                      AC

1 2 3 4 5 6 7 8 9 10
❖
First Edition

The Girls of Lighthouse Lane

Katherine's Story

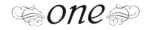
one

Katherine Williams ran across the village green in the center of Cape Light at breakneck speed. Her auburn braids flew behind her as she pulled her friend Amanda Morgan along.

"Wait, Kat!" Amanda gasped. "We're supposed to walk like ladies."

"I can't wait another minute!" Kat said. Her schoolbooks, held together by a leather strap, swung in wide arcs, bumping her leg as she streaked over the grass. "They said it would take two weeks and it's way past that!"

Kat had rushed to the general store/post office every single day after school and she didn't care at all if Mr. Thomas, the postmaster, rolled his eyes when she came in again. It was already Friday, October thirteenth. How much longer could the mail take? "My package just has to be in today!"

All week long—after the usual God bless Mother,

1

Father, my brothers James and Todd, and all the ships at sea—her prayers had ended with "and please give me *patience.*"

But she was all out of patience. Her long skirt whirled around her ankles as she tugged at Amanda.

"All right, I'm coming." Amanda laughed, and they ran across the green to the cobblestones of East Street.

The brilliant fall colors of the oaks and maples surrounding the square passed by in a blur. Kat caught the scent of cinnamon doughnuts as she rushed by the bakery. The slow and steady *clop-clop* of the iceman's horse and the squeak of his wagon rang out from over on North Street.

"Oops." Kat almost ran into a little boy who stood in her way. He had one arm firmly wrapped around the red-and-white pole in front of the barbershop, to keep his momma from pulling him through the door. Her little brother James would do the very same thing and Ma would get so mad! Kat would have slowed down to see the boy and his momma tussle, but not today—not when the postmaster might have her package *right now*!

Two elderly sisters walking arm in arm under a parasol stopped and frowned. "Isn't that the Williams girl galloping by?" one said. "And with the minister's daughter!" the other finished.

Kat and Amanda skidded to a stop in front of the general store's glass door. The bell rang when they opened the door, but Mr. Thomas barely looked up. He was busy talking to some men gathered in front of the potbellied stove.

"Well, I say Teddy Roosevelt will go down in history as one of the great presidents. You can't deny that 1905 has been a year of peace, progress, and prosperity."

"No one thought much of Teddy when he was McKinley's vice president. If it wasn't for McKinley's assassination . . . "

"Imagine, six children in the White House! And all those animals—dogs, rabbits, badgers, even a small black bear!"

"It sure keeps things lively down there in Washington, D.C."

Kat and Amanda stood at the counter and waited. Kat caught the aromas from the pickle barrel and the wheel of cheddar mixed with the fragrance of coffee beans. The counter was piled high with bolts of fabric. Behind it, there were cubbyholes for mail. Kat got up on her toes and leaned far over the counter. She knew Mr. Thomas kept packages on the floor behind it, but she couldn't see any.

Kat tapped her foot.

"I hear Joe Hardy over at the telegraph office got word of a storm traveling up the coast from Hatteras."

Now they were starting a whole *new* conversation! Kat knew she must not interrupt grown-ups, but she was badly tempted.

"Might veer off to sea before it ever reaches us here in New England," Mr. Thomas said over his shoulder as he finally ambled toward Kat and Amanda. "Afternoon, girls. Suppose you're looking for your package again, Katherine?"

"Yes, Mr. Thomas," Kat said. "Did it come? Did it?"

"Well, something came for Miss Katherine Williams, but it's not what you've been waiting for." He bent down to rummage under the counter.

"It's not?" Kat asked.

"Didn't you say you were expecting paint? I guess your father's repainting the lighthouse daymark." He put a narrow package wrapped in brown paper on the counter. "Well, there are no cans of paint in this. Too small and flat."

"It's not for my father, Mr. Thomas." Anyone could see the daymark didn't need repainting! The bright red and yellow stripes painted on the side made the lighthouse a clearly visible daytime landmark for sailors. "It's for *me*." Kat beamed as she grabbed the package. "Four tubes of watercolor paints." She had convinced Papa to give her birthday money in advance—well, only three months, not *that* far ahead—so she could order the paints from an art supply catalog. "Thank you, Mr. Thomas!"

Kat started to rip open the brown wrapping paper. Then she stopped herself. She couldn't bear the thought of one of the tubes falling out and getting lost on the way home.

Kat hugged the package close to her heart as she and Amanda left the store. A few steps along East Street brought them to Lighthouse Lane, the longest road in Cape Light. It ran the entire length of the town all the way to the lighthouse at Durham Point where Kat lived.

"Burnt sienna, cerulean blue! Don't they sound luscious?" Kat said. "Alizarin crimson! Cobalt violet!"

This part of Lighthouse Lane, next to the green, was paved and it had the fanciest houses. Kat's cousin Lizabeth lived in one of the largest homes. Kat glanced at its porch, picket fence, and rose-covered trellis as they passed.

"You paint beautifully with the colors you already have," Amanda said.

"Well, I've been mixing the colors to make new

ones, but I can't always get them right. Now it will be so much easier."

Tall trees arched overhead. Kat studied the turning leaves. Definitely sienna and crimson and a touch of gold, she thought. Oh, she couldn't wait to dip her paintbrush into the new colors! A little voice inside her was singing, "so happy, so happy," and she couldn't help skipping.

"If I keep trying, if I learn more . . . I want to be a real artist someday!"

"Miss Cotter always hangs your pictures in the classroom. And you're the one she picks to help the little kids with drawing," Amanda said. "Everyone in school knows you're the best at art. Doesn't that satisfy you?"

"No! I'm talking about being a *serious* artist. In a big city, where things *happen*. I'd paint and never even think of all my lighthouse chores. I'm so tired of them! I'd go to the great museums and look at the masterpieces close up. I've only seen pictures of them in books and that's not the same at all. And there'd be bright lights and crowds of interesting people doing exciting things and trolley cars—I'd ride a trolley every day!"

They skipped along Lighthouse Lane until it turned

into a dirt road and curved toward the ocean. Kat liked the whalebone decorations on the some of the lawns.

"You wouldn't really leave Cape Light, would you?" Amanda asked.

"I really would. There's never anything new here. Do you know there are *moving stairs* that take you from floor to floor at the R.H. White store in Boston? I want to see that!"

They were almost at Amanda's cottage nestled among tall trees, overlooking the shore. Kat could hear the waves crashing against the rocks below the parsonage.

"Less than half a mile left to go," Kat said. Amanda's house was about halfway between the village green and Kat's home.

"I'm glad that Hannah is playing at Mary Margaret's house this afternoon." Amanda smiled. "I feel as free as anything, without a single thing to do until dinner! I'm not even going to drop off my schoolbooks. I can't wait to get to the lighthouse."

I shouldn't complain about the lighthouse chores, Kat thought. It's so much harder for Amanda to take care of her little sister, Hannah, and keep house for her father.

Amanda glanced at the house opposite the parsonage as they passed by. "Kat, there *is* something new in

Cape Light. You know old Mr. Reynolds, across the lane from me?"

"Yes."

"He's moving out to live with his daughter and her family in Cranberry. So a new family will be moving in."

"Do you know who they are?"

"No. But Father says the house is already sold," Amanda said.

They came to the steep hill where Lighthouse Lane led down to the shore and the docks. In the winter, it was famous as the best sledding hill in Cape Light.

Kat ran down the hill, skidding on pebbles, trying to slide part of the way. *"Whee!"*

Amanda followed more cautiously.

Leaves had drifted down and collected in huge piles at the bottom. Suddenly, Kat whirled around and dove into one.

"Kat!"

"Come on, Amanda!"

Amanda hesitated. "We're not children anymore. We can't be jumping in leaves. I'm *thirteen*."

Kat grinned up at Amanda. "Well, I'm only twelve and three-quarters, so I guess I'm still allowed to have fun."

"Your petticoat is showing! If anyone sees us . . ."

"No one's here but us." Kat grabbed a handful of leaves and tossed it at Amanda. "And I'll never tell."

Amanda looked all around—then jumped in. Kat laughed—she knew Amanda couldn't resist! They jumped from pile to pile, laughing and sliding.

"Got you!" Amanda shouted as she showered Kat with a handful of leaves.

"Got you back!" One of Kat's braids unraveled; the loose hair streamed down her back and tangled with twigs. It blended perfectly with the red and russet leaves.

Kat suddenly stopped. "Oh, no!"

"What? What's wrong?" Amanda asked.

"I forgot! Aunt Sue and Lizabeth are coming over and Ma asked me to tidy up. You know how *perfect* my cousin is, and Aunt Sue will look me over and criticize. Let's brush this stuff off and get going!"

Amanda quickly brushed herself off, but bits of leaves, twigs, and dirt stuck to Kat's rough wool skirt. Kat worked furiously to pick it all off.

Amanda turned back toward the hill. "Kat, I think I hear a horse and carriage."

"It can't be them, not yet! Quick, help me braid my hair. What happened to my ribbon?"

"Too late," Amanda said. "It's them! Coming over

the top of the hill!"

"Oh, no! I'll hide! I'll hide until they pass!"

Kat dove into a pile of leaves before she finished her sentence and buried herself. Just in time, she thought. She could hear the horse's hooves coming closer.

Crumbled leaves tickled Kat's face. The carriage wheels squeaked. They sounded louder and louder, closer and closer. The carriage had to be very near now. She couldn't see a thing. Her nose itched. She was going to sneeze! She couldn't, she just couldn't! She pressed her finger against her upper lip—that helped a little. How long could it take for them to pass by? Please, *giddyap*!

Suddenly, Kat heard Aunt Sue say "Whoa!" The sound of the horse's hooves stopped. One last squeal from the wheels—right next to her! Then silence. What was happening?

"Hi, Amanda." It was Lizabeth's voice. "Are you going over to Kat's? We'll give you a ride."

"Thank you," said Amanda.

Oh, good, Kat thought. I'll catch up with them later.

"Oh, dear!" Aunt Sue's voice rang out. "Over there. Is that a leg? Is that a human leg?"

"Where, mother?" Lizabeth asked.

"Where? Where?" her four-year-old sister Tracy echoed.

"Yes, it is! A leg—a human leg—sticking out of that pile of leaves!"

Kat's face turned hot. She was caught!

"A woman's leg, bare to the knee!" Aunt Sue said. "Oh, dear! We need to get help! We need to get some-one!"

Kat lay still in absolute panic. What should she do now?

"Don't look, children." Aunt Sue's voice was shaky. "It could be a dead body!"

And then Kat heard Lizabeth say, "I think . . . I think I'm going to swoon!"

✎ two ✎

Kat scrunched under the leaves and wished she could disappear. She had to do *something* before Aunt Sue went for help! She didn't have a whole lot of choices.

Kat jumped out of the leaves, shedding a trail of debris.

Aunt Sue's mouth formed an O, exactly like a surprised cartoon character in the Sunday funnies. If Kat hadn't been so embarrassed, she might have laughed.

"Katherine Williams!" Aunt Sue wore a large toque with a satin band on top of her high-piled hair. The hat bobbed as she spoke.

"Good afternoon, Aunt Sue," Katherine said weakly. She knew her face was bright red. She smoothed her skirt down to her ankles.

"What in the world were you doing?" Aunt Sue asked. Lizabeth and Tracy stared.

Kat swallowed. "Just . . . playing."

"What are you playing?" Tracy piped up. "Can I play?"

"Not now," Kat mumbled.

As usual, Kat thought, Lizabeth's long, wavy golden hair looked perfect. Today it was held back with a lavender ribbon to match her silky lavender dress. The dress had puffy shoulders and tight long sleeves and ended with a lavender-and-pale-blue-striped ruffle at her ankles. She had worn the exact same dress to school that day and it was still wrinkle-free and spotless. How did she do it? A soft, pale blue shawl was draped perfectly over her shoulders and her ankle-high patent leather boots were polished enough to really shine. Even Tracy, a smaller version of twelve-year-old Lizabeth, was unnaturally neat for a four-year-old.

Lizabeth's eyes swept over Kat, from her messy head to her wrinkled skirt down to her dusty shoes.

"Katherine—" Aunt Sue shook her head. "Never mind. Get into the carriage, girls."

Kat tried to brush herself off. Awkwardly, she picked up her schoolbooks and her package. Well, at least her cousin Christopher wasn't with them today; he was fourteen and a champion at wisecracks.

Kat glanced at Amanda. She looked as if she was

holding back a giggle. That made Kat's mouth twitch, too. They squeezed into the back of the carriage next to Tracy.

Aunt Sue adjusted the reins and the carriage moved forward. Beyond the hill, Lighthouse Lane curved toward the rocky shore and ran alongside the ocean. Kat kept her eyes on the passing scenery. She knew if she looked at Amanda she'd have a fit of giggles.

There were few houses here and the lane was lined by dense brush, beach plum, and sea grass. They passed by Wharf Way and the busy docks. White sails bobbed in the distance and the smell of fish drifted into the carriage. Then they passed the bait and tackle shed and the rowboat rental sign.

"Your face is dirty," Tracy told Kat.

They passed Alveira & Sons Boatyard. Kat smelled fresh-cut wood and shellac.

Lizabeth turned toward Kat. "What *were* you doing? Honestly!"

"Nothing!" Sometimes her cousin could be so irritating! "Anyway, what was all that about swooning?"

"I don't know." Lizabeth laughed. "I read it in a book. I've never *swooned* in my life."

Kat couldn't help smiling. Just when she was most annoyed with Lizabeth for putting on airs, her cousin could suddenly become real and laugh at herself. By the time they reached the lighthouse and the cottage at Durham Point, Kat, Amanda, and Lizabeth were all laughing together.

They piled into the cottage. While everyone exchanged greetings, Kat's big white dog, part husky and part mystery, barked and ran in welcoming circles around her. "Hi, Sunshine!"

"Jamie! Jamie!" Tracy made a dash for Kat's little brother James. For some strange reason she adored him, and James was as tolerant of her as an eight-year-old could be. Todd, at ten, kept a careful distance.

"Tracy, don't *hug*!" James pleaded. "I'll play with you only if you don't *hug*."

All of them were crowded in the combination living room/dining room/kitchen. A short hall led to Ma and Papa's bedroom. Kat's tiny room was upstairs next to her brothers', tucked under the attic eaves.

It was so different from Lizabeth's house, where there was a separate room for every single thing, even a parlor that the grown-ups used only on special occasions and the children weren't allowed to enter. The parlor had shining parquet wood floors, a grandfather clock, a tufted crimson velvet couch, and a big potted palm.

What was the sense of a room that was just for show, Kat wondered. Anyway, she had the lighthouse tower—it was her special haven where she felt completely at ease. And it had a *round* room, surely the only one in town.

Ma was wrestling the laundry through the wringer in the big kitchen sink. Her feet were firmly braced against the stone floor and Kat could see the strain in her back as she worked. "I'm just about done. I'll hang it up to dry later. There's coffee on. And Kat, please get the muffins out of the oven." Ma dried her hands on her apron and embraced Aunt Sue.

They looked alike, with the same ash-blond hair. Aunt Sue was five years older, Kat knew, but she looked younger. Ma's hands were rough and chapped; Aunt Sue's hands were soft, white, and sparkling with jewels.

Kat was careful at the wood-burning stove; sometimes an ember sparked up suddenly. She popped muffins out of the baking tin and put them on a big blue-and-white enameled plate. "Where's Papa?"

"At the docks helping to tie down the boats. They say there's a squall coming in by morning." Ma raised her eyebrows. "You could rebraid your hair, Kat."

Kat shrugged. What was the point? It was certainly too late to impress Aunt Sue.

Hard work had lined Ma's face, but Aunt Sue had the pampered look of a banker's wife with lots of servants. Two sisters, starting off together—it wasn't fair! Papa had once been the captain of his own whaler. But the ship had been lost in an accident at sea, an accident that injured Pa's leg and kept him from working on the slippery deck of a boat. He had a bad limp when he was tired. He tried to hide it but Kate noticed. She felt a special closeness to Papa and she wouldn't trade him for anyone, but she wished Ma had an easier life.

"Come on, let's go to the lighthouse," Lizabeth said.

That's where they always went as soon as Lizabeth and Amanda arrived at Durham Point. Up in the tower room it seemed as if the rest of the world, with all its rules and judgments, fell away. That's where a peaceful stillness came over Kat. That's where she painted and felt most free to dream.

Ma put some muffins on a separate plate. "Here, take them up with you."

Amanda held the muffin plate and Kat carried her package and a jar of water. She was going to paint today for sure!

They rushed to the lighthouse. Even Lizabeth forgot about taking dainty steps, Kat thought. They hurried up the three wide stone stairs at the base and then climbed the ladder going straight up the dimly lit stone shaft. At the top of the ladder, the sunlight suddenly streaming into the tower room was dazzling.

The small round room, just under the second ladder to the light itself, was their special place. There was just enough space for a few high-back chairs, a low three-legged table, a faded rag rug to warm the stone floor, and a coal-burning stove. Deep windowsill shelves held supplies: a kerosene lantern, a sack of coal, some of Papa's tools, packets of wire and cord, rags and cleanser, a few dog-eared books, and Kat's art supplies.

The room was plain as could be, but the big windows curving all around made it extraordinary. The ocean below stretched as far as she could see. Waves crashed with furious sprays of white foam on the strip of sandy beach. Huge rocks, some half-hidden in the water and some jagged on shore, were as shiny-wet and black as seals. Kat gazed out at miles and miles of sky. This is how it must look from the very top of the world, she thought.

"It's so beautiful," Lizabeth breathed.

"Every time I come here, it feels sort of like I'm coming home," Amanda said.

"Me, too," Lizabeth said. Then she giggled. "If

lighthouses could talk, this one would be saying 'Welcome back, girls,' and 'Come on in.'"

Amanda flopped down cross-legged on the rag rug. "Want to play jacks? I bet I can get up to sevensies."

"Not today," Kat said. "I want to try my new colors."

Lizabeth perched on a chair near the stove. "Let's just talk; it's so nice without brothers and sisters around. Tracy is such a pest!"

"I think she's sweet," Amanda said.

"That's because you don't have to live with her. She gets into all my things. I need a lock on my door. And then there's Christopher. He teases me too much!"

"Well, that's what big brothers do," Kat said. Her cousin Chris was pretty nice and some of Lizabeth's prissy ways almost begged for teasing.

Lizabeth shrugged and nibbled at a muffin. "Mmmm. I love cornbread."

Kat pulled the little table next to her chair and arranged her supplies on it, sniffing at her new tubes when she opened them. She loved that distinctive paint smell. She squeezed spots of paint onto the old plate she used as a palette.

"I'm almost finished with *Jane Eyre*," Lizabeth said. "Who wants it next?"

"I'll take it after Amanda," Kat said. "I want to do nothing but art this week."

"Anyway, I'm a fast reader," Amanda said.

"You'll love it. There's an orphan—that's Jane—and she becomes a governess for Rochester—he's mean and grumpy but she falls in love with him and then he—"

"Stop, don't tell us the whole story!" Amanda said.

"Oops, sorry."

Sometimes Lizabeth is so nice, Kat thought. She buys all the books she wants at the Pelican Street Bookshop and then she gives them to Amanda and me as soon as she's finished.

"Well, I'm not going to read it *twice*," she'd say whenever Kat tried to thank her for a book. "I already know what happens."

"There's a big public library in Boston." Kat gathered some paint-covered rags. "You can borrow books for free, whatever you want. Oh, I'd love to go there!"

"Why bother?" Lizabeth asked. "We have the bookshop right here and they'll order for you if the book isn't in the store. Anyway, who wants a book that's been handled by *strangers*? Maybe someone who just wiped his nose! Yuck!"

Kat dipped a brush in the jar of water and gave it a

little shake. It came to a nice, satisfying point. "Amanda, let me paint your portrait."

"Do I have to sit still? I hate that."

"You can still talk." Kat balanced her block of watercolor paper on her knees. It was thick and solid enough to support her brushstrokes, but what she wouldn't give for an easel!

"Come on, Amanda, I need a model to practice on. Please, please."

"All right." Amanda settled into a chair.

"Turn your head to the side just a little. Don't move."

Kat studied Amanda as she mixed the colors. Amanda's shoulder-length hair was light brown but there were many shades mixed in—bits of gold shining in the brown. And maybe violet highlights?

Most people would notice Lizabeth first, Kat thought. She had elegant clothes and blond hair, blue eyes and rosy cheeks. But Amanda was beautiful; pale skin, hazel eyes, a straight classic nose, a soft, gentle mouth. It took a second look to see her quiet beauty.

"I keep wondering who's going to live in the Reynolds house," Amanda said.

"They'll have to go to my father's bank for a mortgage," Lizabeth said. "So I'll find out."

"Then that's your mission for this week," Amanda said.

"I hope it's a family with children," Kat said. "It would be nice to see some new faces in school for a change."

"A lot of summer people are buying cottages down the coast in Shorehaven," Amanda said. "Maybe Cape Light will get some vacationers, too."

"We could meet interesting people from big cities," Kat said.

Lizabeth shook her head. "No, they won't come to Cape Light. Father says our shoreline is much too rocky. We only have that little strip of beach down below, hardly big enough for one boat to come in. That's not what summer people want."

"Then they don't know what they're missing," Amanda said. "Cape Light is beautiful!"

"Amanda, stop moving! You're changing the shadows!"

"I hate being your model," Amanda said. "You get so bossy."

"Sorry. It's just, well, it's confusing when the shadows on your face shift." Kat had captured Amanda's nose pretty well, but the eyes were all wrong. She had to clear her mind and concentrate on light and dark. Paint what you actually *see*, not what you *think* something looks like, she told herself.

"My neck hurts," Amanda complained.

"One more minute," Kat begged. "Please."

"Let Kat finish." Lizabeth got up for another muffin. "I want to see how it turns out."

Amanda's eyes could change from gray to gray-green in a minute. Kat couldn't get the expression right. She thought she saw sadness in them, even when Amanda was smiling. Six years was a long time to mourn, but maybe when it was your mother, the sadness never went away. Amanda's mother had died in childbirth with Hannah.

Kat remembered when Amanda, who was only seven, came back to school afterward. Everyone rushed to her to say sympathetic things. Amanda looked cornered. Kat could see she was trying not to cry. Kat went to her and took her hand without a word. Amanda gripped hers very tightly and they didn't let go for a long time.

"Kat, I have to move!"

"Just one more second. I promise."

Kat tilted her head back and squinted at the paper. The eyes didn't look anything like Amanda's. She added small flecks of green and a dab of pale yellow to catch the light. Hopeless. They were still flat and expression-less. There were no do-overs with watercolors. This was too hard! But Kat loved the way the white of the paper showed through the translucent colors, the way a spray of water could soften the outlines and get interesting effects—if she was lucky. She didn't know enough. Her little instruction book was too limited. If only she could get some real training.

Kat sighed. "All right, you can move. It doesn't matter."

Amanda stretched. "Let me see."

"No, it's awful." Kat crumpled the paper before Amanda and Lizabeth could look over her shoulder.

Lizabeth picked up some of Kat's old paintings on the shelf. "Why do you paint the same thing over and over again?" she asked.

"You mean the seascapes? Because I'm trying to get it right. Anyway, the sea is *never* the same. It's always changing. Green or black or blue. Peaceful or churning and angry. Tides reaching for the moon. . . ." She gazed out of the window. A tremendous feeling that she couldn't name swept through her. If only she could get it on paper! "Sometimes I feel—I feel as if this is almost a holy place. Even more than church."

Lizabeth nodded.

"I know," Amanda said. "I do love church, though," she quickly added.

"Your father's sermons are always good. I wasn't saying anything about that." Kat grinned. "But *I* know why you love church so much lately."

Amanda looked down at her hands. "There's no special reason."

"What about that boy who's always staring at you?" Kat teased.

"I don't know that he's looking at *me*," Amanda said. "He might be looking at someone in the row behind me."

"I've noticed, too," Lizabeth said. "His head swivels when you go up to sing with the choir."

"And don't think I haven't seen you sneaking looks at him," Kat added.

"I don't know him to talk to, but—don't you think he looks like a nice person?" Amanda blushed. "I do think he's wonderfully handsome."

"Amanda, he's nobody. I bet he's just a deckhand," Lizabeth said. "Probably came to town to work at the docks."

"How do you know? You don't know him at all!" Amanda said.

"That Sunday suit he wears to church? It has shiny worn spots," Lizabeth said.

Kat wished her cousin's snobbishness wouldn't keep slipping out.

"So what?" Amanda's eyes were fiery. "He's still handsome!"

"He must have quit school already. That's why we don't know him," Lizabeth said.

Lots of their classmates quit by age fourteen. Especially the girls. The high school for all the surrounding towns was in Cranberry; there weren't enough continuing students in any one town to fill a high school. Todd would go on for sure—maybe even to college! Papa wanted Kat to have more schooling too, even though she was a girl. Maybe it was Papa's unusual attitude that gave her the courage to dream of something more than being married at sixteen.

"I'd discourage him if I were you," Lizabeth continued.

"You're not me!" Amanda snapped.

Kat was surprised to see even-tempered Amanda flare up. She had to be really sweet on that boy, whose name they didn't even know.

"Well, *I'm* going to marry someone very rich and important," Lizabeth said.

"I believe in marrying for love," Amanda said.

"So do I, but you can decide who to love," Lizabeth said. "A woman has that one chance to have a good life. You want a man who can take care of you, don't you?"

"I don't need anyone to take care of me," Kat said. "I'm going to make my own good life. I'm going to *do* things and go places and when I'm a famous artist, I'll fall in love with someone different and exciting. Someone I'll meet in a great city." She half-closed her eyes. She could almost see it, discussing techniques with other artists in cafes, one of her paintings in a Boston gallery . . .

"Only men are famous artists," Lizabeth said.

"That's not so!" Kat protested.

"Then go ahead, name a famous woman artist," Lizabeth challenged.

"I will!" Kat's mind raced through all the artists she'd ever heard of. Sargent. Whistler. Rembrandt. . . . Not one woman's name came to her. Not *one*!

"I'll think of someone later," Kat mumbled.

Maybe Lizabeth was right. Kat's shoulders drooped. And maybe she was only good enough to be the star artist of a one-room school because she'd managed to draw good Easter bunnies in kindergarten. And judging by the way she'd botched Amanda's portrait. . . . Maybe my dreams are just hopeless, Kat thought. Is there really any way I can make them come true?

three

at watched her brothers grab apples for dessert. They were rushing to their room to work on the telephone they were making out of baking powder boxes, drawing paper, and string. "It says how to do it in the *Handy Book,*" Todd insisted. So far, their telephone didn't work at all. But the *Handy Book* was usually good; Todd had made a nifty war kite following its instructions.

Kat couldn't understand how a *real* telephone worked, much less one made out of boxes. Cranberry already had telephones and switchboard operators called hello girls. The mayor promised that telephone lines would come to Cape Light soon. Wouldn't that be wonderful! Her friend Laurel in Cranberry said her house telephone had two short rings and one long. There were eight parties on a line and you weren't supposed to pick up unless the call was for you, but Laurel listened in anyway. She said it was so funny sometimes.

"Todd, did you clean the glass around the light?" Kat called as he was about to disappear into his room.

"Yes!"

Sunshine curled under the table, with his head resting on Kat's feet. Kat moved her spoon around the last of her chowder. At the end of the month, when money was tight, it was chowder for dinner every night. James and Todd would go clamming at the rocks and come back with a good haul. Sometimes Ma made it with potatoes and milk, sometimes with tomatoes and parsley. She tried every which way to vary it, but it was still chowder and Kat was tired of it.

Ma was at the sink scrubbing the pots. "It's almost time for your watch."

"It's still daylight," Kat said, though she knew darkness could sweep over Durham Point almost without warning. She had the first watch at the lighthouse, from twilight to ten. Papa had the long night watch, then Ma took over for the early morning hours until dawn. "Ma, come sit for a minute."

"Your father will be back soon. I should reheat—oh, I guess that can wait till he gets here. I do want to just *sit*."

Ma smiled, dried her hands with the dishtowel

draped on her shoulder, and sank into a chair across from Kat. "Sorry about dessert. I didn't have time to bake a pie, with Sue visiting this afternoon. I'll make one tomorrow."

"That's all right, I like apples plain." Kat took one from the bowl in the center of the table and bit into it with a crunch. "Ma . . . whenever I see Aunt Sue . . ."

"She looks wonderful, doesn't she? And Tracy— she's growing so fast, the picture of health with those cute rosy cheeks. She's such a bright little girl." Ma laughed. "Though she does bedevil our James."

A log toppled in the fireplace and made a shower of sparks.

"I was thinking . . . about you and Aunt Sue. Ma— are you ever sorry? I mean, about being stuck in a light- house."

"I'm not *stuck*! I can't imagine a more wonderful place than Durham Point!"

"I know, I love it too, but—" Kat turned the apple around and around in her hand. "You work so hard and there's no *end* to it. Ma, didn't you have dreams?"

"Of course. Everyone does, Kat. Do you want to know what my dream was when I was your age?"

"Tell me, Ma."

"Well, I was just fourteen when I first saw him. I

thought Tom Williams was the best-looking, strongest, wisest . . . He had such a smile! He still does, doesn't he?"

Kat nodded. Papa could light up a room.

"Anyway, he was courting someone. That just about broke my heart. I was so young. He'd say hello to me and maybe tousle my hair—you know how your father is, friendly to everyone. But I had the impossible dream that someday, somehow, he would really *notice* me. Well, that dream came true! Of course, I helped it along by being underfoot almost any place he went."

Kat couldn't imagine that. Ma was so proper.

"It was a terrible time for us when your father lost his boat. And it's painful to see how much he still misses going to sea. But think of the women in Cape Light whose men have been taken by the sea forever. And the children lost to pneumonia and influenza and scarlet fever. I have blessing upon blessing."

"I know, but—"

"I don't love getting out of a warm, cozy bed for the morning watch—but I'm happy, Kat. I like making a home, I like puttering in the vegetable garden, I like tending the chickens."

Ma couldn't mean that. The chicken coop behind the cottage smelled!

"Ma, I want so much more! I want to live in a big city. I want my art to be *important*, not just a girlish hobby."

"I think times are changing for women, Kat. Honestly, I don't know if that's good or bad. But you can't forget to enjoy what you already have. Perhaps you could pray for contentment." Ma got up to wipe the table. "It'll be easier for you when you have more free time. Todd will be old enough to take a watch in another year or so."

"I think he's old enough right now," Kat said.

"Todd's the serious one in this family, our scholar," Mom said. "I know that makes him seem older, but he's only ten."

James still had that round, baby face and soft blond hair, Kat thought. But Todd had become tall and lean, with high cheekbones. He still wore knickers and he had that funny cowlick in his dark brown hair, but he'd lost a lot of his boyishness. Why couldn't Ma see he was growing up? It would be nice to have a few evenings off. "I still think he—"

Suddenly Sunshine jumped up and ran to the door. It burst open with a blast of cold and the smell of the sea. Papa's tall rugged shape filled the doorframe.

"Papa!"

He closed the door against the wind, pulled Ma into a bear hug, and leaned down to plant a kiss on Kat's nose. "The best freckle, second from the right," he said. "How's my favorite daughter?"

"I'm your *only* daughter!"

"If I had ten more, you'd still be my favorite!"

They'd said the exact same lines to each other since she couldn't remember when, but Kat still liked it.

"You've had a long day," Ma said.

"We got every boat tied down, every line secured, prepared for anything." Papa scratched behind Sunshine's ears. "I'm bone tired and ready for some hot chowder! Without tomatoes, I hope?"

"You have no imagination," Ma said. "There's life beyond milk and potatoes."

"Not for clams." His eyes squinted with his smile. Papa pulled off his knit wool cap. His auburn hair, the same color as Kat's, tumbled down his forehead. "So they were saying a squall by morning, but the wind feels like it's picking up. My guess is it will hit earlier. We'll lock down the shutters tonight."

"God willing, it'll pass by Cape Light," Ma said.

"And all that work for nothing?"

Kat didn't want to notice how bad Papa's limp was tonight. He sat down to pull off his work boots. "Kat, it's time to stand watch."

"I know."

"It should be a quiet night," he said. "Only a fool would take a boat out with a storm heading this way."

Kat got up reluctantly and took her yellow oilcloth slicker from the hook by the door. She hated to leave the warm circle of firelight, the smell of wood ashes, the scent of baking muffins that still hung in the air. She smiled at Sunshine curled under the table again, this time with his head resting on Papa's feet.

"I'll be up to relieve you at ten," Papa said.

He looked so tired tonight and he'd be able to snatch no more than a few hours of sleep. "You can make it later," Kat said. "Tomorrow is Saturday—no school."

Kat braced herself against the wind as she opened the door. At the base of the lighthouse, it whipped her hair around and into her face. But it wasn't hurricane force. The last time they'd had a hurricane, the outhouse tipped over and wasn't that a mess!

Clouds streaked across a darkening sky. The red and yellow daymark above her stood out in the last bit of daylight. Soon it would become invisible in the night.

Kat climbed up the lighthouse ladder to the tower room, and continued up the second ladder high into the very top to the cramped space where the light was. There was a bell in case she needed to call for help. She checked the glass around the light. Clean and clear. Todd had done a good job.

She wound the spring that made the light revolve. There was hardly room to turn around up here; her elbows bumped the stone walls. She switched on the newly electrified light and watched it turn. Its rays could be seen for miles in all directions.

Kat climbed down the ladder to the room below. They'd had an Indian summer, but the nights were cold. Ma always cleaned the ashes out of the coal stove at the end of her morning watch. It was Kat's job to stoke the new coals and keep the room warm for the long night ahead. She shoveled the coals around with an iron poker and tried to keep her hands clean.

Kat took the kerosene lantern from the shelf. She had to wash and polish the globe once a week, fill it with kerosene, and trim the wick. Well, it looked clean enough and it was full; she'd just filled it on her last shift. She trimmed the wick and lit it. The light was reflected in the dark windows.

She sat in her chair at the window facing the sea. There was nothing left to do but scan the horizon and be alert for a boat in trouble. If the fog rolled in, she would sound the fog horn.

The wind was whistling past and the ocean was choppy. She could barely see the outlines of the rocks. Everything appeared in different shades of black and gray, with no moon at all. Could she do something interesting with that? Daylight was fading too fast to think about painting. The light from the lantern was good enough for doing her arithmetic and spelling exercises, but there was no school tomorrow, so she certainly wasn't about to do homework now!

Kat looked down at the cottage. The shutters were closed. Thin lines of light escaped between the slats.

The sky had become dark. The ocean had turned pure black. Kat could no longer tell the waves from the rocks, except when the lighthouse rays swept by in their steady circle.

She wished Amanda could have stayed to sleep over; they could be sitting here together and talking quietly, just the two of them. But Amanda had too many responsibilities. "I have to pick up Hannah at Mary Margaret's and sort the clothes. The laundress is coming tomorrow," she'd said when she left this afternoon.

Kat's thoughts were interrupted by the sudden absence of sound. The normal background noises were gone. The wind had stopped. She no longer heard waves crashing against the rocks. The air felt heavy in the silence.

Kat got up and went to the window. The ocean was still, waiting. . . . It felt as though the world was holding its breath. This was it, Kat thought. The calm before the storm.

A few raindrops pattered on the glass. Then more ran down in steady streams.

Soon the patter became a thousand drums as rain pelted against the windows. Huge waves battered the shore, smashing and roaring with unleashed fury. It was magnificent. A jagged line of lightning split through the dark.

Inside, Kat felt snug and secure. Papa was always caulking and keeping on top of repairs. The lighthouse was shipshape.

She looked toward the cottage. It was completely dark. Everyone must be tucked into bed and fast asleep by now. Too bad Todd and James were missing this. They'd love the drama of the storm.

Kat turned back to the raging sea. In the lighthouse ray, she caught a glimpse of something. Was it white? Could it be a sail? No, not in the middle of a storm like this!

Kat jumped from her chair and waited for the light to sweep around again. Yes, it was a boat! Her shoulders tensed. It was tossing on the waves like a child's toy. On her watch! This wasn't a night to be out. What should she do? What *could* she do? She watched helplessly as the boat kept heading her way, making for land. Please, whoever is on that boat, let them be good sailors!

The light turned in its rhythmic circle, pinpointing the treacherous rocks. Please, let the light show them the hazards and guide them safely to the beach. The boat looked so fragile! Kat gasped. For a horrible moment, she lost sight of it behind the raging waves. No, thank God, there was the white sail again. It was coming closer on a steady course. Close enough to clearly see the beach each time the light turned. They could make it, they *had* to make it. . . .

Was that a flicker? Kat held her breath. No, she must have blinked, because when she looked again, there was the even beacon sweeping the shore. Kat went limp with relief and watched the rotating ray.

The light flickered again! No, she *wasn't* imagining it! A hissing, stuttering sound came from the top of the tower. What was happening? Kat's skin prickled. Something was terribly wrong! But the light had *never* failed. Another flicker. She froze in panic.

Suddenly the light went out! No! Everything was plunged into darkness. "Papa!" she cried out. "Papa!" She was on her own. All alone. No beacon. And a boat was out there in the night, floundering on the waves.

at's heart pounded. There was no time to get help. The boat was too close! It would never be able to navigate around the rocks in the dark. She pulled the foghorn. Its bleats were a deafening warning, but it couldn't guide the boat in.

What did Papa say to do if this happened? It had *never* happened. Her mind was racing, splintering. She couldn't think. She took a deep, shuddering breath. All right. Steady now. *Think!* The alarm bell!

Kat grabbed the kerosene lantern, its light wavering wildly in her shaking hand. She climbed up the second ladder. Her legs were trembling so, she almost stumbled. She *had* to stop shaking, the kerosene was sloshing around . . . Her hand on the bell's rope was all thumbs. She was clumsy with fear. She pulled the rope, up and down, with all her strength. The peals rang out.

Please, let it wake Papa! Could he hear it over the

roar of the storm? Even if he did, it would be too late! She had to do something *now!*

Kat held the lantern up against the glass facing the ocean. But at sea they'd see only a tiny light high up in the tower. Not enough to illuminate the rocks. Not enough to keep a boat from shattering on them. She had to do something else. But what? *What?*

Take the lantern to the beach, Kat thought. Show them where to come ashore. Their only chance. Hurry!

She grabbed the lantern, scrambled down both ladders, and ran out of the lighthouse. The rain drenched her immediately. She ran onto the strip of beach, tripping on fallen branches, fighting for her balance.

Kat held the lantern as high as her arm could reach. She ran from one end of the beach to the other. A moving light, to show them safe boundaries. Would they understand her signal? Oh please, God, let me guide them in! Please, not a shipwreck on the rocks!

Gasping for breath, she ran back and forth as best she could. Her feet were being sucked into the wet sand. Her blouse and her skirt were soaked and heavy. She remembered her slicker, still on the chair where she'd tossed it. She shivered and held the lantern up. Up and up. Her arm ached. It began to shake, every muscle trembling from effort. The wind threatened to knock her down. The lantern, that was the important thing, she had to hold it high. She couldn't stop, no matter what.

Lightning flashed through the sky. The boat was close enough to see. It was coming her way. Coming to the beach. Please, God, help me save them.

Time had become meaningless. Were minutes going by or hours? The storm, the boat, the rain. Her legs wouldn't run anymore. Walking. The lantern high. Lashing wind. Kat pushed wet hair from her eyes. Pain sliced from her shoulder to her wrist. She gritted her teeth. Walking. Can't trip. Hold the lantern up. Was it rain streaking down her cheeks or tears?

Through misty eyes, as though she was dreaming, Kat saw the boat wash ashore on the sand.

A man and a woman waded through swirling waist-high water and floundered onto the beach. And then she heard a voice behind her. Papa's voice. "Kat!"

"Papa!" Kat sagged against him. "Papa, the light went out!"

"I know, I heard the bell."

The man from the boat stared at her in amazement. "Was that you? Only you and that lantern? I can't believe a young girl—"

"I didn't think we'd make it," the woman sobbed. "Thank you. It was horrifying! Waves swamped the deck and . . . the thunder, the lightning . . ."

"Hush, Evelyn." The man put his arm around her. "We're all right now."

"Those terrible waves." Sheets of rain plastered the woman's hair to her head. Her eyes were wide with shock. "When everything went dark I was sure we were lost. I was sure it was the end."

"Kat, take these people to the cottage." Papa looked up at the lighthouse. "I need to see what happened." The wind snapped his oilcloth. "Please, go with my daughter. My wife has dry clothes and—"

"It was calm when we started. . . ." The man had to raise his voice to be heard over the pounding surf. "We're so grateful—"

"No time for talk now. I've got a light that needs fixing and you need to get out of this storm," Papa said. "Go on, Kat, hurry inside."

In her attic bedroom, Kat dripped puddles on the wood-plank floor. She shivered. I'm safe now, she reminded herself. And those people are safe. And Ma will give us something hot to drink and . . . it's over. It's all over.

She peeled off her wet clothes. Her skirt and blouse were a soaked mess. And her shoes! What she wouldn't give for a hot bath now! But she didn't have the strength left to boil up the water and carry it to the washtub. Anyway, she wanted to see the couple. Evelyn and Kenneth Carstairs, Kat remembered. They had introduced themselves on the way to the cottage. Kat pulled on a heavy sweater and skirt. She toweled her hair. She couldn't stop shivering as she rushed downstairs.

The Carstairses were sitting at the table in front of steaming cups of tea. Papa's fisherman-knit sweater was miles too big for Mr. Carstairs. Mrs. Carstairs was wearing Ma's best cable cardigan. A blanket was draped over her shoulders.

"Katherine," Mrs. Carstairs said, "you were our guardian angel!"

Kat smiled and gulped down her tea. It burned her tongue, but the hot liquid took the chill from her body.

On the table, hurricane lamps flickered. A log was blazing in the fireplace. The Carstairses' cold-weather sailing gear lay in a pile on the hearth.

"We just closed our summer house in Shorehaven," Mrs. Carstairs said. "It was calm when we started out."

"The squall wasn't supposed to hit until morning,"

Mr. Carstairs said. "I thought it was still rounding Hatteras—"

"And we were heading home," Mrs. Carstairs continued. "If it wasn't for Katherine's bravery . . . I'm so sorry for all the trouble we've caused."

"No trouble at all," Ma said. "We'll put Mr. and Mrs. Carstairs in your room tonight." She touched Kat's shoulder. "Set up a bedroll for yourself in the boys' room. I think you need to go to bed."

Soon, Kat thought. She *was* getting sleepy. . . .

"I know it's late in the season, but Shorehaven is so lovely this time of year," Mrs. Carstairs was saying.

"We left in daylight, but we had trouble with a sail. One piece of bad luck after another, and it was twilight long before we could reach our destination," Mr. Carstairs said.

"We decided to dock at Cape Light for the night," Mrs. Carstairs added.

"Please don't think we're completely foolhardy," Mr. Carstairs said. "We're experienced sailors. We've been in any number of regattas along the New England coast and of course, the big one out of Newport." He sighed. "I was so sure we could beat the storm home to Boston."

Boston! Kat sat up straight, suddenly wide awake.

"You live in *Boston*? There's a famous art museum, isn't there?" As soon as she asked one question, ten more popped into Kat's head. "Do the Public Gardens really have swan boats? Do you ride trolleys? Is the Charles River—" Kat bit her lip. Ma's sharp look reminded her that asking too many questions wasn't polite.

Mrs. Carstairs smiled. "I don't know which to answer first."

"Kat, not now. I think everyone's exhausted." Ma glanced at the Carstairses. "We're all about ready to turn in."

Mr. Carstairs nodded. "It's been an eventful night."

But, Kat thought, it's my one chance to hear all about Boston! "Please, may I just ask—is Commonwealth Avenue—"

"Kat, go on to bed," Ma ordered.

"But, Ma—"

"Mr. and Mrs. Carstairs will be here in the morning," Ma added more softly. She handed Kat a hurricane lamp.

"And I'll be happy to tell you anything you want to know." Mrs. Carstairs smiled. "Good night, Katherine. You were wonderful. Thank you again."

"Sleep tight, Kat." Ma smiled.

Kat reluctantly went up to her room. She put on her

flannel nightgown and her fuzzy robe. Sunshine will keep me warm, she thought. Wait. Where was he? Why wasn't he curled up in his usual spot at the foot of her bed? Then she spotted the tip of a white tail poking out from under the bed.

"Come on out, scaredy dog. A big dog like you. . . . There's no lightning indoors, silly."

Sunshine wriggled out from under the bed. Kat could swear he looked embarrassed.

She took the bedroll and an extra quilt from the cupboard, the star quilt made by Grandma Williams long ago. She tiptoed into her brothers' room with Sunshine following close behind.

The light of her candle showed Todd asleep on the top bunk. He turned over, but he didn't wake up. James was in the lower bunk, his arms and legs spread out. His breath whistled softly. They'd slept through all the excitement!

Kat arranged her bedroll on the rag rug. Though she was worn out, she didn't lie down. Not yet. She wrapped the quilt around her and went to the window. She opened the shutters just a bit. All she could see was blackness.

She waited at the window; waited and worried. Then her heart jumped. The light went on! Its steady ray was revolving again.

Now she could rest.

She blew out the candle and burrowed into the comfort of the bedroll, but her thoughts drifted in all directions. The Carstairses. Boston. The lightning and her terror . . .

The door creaked open.

"Kat? Are you still awake?" Papa whispered.

"Yes."

He came close and squatted next to her. "Some wiring came loose," he whispered. "I soldered it. The light's working fine again."

"I know. I saw."

"I found your slicker on the chair. You could have used it."

"There wasn't time," she said.

"I know. . . . Kat, you saved those people. All by yourself." His callused hand stroked her cheek. "I'm proud of you, Kat. I couldn't be more proud."

Kat knew he was smiling at her in the dark. She smiled back and closed her eyes.

"I thank God you're safe, kitten. When I think of— "

Exhaustion washed over her and she didn't hear anything else.

The next thing Kat knew, the shutters were wide open and sunlight was streaming into the room. It was morning already! Todd and James were gone and their beds were neatly made. It had to be late. The Carstairses might have left!

Kat jumped up and threw on her bathrobe. She brushed her teeth slapdash and splashed some water over her face. There was no time to bother with braiding her hair. She tied back the tangled mass in one big bunch and clattered down the stairs.

If she'd missed the Carstairses, she would die!

h, good! Mrs. Carstairs was still here, sitting at the table.

Ma, at the stove, raised her eyebrows. "Kat! Your hair. A dress would—"

"Why didn't anyone wake me?"

"You needed your sleep," Ma said. "After last night."

Mrs. Carstairs smiled. "Besides, we'd never leave without saying good-bye to you."

Kat suddenly felt awkward. Why hadn't she stopped to get dressed? She was a complete mess and in front of a lady from Boston.

Mrs. Carstairs looked very different this morning. She was relaxed and her hair was in a neat bun. "Katherine, come sit with me," she said. "Your mother made the most delicious flapjacks."

Ma put a plate in front of Kat. "Here, I kept them warm for you."

"Where is everybody?"

"At Alveira's boatyard," Ma said, "getting work done on the boat."

"Thanks to you, there's very little damage," Mrs. Carstairs said. "It looks like we can sail home today without a problem."

Kat poured maple syrup on her pancakes, but her fork remained in midair. She was too excited to eat. "Home to Boston! Do you live right in the city?"

"Yes, we live in a row house close to Beacon Hill. It's an historic area. Well, Boston is an historic city. You can follow the path of Paul Revere's ride."

"And there's a famous art museum?"

Mrs. Carstairs smiled. "Yes, it has quite a collection—Corots, Turners, many of the Dutch masters, including van Eycks and some Rembrandts, I believe. Even some of those modern French painters . . . Impressionists, I think they're called. Renoir, Matisse . . ."

"Oh!" Kat said breathlessly. Oh, to see those paintings in person!

"Kat likes to draw," Ma said. "They always hang up her pictures in school." She gestured to the seascape over the fireplace. "That's one of Kat's."

"Why, that's lovely," Mrs. Carstairs said. She got up

for a closer look. "The way the sea blends into the sky, the shadows of the rocks . . . You are remarkably talented."

"Oh! Oh, thank you!" This was a lady from Boston who would *know*! Well, maybe she was just being polite. But she didn't have to say "remarkably"—so maybe she meant it! Kat was filled with a warm glow.

"Are there . . . are there any famous women artists in Boston?"

"Women artists?" Mrs. Carstairs frowned. "Let me see . . . I can't think of any. I suppose women in art are mostly the artists' models or wives," Mrs. Carstairs said.

"Oh." Kat felt heavy with disappointment. "Maybe . . . maybe it'll be different by the time I grow up."

"I hope so." Mrs. Carstairs looked closely at Kat. "Do you want to be a *professional* artist?"

Katherine nodded, embarrassed. Did Mrs. Carstairs think that was silly? Or even worse, hopeless?

"Perhaps women will be taken more seriously if we ever get the vote," Mrs. Carstairs said. "It's beginning. . . . I've seen suffragettes parading on Commonwealth Avenue. Of course, a lot of people make fun of them. Some even throw rotten fruit!"

"They're so brave," Kat said. "I'd like to be a suffragette."

"Kat, you don't mean that!" Ma said.

"Commonwealth Avenue is the main street, isn't it?" Kat asked.

"Yes," said Mrs. Carstairs. "But it's getting too crowded and busy, with more and more of those automobiles. Too noisy, and they really do scare the horses."

Ma put an arm around Kat. "I hope my daughter isn't pestering you with too many questions."

"Oh, no, not at all. It's nice to meet someone so bright and curious," Mrs. Carstairs said.

"I'd give *anything* to live in Boston! There'd be so much to see!"

"I hope you'll come to visit. I'd love to show you around," Mrs. Carstairs said. Suddenly she exclaimed, "Mary Cassatt!"

"Pardon?" Kat asked.

"I just remembered. Mary Cassatt is a famous woman artist. She was discovered by Degas. She's an American but she's lived in France for many years."

So there *is* someone, Kat thought. Wait till I tell Lizabeth and Amanda!

Kat's flapjacks were cold and forgotten. And later—when Papa and Mr. Carstairs came in, when the boys made their noisy entrance, when the Carstairses were getting ready to leave, when the good-byes and thank-you's were said—Mrs. Carstairs's words were still going round and round in Kat's head. Visions of Boston danced before her eyes.

Somehow I'll get there, she thought, no matter what it takes.

~six~

After the Carstairses left, Kat helped Ma hang the laundry on the line outside the cottage.

"A nice sunny day," Ma said through the clothespin between her teeth as she lifted a sheet from the laundry basket.

Kat took the other end of the sheet and fastened it to the line. Once the clothespin held it securely, Kat took a step back. She hated it when a breeze flapped wet laundry into her face!

"Look at the ocean, Ma. You'd never know we had a storm." The sea was calm. Waves splashed lazily against rocks that didn't look menacing today. Off in the distance, boats were out again. Except for some broken tree branches on the ground, there were few reminders of last night's nightmare.

"Your father said some of the roof shingles were broken." Ma shook out one of Todd's shirts.

Kat pinned a pillowcase to the line and glanced back at the cottage. She couldn't see much of the roof from where she stood.

"He'll take a closer look when he gets back," Ma said. Papa had taken the horse and wagon to see if there had been damage in town. "I hope everyone came through without trouble."

Kat and Ma automatically took opposite ends of the larger items. Sheets, towels, clothespins, shirts, napkins, clothespins. Kat didn't mind hanging the wash; it was the ironing she hated. When the laundry was not quite dry, it would be time to heat the five irons at the fireplace. As soon as one iron cooled too much to be of any use, Ma needed the next hot iron. It was Kat's job to keep them coming. Ma was teaching her to iron. It was maddening. If Kat was careful not to scorch their things, she couldn't iron them smooth enough. And shirts were impossible! What was the point, anyway, if everything was going to get wrinkled all over again? Though Kat had to admit she loved sleeping on freshly ironed sheets smelling of sunshine and sea breeze.

Women's work was no fun. Kat knew exactly the kind of work she wanted to do. Mary Cassatt, she thought. She just had to see her paintings! If there was one famous woman artist, there could be others. And one of them could be *Katherine Williams*!

"Kat! You're letting that towel trail on the ground!"

"Oh! Sorry." Kat quickly pinned it to the line. Tablecloths, shirts, clothespins . . . "Ma, Mrs. Carstairs was so nice, wasn't she?"

"Yes, I liked her very much. Kat, for you to come downstairs in a bathrobe—it just wasn't proper."

"I was so anxious not to miss the Carstairses. . . . I'm sorry, I didn't stop to think."

Kat held up two corners of a cotton blanket and Ma held the other two. They moved together to hang it.

"Kat, you're growing up and certain things are expected of a young lady. You *have* to stop to think. You have to be less impulsive and—"

"I know, Ma. I'll try. I really will."

"Last night, you showed so much character and responsibility. A grown man couldn't have handled it better. I'm very proud of you. But sometimes I don't know what you're going to do next." Ma picked up the empty laundry basket and balanced it against her hip. "And there was something Aunt Sue mentioned to me. Something about finding you buried in leaves? What was that about?"

Kat shrugged. "Um . . . nothing."

Ma raised her eyebrows.

"Nothing important," Kat mumbled. She whirled around at the sound of approaching wheels. "Here comes Papa!" She ran to the horse and wagon on the lane and Ma followed.

"Hello, Papa!" Kat petted the horse's velvety nose.

"What happened in town?" Ma asked.

"Bad news. The Hallorans' barn was hit by lightning." Papa jumped off the wagon. "Burned to the ground."

"Oh, that's terrible." Ma shook her head. "I'll call on Mrs. Halloran after church tomorrow."

"Bad as it was, thank goodness it didn't spread to their house," Papa said. "And we lost that big maple by the side of the courthouse. It's covering the village green."

"That was a beautiful old tree," Ma said.

"It'll be a job to cut it up and haul it away. I was just coming back for my ax." Papa sighed. "It's a shame. Well, there'll be more firewood for everybody this winter."

"What about the Hallorans' cows?" Kat asked.

"They made it out. They're stabled at the Whites' for now." Papa was heading for the cottage. "So there'll be a barn raising next week."

"And a barn dance after?" Kat asked.

"Next Saturday night."

"That will be such fun!"

Kat loved square dancing, loved whirling in circles with the caller's "Swing your lady, swing her down, allemande left, promenade to town. . . ." She wished she didn't have to wait a whole week for it. But it would take the week for Mr. Halloran and his boys to assemble the timbers and have them ready to go. Then on Saturday, all the men would come to raise the framework into place, something that one family could never do alone. All the women would bring pots and pans of their best recipes in the evening. Ma would bring her special potato salad for sure, and probably apple pie. . . .

"I ran into Amanda and Lizabeth in town," Papa said.

"I can't wait to see them," Kat said. "I have so much to tell them!"

"You can tell them after church tomorrow," Ma said. "Kat, please see about collecting the eggs."

In church on Sunday, Kat turned every once in a while to see if that boy was still staring at Amanda. But she paid attention to Reverend Morgan's sermon, too. His words always inspired her to be the very best person she could.

After the service, Kat saw Amanda holding Hannah's hand, and Lizabeth waiting for her at the bottom of the church steps. She was dying to run right to them, but she was expected to file out with her family. Reverend Morgan stood at the door to say a few words to everyone as they left.

Kat didn't know how he did it—he remembered the name of every single child in the congregation. Even all ten of the Hallorans, and Kat wasn't sure the Hallorans themselves could keep them straight! Reverend Morgan was such a kind man, Kat thought. He was always calling on people who were sick or troubled, and helping in every possible way. The only fault Kat could see was that he didn't have much time left over for Amanda and Hannah.

After he greeted Ma and Papa, the Reverend's dark, serious eyes were on Kat. "You're the talk of the town, Katherine."

"I am?" Kat was startled. *What did I do now?*

"Saving a life earns a special place in heaven."

Oh, the Carstairses! Kat blushed with pleasure. "Thank you, Reverend Morgan."

He smiled at her. "I see Amanda and Lizabeth are waiting very impatiently. . . .Well, Todd, how is that project coming along?"

Kat flew down the steps to her friends.

"We couldn't wait to see you!" Lizabeth said.

"Out in the lightning!" Amanda said. "Weren't you scared?"

"I wasn't scared," Kat said. She looked at her friends. "I was *terrified.*"

"You're a hero." Hannah's little face was awestruck.

"And wait till I tell you—Mr. and Mrs. Carstairs are from *Boston*," Kat continued. In a rush of words, she tried to make them see all that Mrs. Carstairs had described. "And there *is* a famous woman artist. Mrs. Carstairs told me. Mary Cassatt!"

"I've never heard of her," Lizabeth said.

"That doesn't mean she's not famous," Amanda said.

"Anyway, I have some news, too." Lizabeth paused dramatically until the other girls stared at her, waiting. "I know who bought the house across the way from Amanda's."

"Go on!" Amanda said. "Who are they?"

"They're from New York City. Dr. and Mrs. Forbes."

"Why would they ever come here all the way from New York City?" Kat asked. New York was even bigger than Boston. It had to be full of wonders.

"Mrs. Forbes's sister lives in Cape Light. Maybe that's why. You know the Claytons, don't you? They own those stables out past the orchard? Well, Mrs. Clayton is Mrs. Forbes's sister." Lizabeth was puffed up with importance for knowing all the facts. "Anyway, they're going to turn part of the Reynolds house into Dr. Forbes's medical office and waiting room. They're moving in March."

"Cape Light needs a doctor," Amanda said. "Maybe if my mother had . . ." She glanced at Hannah and bit her lip.

Kat knew what Amanda was thinking. But Annie Albright was an excellent midwife, everyone said so, and later the doctor from Cranberry came. . . .

"And the Forbeses have a daughter," Lizabeth continued.

"Is she six years old?" Hannah asked hopefully.

"No. One daughter, that's all. Her name is Rose. And guess what? She's around our age. Fourteen."

"I hope she's nice," Amanda said.

"I hope she's fashionable," Lizabeth said.

Typical Lizabeth, Kat thought.

"Rose is a pretty name," Kat said. Maybe one day she would have a friend from a big city. She couldn't wait until March to meet her.

❦ seven ❦

M iss Cotter, the teacher, said, "If you've finished your work, you must wait silently with
your hands folded on your lap until I come
around to you." Kat couldn't really blame Miss Cotter;
with sixty students in grades one through nine in the
same room, she had to keep the class in control.
Especially with the assistant teacher, Miss Harding, out
for the week with influenza.

But how could Kat *possibly* remain quiet for hours?
She always had so much to say!

The littlest children—Hannah, Mary Margaret,
Betsy, and Joseph—whispered while they were working
with wooden alphabet blocks. Todd was always good,
but James got into trouble for talking to Roger and
Francis.

That week everyone was thinking about the barn
dance. The boys talked about the food. "I hope Mrs.

White brings that lemon meringue pie." "I love ice cream. You think someone will bring ice cream?" "Dummy, it would melt."

"James and Francis!" Miss Cotter said. "Maybe your penmanship would be neater if you talked less and *concentrated more.*"

Well, Kat thought, at least Miss Cotter didn't rap their knuckles with her ruler—that hurt!

Kat, Lizabeth, and Amanda sat at a table with Joanna, Mabel, and Grace. They were practicing their sewing: two small running stitches forward and one stitch back to make a tight seam. Amanda's seam was neat and even. Kat didn't have the patience. Her running stitches galloped ahead.

"Much too large, Katherine," Miss Cotter corrected. "Please take them out and start again."

"Why do we have to learn this, Miss Cotter?" Lizabeth put down her practice cloth. "You can make a tighter seam with a sewing machine. With your foot on the treadle, it goes so fast."

"Not everyone has a sewing machine, Lizabeth," Miss Cotter said.

While Miss Cotter was busy teaching division to the third graders, Lizabeth whispered, "What's everyone wearing?"

"To the barn dance? I got the prettiest dress from Montgomery Ward. It just came last week," Amanda said. "It's dark red—the catalog calls it burgundy—and it has puffy shoulders and long, tight sleeves and a big sash."

"I don't understand clothes from a catalog." Lizabeth sniffed. "They're made in factories, with one person just doing sleeves and another just doing collars and . . . I don't see how they can possibly fit. I always have at least two fittings."

"Mine fits," Amanda said.

"I'm wearing my Alice-blue dress," Lizabeth said.

The whole country was in love with the president's beautiful oldest daughter, Alice; she was so lively and full of fun. Kat had read in the newspaper that Teddy Roosevelt himself had said, "I can do one of two things. I can be President of the United States or I can control Alice. I cannot possibly do both." That had to be said with a smile, of course. Alice was the ideal American girl.

"It has a wonderfully wide skirt," Lizabeth continued, "so when I swing around, it'll twirl and twirl. It has the tiniest tucks in the front. And I'm getting a rat for my hair."

"A rat?" Grace laughed. "Watch it doesn't bite you!"

"You know what I mean," Lizbeth said impatiently. "That padding to puff up my hair on top for a pompadour."

"Momma says pompadours are for older girls," Joanna said.

"I don't care—I'm having one for the dance," Lizbeth said.

Lizbeth was in a hurry to grow up, Kat thought. Next thing, she'd be lacing herself up in corsets! How could Ma and Aunt Sue move—or even breathe—in them?

"What are you wearing, Kat?" Lizbeth asked.

Kat shrugged. She didn't care much about fashion. Lizbeth would get all excited about her new dresses, made by a dressmaker with special fabric from the city. Amanda ordered hers from Sears and Montgomery Ward. She loved looking through the catalogs. Ma made Kat's dresses from Butterick patterns. She always picked the most durable fabrics from the bolts at the general store.

"My Sunday dress, I guess." Kat hadn't given it much thought before. But was it too plain? "You know the striped one with the pinafore? Do you think—"

"Lizbeth and Katherine!" Miss Cotter called. "I see your mouths moving but not your needles."

At recess on Wednesday, Amanda was helping Hannah and her friends skip rope.

Kat roamed the schoolyard with Lizabeth and Grace. She spotted James with the big boys who were playing mumblety-peg.

"James!" she called. He knew he wasn't allowed to play that game! He was too young to be flipping a pocket knife. There was a chance he'd flip it right into his foot instead of the ground!

James made a pleading face at her, but Kat shook her head "no." She kept her eye on him until he wandered over to see Roger's new wooden top.

". . . and gray suede boots with tiny little buttons going past my ankle and . . ." Grace was saying.

They were *still* talking about clothes. What a waste of recess! Soon it would be too cold to play outdoors.

"See you later." Kat headed for a group playing tag.

Lizabeth followed her. "Wait, Kat. I was thinking . . . I have a new dress. It's sort of jade green and it's really pretty, with the nicest ruffle at the bottom," Lizabeth said. "But the color's all wrong for me. It makes me look pale as a ghost."

What was Lizabeth talking about? She looked perfectly fine in green.

"It's a perfect color for *you*, though," Lizabeth continued. "Want to have it? You could wear it to the dance."

"Your dress?"

"I'll bring it to school for you tomorrow," Lizabeth said. "I can't wait to see how you look in it!"

"Thank you!" Kat gave her cousin a big hug. "Thank you, Lizabeth!" Kat didn't care much about clothes, not really. But when she heard Amanda and Lizabeth talking about their new dresses this morning . . . it would be nice to have a new dress to wear. And all of Lizabeth's things were so *pretty*!

Finally, it was Saturday night!

Lizabeth's dress was the most wonderful color, Kat thought, as if she'd mixed vermilion green with just a touch of cerulean blue. It had a deep ruffle at the bottom that swished around her feet. Kat couldn't help stroking the fabric—it was the smoothest, softest wool. It fit perfectly, too. It made her feel . . . well, different, in a new, good way.

Now that she was almost thirteen, it wouldn't hurt to do something more than braids, would it? That beautiful dress needed something more. Not a pompadour, but . . .

"Ma, would you curl my hair?"

Ma looked pleased. "You've never let me before. You really have beautiful hair, Kat. Come into the kitchen."

Ma heated the curling iron in the stove and wound strands of Kat's hair around it. Ugh, that thing was hot and it pulled and took forever.

"No more!" Kat said.

"I can't stop now," Ma said. "You can't have one side curled and the other straight."

"All right," Kat grumbled. "Are we almost finished?"

"Almost." Ma smiled. "They say you have to suffer for beauty."

"Almost" took a long time—but when Ma was done, Kat's hair flowed down her back in long, soft ringlets. As she entered the barn with Ma, Todd, and James, she found herself walking more slowly, letting the ruffle flutter gently around her legs. She felt pretty!

She heard the toe-tapping music and the fiddler calling, "Swing in the center, then break that pair; lady goes on, and gent stays there. . . ."

Papa met them at the door. He took Ma's hand and whirled her into the square dance. He was a surprisingly graceful dancer, even with his limp. Todd and James rushed to join the crowd at the long table on the side. It was piled high from end to end: potato salad, cole slaw, fried fish, fried chicken, beef hash, green beans, baked beans, a whole ham, deep-dish apple pie (that was Ma's), peach cobbler, and on and on. James was helping himself to a huge chunk of Mrs. White's famous lemon meringue pie. Out of Ma's sight, he always went straight for dessert.

Kat made her way through the barn, skirting around the lively dancers. The reverend was swinging a thrilled, laughing Hannah off her feet. Neighbors mingled on the sidelines and little children spun each other around with abandon. She said hello to many freshly scrubbed classmates and quickly found Amanda and Lizabeth.

"I don't think he'll be here," Amanda was saying.

"Well, he is," Lizabeth said. "Right there!"

Kat followed her glance. There was that boy from church standing across the room. He was tall, with brown hair and a firm chin. Amanda was right—he *was* handsome!

"Don't look," Amanda pleaded.

"He's staring at you," Kat said.

"Is he? Don't look, Kat!"

"And . . . he's coming over!" Kat said. She heard Amanda catch her breath.

And then he stood in front of them. He shifted awkwardly from foot to foot. Amanda looked at him, looked down, looked at him, looked away. If they're *both* going to be that shy, Kat thought, we'll be standing here in total silence forever!

"Hello, I'm Kat," she said.

"And I'm Lizabeth."

"I'm Amanda." Her words came out breathlessly.

"I know," he said. "Amanda Morgan. I—uh—found out."

Amanda blushed.

There was a long pause.

"You must have a name, too," Kat finally said to the boy.

"I . . . um . . ."

Had he forgotten his own name, Kat wondered. She and Lizabeth could have been invisible. His eyes were glued to Amanda.

"Um . . . do you think . . . um . . . Would you like to dance?" he asked.

Amanda nodded. She seemed to have lost the ability to speak, too. Kat grinned as she watched him take Amanda's hand and lead her to the dance area.

"Well, he's handsome," Lizabeth said. "I'll say that much for him."

"They look nice together," Kat said. "But does love

have to make you senseless?" Both girls giggled.

Kat would have kept watching them, but Billy from school asked her to dance. Then Mark, the blacksmith's son, who'd been her friend forever. Promenade. Do-si-do. Kat danced and danced, with Papa and then with Todd. With Mr. Thomas from the general store and more friends from school. To "Turkey in the Straw." To "The Arkansas Traveler." "Allemande left and allemande right," the fiddler called. Kat whirled and twirled, hair flying behind her, loving every minute of it. Finally, flushed and perspiring, she collapsed on a chair at the side.

That's when she saw Amanda. She was still dancing with that boy, in the center of the Virginia reel line. Her smile was radiant. Everything about Amanda was shining.

Kat wished she had someone to like, too. Someone she hadn't known her whole life, someone who could make her glow like that.

Lizabeth collapsed on the chair next to Kat's. Strands of hair were escaping from her pompadour. "I had the best time, didn't you?"

"Uh-huh." Kat glanced around the barn. It was emptying out. Soon Papa would be taking them home. Some of the women were gathering their pots and dishes. Her gaze stopped at a boy standing next to her cousin Christopher. She'd never seen him before. His eyes were a startling blue.

"Who's that?" Kat asked. "With your brother?" He had the blackest, shiniest hair.

"Oh, that's Michael," Lizabeth said. "Chris's friend from Cranberry. He's staying over this weekend."

Kat wished she had seen him earlier. She wished he had asked her to dance.

The next day the girls gathered in the tower. Half of the fun of the dance was talking about it later!

Amanda sat on the rag rug with her smoke-gray Sunday skirt billowing out all around her. ". . . and his name is Jed Langford," she was saying. "Isn't that the most beautiful name you ever heard?"

"It's a *name*, Amanda." Lizabeth had picked the chair nearest the warm stove. Kat was stoking the coals. It was cold even in the daytime now.

"He has four older brothers," Amanda went on, "and he *is* a deckhand, but he plans to be the captain of his own ship someday." Her eyes were glowing green. "And he has a pet goat and—"

"He seemed awfully shy last night," Lizabeth said.

"Oh, no, not at all—not once we got to talking," Amanda said.

"Looks like someone is going to come courting," Kat teased.

"Father would never allow that." Amanda's face fell. "I'm too young for courting. Not until I'm at least fifteen."

They had dozens of other things to talk about, but there was one sentence that Kat replayed in her mind later, over and over again.

"Michael asked Chris about you last night," Lizabeth had told her.

"He did?" Kat shrugged. She tried to sound just mildly curious. "What did he say?"

"'Who was that pretty redhead with your sister?'"

"He said that?"

"His exact words."

Who was that pretty redhead! Kat hugged the words to herself. That was *me*! Cranberry was close by. Maybe, cross her fingers, maybe she would see Michael again.

eight

By early November, it was freezing. Kat rushed home from school. She kept her hands in her coat pockets, but her fingertips still felt frozen. Mitten weather, she thought. She'd have to remember to wear them to school tomorrow.

She ran into the cottage, thinking of the blazing logs that would be in the fireplace. The door banged shut behind her.

"Kat," Ma said, "please don't slam the door."

"Oops, sorry." She didn't want to think about how often she'd been reminded to close the door quietly.

"You left your scarf and mittens home again."

"I know. I forgot." Kat shrugged off her coat.

"Where are the boys?"

"Coming along the lane. They've been dawdling all the way."

"I received a lovely gift from the Carstairses." Ma

opened a white cardboard box. "Look at this tablecloth, Kat. Isn't it lovely? Please don't touch unless your hands are absolutely clean. They shouldn't have; it wasn't at all necessary."

"It's really beautiful," Kat said. The fine beige linen had delicate lace inserts.

"And they sent something for you, too. On your bed."

"For me?" Kat ran up the stairs two at a time. The box on her bed was covered by the most beautiful paper, gold with red and blue designs. She'd never seen such fancy gift paper. In Cape Light, people wrapped presents in white paper from the general store or the bookshop.

Kat couldn't wait to open the package—but she did it slowly so she wouldn't tear that special paper, Then she folded it carefully to save it. A box of chocolates! Before dinner? Oh, well. She couldn't resist.

She popped a chocolate into her mouth. Mmmm, it had a delicious creamy filling that tasted of vanilla. Then another. This one had a different filling, cherry. She wanted to try them all, though she knew she really should save some for her family. Maybe just one more, just to see . . . That's when she noticed the envelope. A letter from the Carstairses!

Dear Katherine,

There is really no way to thank you for saving our lives. We owe everything to your quick thinking and courage.

We were most impressed by how very bright, talented, and curious you are. A close friend of ours is the headmaster of the Bartholomew School in Boston and we told him all about you. The Bartholomew School is well known for excellence and has an extremely selective admittance process. However, the headmaster agreed to admit you for the January semester if you would like to go. The school has challenging academics and an outstanding art program—we thought that might be of special interest to you.

They would waive room and board; that leaves the tuition of $50 per semester. Your tuition and the enclosed application, to be sent directly to the school, would be due by December 15th to hold a place for you for January. Of course, you'll want to talk this over with your parents and we'd be happy to answer any questions.

If you would rather remain in your school in Cape Light, we still hope that you'll visit us in Boston. We'd be delighted to welcome you to our city and our home.

With sincerest thanks,
Evelyn and Kenneth Carstairs

Katherine sat on her bed, stunned. She read the

Carstairses' words again. For a moment, she couldn't breathe.

Then she jumped up. "Ma! Papa! Everybody!" she screamed.

She heard Papa running toward the stairs. "Kat? What's wrong?"

"Nothing's wrong!" She raced down. Sunshine ran toward her, barking. "Everything's right! Everything's wonderful!"

Papa, Ma, Todd, and James had gathered at the foot of the stairs. "What?" "What is it?" "Kat, say something!"

"Papa, read this!" Kat's hand was shaking as she handed him the letter.

Papa read it. He frowned and silently passed it to Ma.

"What happened?" Todd said. "Isn't anyone going to tell me?" He grabbed the letter from Ma when she finished.

"That's a very nice gesture," Papa said. "But—"

"You're so young; you belong here with your family," Ma said. "Kat, write them a note. Say you appreciate the thought—"

"Appreciate the thought?" Kat exploded. "I'm going to Boston!"

"Kat, you know that's impossible," Papa's voice had become very quiet.

"It's not impossible! It's my dream come true!" Kat looked at their faces. "Why isn't everyone happy?"

"I'm happy," James piped up.

"I just wish they'd written to us first," Ma said, "instead of getting you all excited."

"Of course I'm excited! Why shouldn't I be?" Kat trailed Papa and Ma to the kitchen table. "They said they'll answer any questions you have. . . ."

James wandered away. Todd stayed in the doorway, listening.

"Fifty dollars for tuition. And that's just for one semester." Papa sighed as he sank into his chair. "Kat, we don't have that kind of money."

"Even if we were willing to send you so far away," Ma added.

"But Papa, they'll waive my room and board!" Kat sat down opposite him. "You read the letter. There's an outstanding art program! I'll get art training—the training I need and—and I'll live in a big city and I'll . . . it's everything I've always wanted!"

"What about the lighthouse?" Ma said. "We do need you here."

"I could take Kat's shift," Todd said. "If she went to Boston."

Kat looked at Todd gratefully. She knew he'd much rather read or play in his room. He was on her side.

"No, Kat. I can't pay for a private school," Papa said.

"It's my big opportunity!" Kat said. "You *can't* take it away from me! You can't!"

"Do you think I want to take anything away from you? Don't you know I'd give you the moon if I could?"

Kat had never seen her father look so defeated. It broke her heart to see it. She knew she should stop now—but she couldn't.

"All I'm asking for is a good school and—and a chance to make something of myself! Fifty dollars. That's not the moon!"

"I didn't raise you to be disrespectful. Stop badgering your father right now." Ma had placed a protective hand on Papa's shoulder. "You can make something of yourself without the Bartholomew School."

"But I *have* to go!"

"We get the cottage for free because we're the lighthouse keepers." Papa sounded very tired. "But we're responsible for maintaining it—you know that. And some months our stipend barely stretches to cover our expenses."

"But they'll waive room and board—"

"I'm sorry. The answer is no. End of discussion."

Kat didn't want to make her father feel bad but she couldn't give up. "We can save fifty dollars somehow, there must be a way and—"

"That's enough, Kat! Leave your father alone," Ma said.

"And I'll eat clam chowder every night of the week, I don't care, I don't need clothes or—"

"Katherine, I've always provided for this family!" Papa's voice had turned icy. He never called her "Katherine" unless he was furious. "There's always food on the table and shoes for my children. You've never wanted for anything!"

"I didn't mean . . ." Kat whispered. "I just thought . . . there must be a way we can—"

"Enough!" Papa thundered.

Two red circles formed on Kat's cheeks. She had hurt Papa's pride and she felt guilty. But he was hurting her, too. He wouldn't even listen!

She bit her lip as she helped Ma snap the beans.

Later, the dinner conversation flowed around and past her, and she didn't say a word. Papa said there might be more damage than broken shingles. Ma hoped not. Papa had to check the roof more carefully. Todd wanted to enter the spelling bee this year. James said his *real* best friend was Francis. . . . Everyone was acting normal, as if her dreams hadn't just been crushed!

It would be too terrible for this opportunity to come, just to be snatched away! She glanced at her father. All right, fifty dollars was more than he could afford. . . .

"Kat!"

"What, James?"

"I said, 'Please pass the bread.' *Twice.*"

Kat passed the basket. She nibbled at her food without tasting it. If only there was less tuition for Papa to pay. . . . If only . . . Maybe she could earn some of it herself!

Papa was starting on the bread pudding, his favorite dessert. He looked relaxed now. He was never angry for long. Did she dare?

"Papa?" Kat said.

He turned toward her.

"If it was less than fifty dollars—"

"But it's not," he interrupted. "Stop it, Kat. I want to eat my dinner in peace."

"Please, just listen," Kat pleaded. "What if I earn half of it by myself? If you only had to pay twenty-five dollars? Then could I go to the Bartholomew School?"

"How can you possibly earn twenty-five dollars? And by December fifteenth?" Papa said.

"But if I do," Kat said. "*If.*"

"If pigs had wings, they'd all fly." Papa poured fresh cream on his pudding.

"Kat, I think you need to give up on this," Ma said.

"Papa, if I have twenty-five dollars by December fifteenth, would you pay the rest?"

He sighed. "I suppose. But I don't see how you—"

Kat caught her breath. "Do you promise?"

"You certainly know how to wear a man down, Kat." Papa passed his hand across his forehead. "All right, I promise. If you can come up with twenty-five dollars, I guess I can, too."

Kat jumped up out of her seat and hugged him. "Thank you, Papa! Thank you!"

"I hope you're not planning to rob your uncle's bank." Joking, Kat knew, was her father's way of making up for yelling at her.

"No." Kat giggled.

She ran upstairs to write a letter to the Carstairses.

She wrote slowly, concentrating on good penmanship. She was very careful to avoid splotches when she dipped her pen in the ink bottle.

Dear Mr. and Mrs. Carstairs,

Thank you very much for the delicious chocolates. I love chocolate and these are the best I've ever had. And thank you for the wonderful opportunity to go to the Bartholomew School. I'm very happy to accept the offer and I'll send the application and the tuition to the school by December 15th.

Kat chewed on the pen as she thought about what to write next. She reread her last sentence and suddenly a prickly feeling came over her. How was she ever going to earn twenty-five dollars? It was already November seventh and she had no plan at all!

∽*nine*∾

The next morning, Kat walked to school with
Todd. For a long stretch of Lighthouse Lane,
they were quiet, deep in their own thoughts.
James ran ahead with his friend Francis.

"I can give you five dollars," Todd suddenly said.

"What? What do you mean?"

"For that school. I have the five dollars I saved
up from yard work last summer. And from my paper
route."

"Oh, Todd! I can't take your money," Kat said. "You
worked so hard for it."

"I want to give it to you," he said. "You'd help me
out, wouldn't you? If I needed it? For something really
important?"

"You know I would." Kat looked at him and smiled.
"You really understand, don't you? I think you're the only
one in the whole family who does. Todd . . . thank you."

Todd nodded. "You're welcome. Now you only need twenty."

"It sounds like a lot less that way, doesn't it? Thank you! I promise I'll pay you back someday."

"See, I have a dream, too, but I never say anything to anyone. All my friends want to be captains of their own boats or own their own farms. I want something different."

Her brother was the quiet, thoughtful one in the family. "What's your dream?" Kat often wondered what was going on in his mind. "Come on, Todd, what is it?"

"I want to be an inventor! Like Alexander Graham Bell and Thomas Watson. Well, they've already invented the telephone . . ." Todd grinned. "Beat me to it! But I want to be an inventor like them and I'd think up my *own* ideas."

They left Lighthouse Lane and turned south onto William McKinley Road. Kat checked on James. He was still in sight, running toward the school with his friend.

"See, everything's changing so fast now," Todd said. "Electricity, flying machines . . . Something new every single day! I bet there'll be things no one can even imagine yet. So I want to invent some of them. Well, what do you think? You think it sounds impossible or conceited or—?"

"It sounds just right. I think you can do just about

anything you put your mind to." Kat took Todd's hand and squeezed it. "Thank you for telling me about your dream."

Lizabeth and Amanda were standing on the front steps of the school. Miss Cotter hadn't rung the big brass bell yet.

"Twenty dollars?" Amanda's eyes opened wide when Kat told them her news. "That's a lot!"

Kat's shoulders sagged. "I don't even know where to start."

"We'll help you," Amanda said.

"Here's how my father says you make money," Lizabeth said. "You make a product that everyone wants and sell it a fair price."

Miss Cotter was in the doorway, swinging the bell in her hand.

"I don't have a product." Kat slowly started up the steps.

"Girls, come along!" Miss Cotter called.

"Don't worry, we'll find a way," Amanda said.

Miss Cotter kept them busy all morning. She drilled them on the multiplication tables. Then the older boys did woodwork while the girls sewed. Miss Cotter asked

Kat to help the second graders draw with crayons. Crayons were new to Cape Light. Kat didn't like them that much. They were too waxy and didn't blend well. At least they didn't drip all over the second graders the way paint did.

Amanda, across the room at the sewing table, mouthed, "I have an idea."

"What?" Kat mouthed back.

There was no chance to talk. Everyone, except for the very youngest, was asked to line up in front of the room to practice for the spelling bee.

"Children, this year the spelling bee will be held in the courthouse! It's going to be a big event."

A buzz of excitement filled the room. Everyone in town would come out to be entertained by the spelling bee.

"The Cranberry schools will be taking part, too," Miss Cotter continued. "And Mrs. Cornell will be donating a prize from the Pelican Street Bookshop."

She'd probably be gone by then, Kat thought, but it didn't matter. There had to be a lot more going on in Boston than a spelling bee! She wasn't a great speller anyway.

Finally, it was recess. Kat and Lizabeth ran to Amanda in the schoolyard. "What's your idea? What is it?"

"*Everyone* loves ice cream," Amanda said. "It's the perfect product!"

"But how can we—?" Lizabeth started.

"There's a lady named Nancy Johnson—I read about her in the *Saturday Evening Post*," Amanda continued. "She invented a hand-cranked freezer that allows ice cream to be made at home—very easily, the article said."

"That's brilliant!" Kat said.

Lizabeth frowned. "But who has a hand-cranked freezer?"

"Cranking just means turning it, doesn't it?" Kat said. "Stir it, that's all it means."

Lizabeth brightened. "And freezing—ice from the icebox."

"All we need is cream, ice, and flavoring, and we'll keep mixing until it turns into ice cream," Amanda said. "Delicious!"

"And profitable," Lizabeth added. "Everyone loves ice cream."

"Exactly." Amanda smiled.

"If we sell it on the village green and charge fifteen cents, and suppose that thirty people come by . . . I bet we get lots of repeat customers," Kat said. "Thirty times fifteen is—"

"We can't charge that much," Amanda said. "At the restaurant in Cranberry, ice cream costs ten cents a dish."

"All right. Ten cents," Kat agreed.

"Thirty times ten . . . three dollars in one afternoon," Lizabeth said.

"It's November eighth—I have plenty of afternoons left before December fifteenth!" Kat felt as though a huge weight had been lifted from her shoulders.

"I bet you'll have a lot extra left over," Lizabeth said. "You could buy beautiful elbow-length kid gloves or . . ."

"We should get started right away," Kat said.

"My house tomorrow after school," Lizabeth said. "Mother is taking Christopher and Tracy to the dentist and it's the cook's day off, so the kitchen will be ours. I'll ask Ada to get lots of cream for us before she leaves."

"I'll arrange for Hannah to play at Mary Margaret's tomorrow," Amanda said.

"Wonderful!" Kat beamed. Anything was possible when good friends put their heads together.

"First, the bowl." Lizabeth reached to the top of the cupboard for a large, deep bowl.

"Next, the cream," Kat said. There were three big

pitchers. Ada had actually followed Lizabeth's instructions and had all that cream ready and waiting for them. The girls poured it into the yellow ceramic bowl. "Well, that's easy!"

"Now for the ice," Amanda said.

They looked at the large blocks of ice in the icebox. "We've got to chip some off," Lizabeth said.

That wasn't so easy. They tried chipping it with kitchen knives but it was too rock-hard. Lizabeth found a hammer in a drawer and they took turns swinging it. Shards of ice flew wildly onto the floor. The girls slipped and slid.

"We *can't* use it off the floor," Amanda said.

"But there's so much of it, all our effort is wasted. . . ." Kat moaned.

"We *can't.*"

"All right. I know what, put clean towels down to catch it." Kat banged the hammer and loosened some big chunks. They were collected and added to the bowl.

Lizabeth took some big swings at the ice and massaged her arm. "I think that's enough."

"No, we need more to make it freeze." Kat landed the hammer again and again. She switched from her right hand to her left. Pieces of ice of all sizes swam in the cream. "Now *that* looks like enough."

"What flavor do we want?" Lizabeth rummaged in the cupboard. "There's strawberry jam and apple jelly and . . . squash preserves, no! Wait, here's some baker's chocolate! The package says it's from San Francisco."

"Oh, good, everybody likes chocolate," Amanda said.

They stared at the dark thick bars on the wooden counter.

"I guess we ought to chop it up," Lizabeth said.

"Some," Kat agreed, "but we don't have to do that much. It'll all blend in with the cream when we mix it."

Lizabeth found two large serving spoons and a soup ladle. First they took turns mixing. Then they all crowded around the bowl and stirred in unison. They mixed until their arms ached, with big sweeps of the bowl and little ones. Kat tried using her spoon as a beater. So then they beat and mixed. Strangely enough, the contents of the bowl didn't look much like ice cream. Big chunks of ice floated next to chunks of chocolate. The cream took on a brownish hue. It became more liquid as narrow ice shards melted.

Amanda stopped. "Something's wrong."

"I know!" Kat snapped her fingers. "It needs salt! I'm sure I've heard something about salt and freezing."

"Well, let's see." Lizabeth emptied a big salt shaker into the bowl.

They stirred it around and around. The strange brownish color of the cream became somewhat darker.

Kat's face fell. "It's not setting. It's definitely still liquid."

"So it's not ice cream," Lizabeth admitted. "We'll call it an ice cream *drink*!"

Kat brightened. "*Chocolate ice cream drink.* Doesn't that sound good?"

"And then we won't even need to hand out spoons. Only cups," Lizabeth said.

"I think we'd better taste it first," Amanda said.

"Go ahead."

Amanda dipped a spoon into the mix and sipped. She swallowed hard.

"Well, what? What?" the others prompted.

"It's, um, salty."

"Oh. Well, yes. I guess it needs sugar," Kat said.

"Lots of sugar," Amanda added. "The chocolate is bitter!"

Lizabeth poured a one-pound bag of sugar into the bowl. They stirred some more.

"We'd better get it out to the green now," Kat said. "I have to be home in time for my lighthouse watch."

At the village green, the girls set up a card table. They

lined up paper cups around the big bowl and chanted, "I scream, you scream, we all scream for ice cream! A brand-new chocolate ice drink! Come one, come all. Only ten cents a cup!"

A lot of people scurried past through the blustery wind. Mr. Thomas paused for a moment on his way across the lawn.

"Now if you were selling *hot* chocolate on a day like this, I'd be a customer," he said.

"I never thought of that," Amanda mumbled. "It is kind of cold for ice cream."

"Especially ice cream that isn't . . . quite ice cream," Lizabeth added.

"Don't give up, we're just getting started!" Kat insisted. "Come one, come all! A new chocolate ice cream drink! Chocolate all the way from San Francisco! Only ten cents a cup!"

A few people stopped, peered into the bowl, and hastily went on.

"A brand-new chocolate ice cream drink! Only eight cents a cup!" the girls chanted.

And after a while, "Step right up and try our chocolate ice cream drink! Only five cents a cup!"

Mr. Alveira, from the Alveira & Sons Boatyard,

stopped. He smiled at them sympathetically. "Well, if you girls are working so hard, I'll have to try a cup. Here you go." He handed a nickel to Kat. Then, as Lizabeth poured for him, he took a closer look into the bowl. "It looks like, um, exactly what's in that?"

"Only the freshest ingredients, Mr. Alveira," Kat told him. "Fresh dairy cream and chocolate from San Francisco and—"

He hesitated. Three pairs of hopeful eyes were glued to him. Bravely, he raised the paper cup to his lips and took a sip. He sputtered and coughed. Kat was alarmed. Was one of the chocolate chunks stuck in his throat? Or even worse, a shard of ice *piercing* it?

"Are you all right, Mr. Alveira? Nod if you want me to pat your back!"

He caught his breath. "No, thank you," he managed to cough out. He handed the half-full cup back to Kat and cleared his throat. "I'm not . . . very thirsty." He walked away as fast as he could without actually running.

Kat followed him. "Mr. Alveira? Do you want your nickel back?"

"No, that's quite all right, Katherine. . . . Good luck with your, er, concoction."

Kat went back to Amanda and Lizabeth. "I think . . .

I think we'd better stop."

"I vote for pouring the whole thing down the sewer," Lizabeth said.

"Oh, no!" Amanda said. "It's wrong to waste food. I mean, all that cream and chocolate! My father teaches us to respect good food, especially when there are so many needy people."

Kat agreed. "It's sinful to throw it away. Just the cream alone— It should be put to use."

"Well, what do you plan to do with it?" Lizabeth asked. "If you give it to charity, I don't think they'll be grateful."

"We have to drink it ourselves," Kat said.

Amanda nodded.

"Count me out," Lizabeth said. She watched as they drank their first cup. "What does it taste like?"

"Very rich," Kat said.

"And very sweet," Amanda said.

"With a kind of salty thing around the edges," Kat added.

"And very, *very* rich," Amanda repeated. "With lumps."

They each forced down a second cup. It seemed as though they hadn't even made a dent in the brimming bowl.

"You're not going to finish all of it, are you?" Lizabeth asked.

"I'll try." Kat's voice had become very small. "Waste not, want not." She glanced at Amanda. Amanda downed her third cup. Her face looked drawn; her skin had taken on a greenish pallor. Kat suspected she looked the same way.

Kat started another cup. The excess sweetness made her mouth pucker. A lump of bitter chocolate sat in her mouth. "I can't do this," she whispered.

"Me either," Amanda moaned. "I'm . . . I'm sick to my stomach."

Kat and Amanda reeled along Lighthouse Lane to their homes. Kat continued on alone, taking deep shuddery breaths all the way. She skipped dinner that evening. At the sight of the remaining chocolates from the Carstairses, she clapped her hand over her mouth.

It was November ninth and she was exactly one nickel closer to her goal—at the cost of feeling horribly guilty about nice Mr. Alveira. On the bright side, she thought, she was forever cured of her sweet tooth.

fter school the next day, the girls walked along Lighthouse Lane.

"Were you sick last night?" Amanda asked Kat.

"Well . . . not seriously," Kat said.

"Father was upset that I didn't eat dinner," Amanda said.

"Let's please forget about ice cream drinks," Kat said.

"Are we really going to do *yard work* all afternoon?" Lizabeth asked.

"I can't think of anything else right now," Kat said. "You don't have to."

Lizabeth sighed. "I said I'd help, so I will."

"The good thing about raking leaves," Kat said, "is that new ones keep falling. So we'll have lots of repeat customers."

"We'll need dozens of customers to earn twenty dollars," Lizabeth said.

"Twenty dollars minus a nickel," Kat corrected. "I'll have to work every single day." It was already November tenth and December fifteenth wasn't that far off. "Look, that front yard is drowning in leaves! Let's go."

Kat led the way up the front path and rang the doorbell.

Mrs. Peterson opened the door. "Katherine, Amanda, and Lizabeth, my three favorite young ladies. You all looked lovely at the barn dance, all grown up."

"Thank you, Mrs. Peterson," Lizabeth said.

"Mrs. Peterson? We saw the leaves in your yard," Kat said, "and we could rake them up for you. It's only twenty cents for all three of us."

"I don't think so, Katherine."

"Or fifteen cents," Kat pleaded.

"We'd bag them neatly," Amanda said, "and do a clean job for you."

"They do need raking, but it's not a job for girls," Mrs. Peterson said. "I'm sorry, but I'd feel very uncomfortable."

"But Mrs. Peterson—"

Mrs. Peterson shook her head. "It's just not appropriate."

Kat, Amanda, and Lizabeth went from house to house along the lane.

Mr. Whipple looked amazed at the idea. "Girls raking? I don't think so!" He turned to Lizabeth. "I could use some help if your brother Christopher's interested."

"Young Jimmy Hanlon does all my odd jobs." Mrs. Killigrew frowned. "Amanda, does your father know you're doing this?"

Mrs. Lee said, "Young ladies asking for yard work? I never heard of such a thing!"

The three trudged on. At one house, there was a compliment for Lizabeth's new coat. At another, someone sent regards to Kat's mother. But everywhere they went the answer was no.

Mr. Justin turned them down, too, but then he said, "Try Potter's orchard. They had a huge crop this year and they're desperate for more pickers. They might even take on girls."

"Thank you, Mr. Justin!" The bounce was back in Kat's step on her way down his path. "I never thought of that. We can pick apples!"

"Potter's Orchard! That's at least a mile from here," Lizabeth complained.

"One mile isn't that far," Amanda said.

But the mile ran mostly uphill along curving roads. And what made it seem extra far to Kat was having to listen to Lizabeth all along the way. "This is ruining my new shoes," and "I'm not dressed for hiking," and "I'm used to riding in a horse and carriage."

"Lizabeth, we're almost there," Kat said wearily.

They passed farmland with widely spaced houses. They passed by a red barn and a pasture with grazing cows. They passed neat haystacks. Kat was about to jump into one, but no, she had serious business to take care of today.

Kat didn't want to admit it, but by the time they reached Potter's, she was worn out. Amanda said, "I feel like we've done an afternoon's work before we've even worked."

At the orchard, they made their way through long aisles of apple trees. The winey fragrance of ripening apples drifted through the air. They passed groups of men and boys hoisting baskets of apples and climbing up ladders. They found Mr. Potter near the main house.

"Mr. Potter, we heard you need pickers," Amanda said.

"And here we are, all ready to work," Kat added.

"*Girls* picking?" Mr. Potter scratched his white beard. "I don't know about this."

"Please, Mr. Potter," Lizabeth said. "We came a long way."

"We're good workers," Kat said.

"It's a sin to let the apples rot on the trees," Amanda said.

He hesitated and cleared his throat and hesitated some more. Finally he said, "All right. Bushel baskets, ten cents for each full basket."

Kat nodded eagerly.

"Get your baskets from Hiram over there—the tall man in the checked shirt—and bring them back to me when they're full."

"Yes, sir!" Kat said. "Where do we get the ladders?"

"I don't want you on ladders," Mr. Potter said. "Pick whatever you can reach."

"But—but why can't we use ladders?"

"I have daughters of my own and I'm not about to have any girls climbing ladders! If I wasn't so short-handed today . . ." He pointed to the far edge of the orchard. "Start over there, by the fence."

The man named Hiram looked surprised as he gave them baskets.

The fence was far away from any of the other workers. "I guess Mr. Potter doesn't want anyone to see that he hired us," Amanda said.

There weren't many apples on the lowest branches and they had to reach up high to pick even those. Kat's shoulder began to ache from the constant stretching. Amanda stood on tiptoe; her lips were set in a grim line. After a few tries at reaching for the crop, Lizabeth sat down against the trunk of the tree and munched on a McIntosh.

Kat glanced at her. "We'll never get anything done that way."

"We're not getting anything done anyway," Lizabeth answered.

It was true; apples barely covered the bottom of one basket.

"What if I shake the tree?" Kat asked.

"It's too big to shake and if the apples fall, they'll be bruised," Amanda said.

"I know, I'll climb up and hand them down to you," Kat said. She found a toehold and shimmied up to a crotch in the trunk. It had been a lot easier to climb when she was younger, when she could still wear tights and skirts to just below the knee, like Tracy and Hannah. Kat handed a few apples down to Amanda and Lizabeth, but the big crop was still too high to reach. She had nothing to show for her effort but a skinned ankle.

Kat jumped down to the ground. "This doesn't make sense. I need a ladder."

"But Mr. Potter said—" Amanda started.

"You can't climb up a ladder. Your *unmentionables* will show!" Lizabeth said.

"So what? There's no one here but us." Kat looked around the orchard. "I'm going to look for one!"

Kat walked through aisles of trees. The other crews were almost out of sight. Far off in the distance she saw a shed and a boy going toward it, carrying a ladder over his shoulder.

She ran down toward the boy. "Hey! If you're through with it, I want it!"

The boy turned around. His hair was as black as a raven's wing and his eyes were startlingly blue. It was *him*! The boy from the barn dance, Christopher's friend Michael!

"What do you want with a ladder?" he asked. "Wait a minute! You're Lizabeth's friend, aren't you? Is it Cat, as in 'meow'?"

"K-A-T, short for Katherine."

"Oh. Then I can call you Katie."

"You can call me that but I won't answer," Kat said.

"What?"

"That's not my name. I mean, no one calls me Katie. Well . . . I guess you can . . . if you want to. I don't mind if . . . I mean, maybe I'd answer if—" She stopped short; she was babbling like an idiot!

Kat squirmed under his blue-eyed stare. She didn't know what to do with her arms and legs. She had to say *something*. "What are you doing here? I thought you lived in Cranberry."

"How do you know where I live?"

Oh, no. Now he knew she'd been asking about him! She could tell by his big grin. Kat prayed she wouldn't blush.

"Mr. Potter's my uncle. I come here to help out in picking season. What are *you* doing here?"

"Picking," Kat said. "Apples."

"You?" His eyebrows lifted. "No, seriously."

"Yes! What's so strange about that?" All day long people had been telling her what girls shouldn't do. She was sick and tired of it! "And I need the ladder," Kat said.

He took in the long skirt that reached her ankles. "You're planning to climb up in that?"

"Of course I am! What's the problem? It's not my fault if I don't have trousers!" She'd have to hike up her skirt and her petticoat. Lizabeth's warnings came back to her. "But don't look, all right? Promise."

"I promise." He looked confused. "But . . . don't look at what?"

"Oh, never mind!" Kat wanted to kick herself for saying anything. She sure wasn't going to explain! "Please just give me the ladder!"

"You can't carry it by yourself."

"I can so carry it! As well as anybody! Why does everyone think girls are so helpless?"

"Listen, Katie, I'm only trying to act like a gentleman."

"Just put it up on my shoulder!"

Michael laughed. "All right! I'm not about to fight with a prickly redhead." His hand grazed her shoulder to adjust the ladder and Kat was surprised by the shivery feeling that ran up her back.

"I swear, I've never met a girl like you before."

Was that good or terrible, Kat wondered. Just possibly, just maybe, it was good because he said it with such a friendly smile. As if, maybe, he liked her! Wait, was that a nice smile, or was he *laughing* at her? How dare he!

Kat carried the ladder back to Lizabeth and Amanda. *Prickly*, on second thought, definitely wasn't good. Well, she didn't care a bit. Michael was horrible!

She steadied the ladder against the trunk and pulled her skirt up out of the way in spite of Lizabeth's shocked expression. Kat took a cautious look around. Michael was way off in the distance somewhere. She couldn't see the shed through the trees. She climbed up to a big bunch of apples.

The girls fell into a work rhythm. Kat handed apples to Amanda, standing on a lower rung; Amanda gave them to Lizabeth, who placed them in the basket.

They didn't know she'd met Michael, Kat thought. She never kept anything from her friends but there was nothing at all to tell, was there? Except that Michael made her feel bewildered and jangled. Maybe if she saw him again . . . How could she have forgotten? She'd be far away in Boston.

As the afternoon light began to fade, three very tired girls dragged three baskets of apples to Mr. Potter at the main house.

Mr. Potter examined the baskets. "*Almost* full, but not to the top. All right," he said. "I'll give you ten cents for each. Thirty cents."

"Thank you!" Kat said. "We'll come back tomorrow."

"No, I have some other crews coming tomorrow."

"But we did a good job," Kat protested. "We'll start earlier—we'll fill them all the way."

"No. Thank you, girls. You did fine, better than I expected, but this isn't women's work."

If Kat heard that one more time! She glanced at Lizabeth and Amanda; no reaction at all. If "women's work" seemed normal to everyone else—to Ma, even to her best friends—then maybe she was truly odd to object.

On the long walk back to Lighthouse Lane Kat did the arithmetic. "Thirty cents from twenty dollars leaves nineteen dollars and seventy cents. Minus one nickel. . . . Nineteen dollars and sixty-five cents to go." She sighed. "I have nowhere near enough."

"We'll find something else to do," Amanda said.

"Ten cents each," Kat said slowly. "The two of you earned your share. It's really yours, and I don't know if I should—"

"Of course you should," Lizabeth said. "We *want* to help."

"That's what friends are for," Amanda added.

"I spent all my savings on a new parasol," Lizabeth said. "It's aquamarine with the prettiest ruffle. But now I wish I still had the money to give to you."

"I love you both so much!" Kat pulled them into a big bear hug. "I'm so lucky to have such good friends."

As long as she was with Amanda and Lizabeth, Kat didn't feel too discouraged. But when they separated at Lighthouse Lane and Kat walked on to Durham Point by herself, reality washed over her. It was November tenth and she had to allow time for the mail to reach Boston by December fifteenth. She had only four weeks left.

Kat came home from the orchard barely in time for her lighthouse shift. She gobbled down a quick supper and automatically started to reach for an apple from the bowl on the table to take up to the tower with her. Wait, the last thing on earth she wanted was an apple!

Kat settled into her chair and scanned the horizon. The sun was setting and turning the sea into glorious shades of rose and gold. It was a scene begging for her watercolors. The light of the kerosene lantern was too dim for mixing colors, but at least she could sketch. She had read somewhere that the human hand was the hardest thing to draw well. She could use her left hand as a model and sketch with her right. The more she practiced, the better she'd be when she arrived in Boston. *If* she arrived in Boston. No, she wouldn't allow herself to doubt. She *had* to think of something she could do to make money.

Kat crossed to the shelf where she kept her art supplies. She picked up her sketch pad and the Carstairses' letter peeked from between the pages. The letter was grimy and wrinkled from her many rereadings. Next to it was the carefully folded gift paper that had wrapped the box of chocolates. Kat touched it gently.

Suddenly, Kat's eyes widened. Yes, this was it. She had the answer right in front of her nose!

∼eleven∼

The gift paper, with its red and blue designs over a shiny gold background, was beautiful. Any gift, even the simplest, would seem special wrapped in paper like that. So different from the plain white paper they had in Cape Light.

Kat examined the paper more closely. The red and blue were curlicued squiggles, pretty, but not hard to imitate. Could she? Of course! She didn't have shiny gold paper like that, but she could paint designs all over a white background, pale blue and lilac snowflakes for winter, red and green bells for Christmas. Or red-striped candy canes, or green pinecones! Winding yellow or pink ribbons for birthdays, red hearts for Valentine's Day, colorful dots for any-occasion gifts. . . . Kat caught her breath as ideas kept coming. This was something she could do and surely the people of Cape Light would want it. Maybe she could sell her gift paper to the general store and the Pelican Street Bookshop! She needed to make samples.

For the rest of the evening, Kat squinted in the light of the lantern and painted designs on the pages of her watercolor tablet. She labored over the pale blue and lilac snowflakes, each one different. She was pleased with the results. Next, she painted scattered red balloons with trailing strings. There was a flutter of excitement in Kat's stomach. This was going well! Oh, she wished she didn't have to keep stopping to scan the horizon! But it was her job and she did it, however impatiently. Yellow stars . . . she redid them; they looked nicer if they weren't too crowded. The bright red hearts were easy. They went fast.

At the end of her shift, Kat nodded with satisfaction. Almost a dozen pages of designs were propped up to dry on the shelf.

The next day, Kat was anxious as she climbed up the ladder to the tower. Would her designs still look as good in daylight? In the tower, she examined them critically. She tore up the green pinecones: the color was muddy and you couldn't tell what they were supposed to be. The stars, well, chrome yellow was too garish; pale yellow would be prettier. She'd redo them. The rest had turned out well, she thought. Kat picked the best samples to show.

On her way to Lighthouse Lane she waved to Papa on the roof of the cottage. He'd been working up there for days.

"Morning, Papa," she called.

"Morning, Kat," he called back. "I saw your pages on my watch last night. Different from the things you usually paint. Nice, though." He moved gingerly from one part of the roof to another. "What are they for?"

Kat hesitated. Her gift paper might go the way of the ice cream drink and the raking project. It would be better to surprise him later, if this worked out. "Just something I'm trying," Kat called back.

At the general store, Mr. Thomas studied the snowflake page. "Hmmmm," he said.

Kat held her breath and crossed her fingers.

"Gift paper, eh?"

"Yes, sir." Kat's mouth was dry. She fidgeted nervously.

"Just the other day Mrs. White was in for the mister's birthday present and she was pining for some fancy wrapping. I'll tell you what, Katherine, I'll try the snowflakes. And the ribbons. And . . . hmmm . . . the dots, too. I'll try a dozen sheets of each. Thirty-five cents a dozen."

"Thank you, Mr. Thomas! But Mr. Thomas, they're hand-painted." There was a sudden catch in Kat's voice. Was she pushing too hard? She'd never done anything like this before!

"Hmmmm. All right, forty cents a dozen, paid on delivery."

"Thank you!" Her first sale! "I'll have them ready for you in no time! I'll need some of your white wrapping paper to paint on."

Mr. Thomas unrolled the spool of wrapping paper behind the counter. "Let's say . . . two feet for each sheet. That should be big enough to wrap most anything."

Kat watched him cut the paper into two-foot sections and place them in a brown paper bag. Forty cents for a dozen sheets, times three. One dollar and twenty cents!

Flushed with success, Kat stopped in at the bakery.

Mr. Witherspoon stood behind the counter in a smock dusted with flour.

"Hello there, Katherine. Was there much storm damage out your way?"

"Some broken shingles on the cottage roof."

"Not too bad, I hope. Well, what'll it be today? I have some nice chocolate cookies still warm from the oven."

"No, thank you, Mr. Witherspoon, I've sort of given up chocolate. I'm here to show you my samples."

"Samples? What kind of samples?"

"For gift wrapping paper." She spread her pages out on the counter. She was less nervous now that she had practiced on Mr. Thomas. "I thought you might want some."

"Nice, but what do I need with wrapping paper? Everything here goes into cardboard boxes."

"Mr. Witherspoon, lots of people bring a box of cookies when they go visiting. If they wrapped the box in pretty paper . . . well, that's more of a gift, isn't it? Or cakes for special occasions?"

"That's not a bad idea." Mr. Witherspoon cleared his throat as he thought. "Those dots . . . They're cheerful, aren't they? And the Christmas bells, though Christmas is still far off."

"It'll be here before you know it," Kat said.

"How much do you want for it?"

"Only forty cents for a dozen sheets. Two-foot sheets."

Mr. Witherspoon frowned.

"Mr. Witherspoon, it's all hand-painted."

"I don't know . . . I don't know . . . Well, all right. I'll see how it goes over with my customers. I'll try the dots and the Christmas bells."

Forty cents times two is eighty cents, Kat thought, plus one dollar and twenty cents from Mr. Thomas. She'd be getting two dollars!

On her way to Pelican Street and the bookshop, Kat hummed a bit of the popular song "Meet Me in St. Louis, Louis" but the words in her mind were "Meet Me in Boston, Boston. . . ."

Mrs. Cornell at the Pelican Street Bookshop didn't hesitate the way Mr. Thomas and Mr. Witherspoon had.

"These are lovely, Katherine—especially the snow-flakes," she said. "Each one is different; you can see immediately that they're handmade. I'll take three dozen of the snowflakes and three dozen of the ribbons. The hearts would be nice for Valentine's Day. Maybe I'll order them later."

"Thank you, Mrs. Cornell. I'll just need some plain wrapping paper to paint on."

Mrs. Cornell unrolled her white paper. "Have you thought of making matching gift cards, too, Katherine?

I'd add twenty-five cents for each set of twelve cards."

"All right! I'll get it all to you by the end of the month."

"That's fine. Katherine, can you make Valentine's cards, beautiful lacey ones with ribbons and trimmings, roses and forget-me-nots, something obviously hand-made? I'd pay fifty cents each for something spectacular. They'd have to be truly special."

"I can do that, Mrs. Cornell." Could she? Kat bit her lip.

"Show me a sample and I'd order in February."

"Mrs. Cornell, I'll get the samples to you fast. If you like them—if you could see your way to ordering them ahead of time—I need to earn a lot before December fif-teenth."

"You have a real talent for design, Katherine. I'm betting they'd be wonderful. All right, if you deliver two sets of heart paper and matching gift cards, and when I see your Valentine card sample I'd order say, twenty-five of those. You may deliver early and I'll keep them in stock."

"Thank you, Mrs. Cornell. Thank you so much!"

Numbers and orders were dancing in Kat's head. She rushed home to write it all down.

Mr. Thomas, general store

1 dz snowflakes	.40
1 dz ribbons	.40
1 dz dots	.40

Mr. Witherspoon, bakery

1 dz dots	.40
1 dz Christmas bells	.40

Mrs. Cornell, bookshop

3 dz snowflakes	1.20
3 dz matching gift cards	.75
3 dz ribbons	1.20
3 dz matching gift cards	.75
2 dz hearts	.80
2 dz matching gift cards	.50
25 Valentine's cards @.50	12.50
Total	$19.70

Kat added it up twice to make sure she wasn't making a mistake. A total of $19.70 plus thirty cents from the orchard, five dollars from Todd, and one nickel: twenty-five dollars and five cents. Even one nickel extra! She'd have to make her deliveries before December fifteenth. Well, by December seventh to allow for the mail. Less than one month to go.

Boston, here I come!

❧ *twelve* ❧

That afternoon, Kat rushed to the tower and painted snowflakes. The first three sheets were fun. She stretched her arms and back muscles before she started the fourth. And again before the fifth. And the sixth. Kat rolled her shoulders and checked the list of orders. Four dozen sheets of snowflakes. Forty-two more to go!

Ma called her to the cottage for supper. Kat ate quickly, with snowflakes swimming before her eyes.

"You're so quiet tonight," Ma said.

"I'm tired, I guess," Kat answered. Forty-two more plus thirty-six matching gift cards! She ate the chicken potpie in front of her automatically. She still had ribbons, dots, and hearts to do—and Valentine's cards. Getting the orders was the *easy* part!

Kat took a hurricane lamp from the kitchen back to the tower so that along with the kerosene lantern, she would have more light. She diluted cobalt violet with lots of water and a touch of gray for soft lavender snowflakes. She dipped her brush in cerulean blue with just a drop of violet for other snowflakes. Together, the colors were ethereal, until they blurred in front of her eyes. Snowflake after snowflake. Kat put down her brush and stretched. She scanned the horizon. The sea was calm tonight and a full moon floated in a starry sky. How strange it would feel, not being here to see this! But each snowflake was one step closer to Boston. Kat picked up her brush again. She painted until Pa came up for his shift.

"You look tired, Kat. Go on to bed."

"I will. You look tired, too, Pa."

"I've been working up on the roof all day." He sank into a chair. "Good night, kitten."

In her room, Kat moved Sunshine over to the foot of her bed and got under the covers. She fell asleep as soon as her head touched the pillow. She had disturbing dreams of dancing snowflakes pinching and poking her with sharp crystal edges.

After school on Monday, Amanda said, "I'll help you. Tell me how."

"Me, too," Lizabeth added.

They were sitting cross-legged on the floor of the tower, watching Kat paint multicolored dots.

"Thank you, but there's nothing I can think of right now." Kat sighed. "Except for keeping me company." She still had more snowflakes to finish and she hadn't started on the ribbons and Christmas bells yet. "But if you have any bits of lace and red or pink ribbon, for when I start on the Valentine's Day cards . . . the Valentine's cards will be the hardest," Kat said. "And twenty-five of them! How will I ever get them done in time?"

Kat painted the gift paper while Lizabeth and Amanda were there, and continued to paint after they left. She painted every afternoon after school and all during her watch by the light of the lantern and two hurricane lamps. November fourteenth, November fifteenth, November sixteenth. The week went by in a blur of ribbons, snowflakes, dots, Christmas bells.

On November seventeenth, Kat's hand cramped from holding the paintbrush for so long. She soaked her hand in warm water and wriggled her fingers. There, that felt better, but she definitely needed a break!

On November twentieth, Amanda gave Kat an idea. They took a raw potato from the kitchen and cut it in half. Kat carved the shape of a heart into it. Amanda dipped it into red paint and pressed it onto scrap paper. If it worked, Amanda and Lizabeth could do some sheets and it would go so much faster. Kat examined the scrap. No, the hearts' edges didn't come out sharp enough and making every heart an exact duplicate didn't look as good. She had promised hand-painted designs and she had shown samples of her very best work. It wouldn't be fair to deliver any less.

Just when Kat thought she couldn't face one more Christmas bell, a letter came from the Carstairses.

Dear Katherine,

Thank you for your letter. We're delighted that you plan to enroll in the Bartholomew school. We think you'll love it.

The brochure we sent gives you and your parents some basic information, but we thought we'd add some of our impressions.

The school is in Back Bay, one of the nicest residential neighborhoods of Boston. The girls' dormitory is across from the main building on Clarendon Street. There are six girls to a room. The rooms are not luxurious, but they seem spacious. The girls' dining hall downstairs was changed very little when the building was converted from a private townhouse. It has beautiful wood carvings, a huge fireplace, and a crystal chandelier. One evening a week it is the setting of a tea for the girls and a visitor, perhaps one of Boston's many writers or artists. Once a month or so the girls are taken to the Music Hall, the opera, or the theater.

The art studio is on the top floor of the main building, with lots of natural light from the skylights. You can use the studio for your own projects when a class is not in session.

We thought you might like to see the school for yourself before you enroll. You're very welcome to stay at our house. Let us know and we'll work out a convenient time for your visit. We're looking forward to seeing you in Boston.

Your friends,
Evelyn and Kenneth Carstairs

Visiting the Carstairses in Boston would be wonderful but what would she use for the fare? She'd write back to them as soon as she finished her job. Maybe she could get more orders. . . .

Skylights in the studio! The Music Hall, the opera . . . Back Bay sounded so—so Bostonian! Kat had a burst of new energy. Bring on the Christmas bells and the hearts!

On November thirtieth, Amanda and Lizabeth raced up to the tower. "Kat! Kat, look at this!"

Amanda's hands were full of small roses and rose-buds made out of pink and red satin ribbon. "What do you think, Kat?"

"They're beautiful!" Kat beamed. "For Valentine's cards?"

"Exactly!"

"You made them yourself, Amanda? How did you—"

"I was over at Lizabeth's and she had lots of ribbons and I just played around with them and twirled them and sewed them in place. Abracadabra—roses!"

"I love them! I couldn't have done anything like that."

"I can make lots more," Amanda said.

"And I brought leftover lace trim," Lizabeth said. "I'm not exactly artistic, but I can paste."

Kat designed the cards. She cut out and painted hearts, Lizabeth pasted lace borders, and Amanda attached roses and rosebuds. "It goes so fast with the three of us," Kat said.

"Like mass production in one of those new factories." Lizabeth laughed.

"They turned out much better than my sample. Thank you!"

By December first, Kat was ready to deliver her gift paper to Mr. Thomas.

On December second, she delivered Mr. Witherspoon's. On December fifth, Kat, Amanda, and Lizabeth put the finishing touches on the last Valentine's Day card. "I think Mrs. Cornell will love these," Kat said. The next day, Amanda and Lizabeth helped her carry everything to the bookstore.

"They're so charming!" Mrs. Cornell said. "With those sweet rosebuds. Even nicer than your sample!"

"I had a lot of help from my friends," Kat said. Amanda and Lizabeth beamed with pride.

On Pelican Street, outside the bookshop, Kat put her hand in her pocket and touched the money from Mrs. Cornell. "So now, altogether, I have twenty-five dollars and five cents! More than I've ever had in my whole life."

"I've never seen anyone work so hard," Amanda said.

Kat's eyes were shining. "I still can't believe I did it!"

"Kat, I can't believe you're really going," Amanda said. "I can't imagine Cape Light without you."

Kat suddenly felt shaky. "I can't believe I'm going either," she whispered. Her dream was becoming reality. She'd actually be leaving her home and her friends!

"The semester doesn't start until January," Kat said,

"so it's still far off." That was enough time to get used to the thought of living in a new place. She'd just keep thinking of how wonderful the Bartholomew School would be. And to have all of Boston outside the door!

"When are you telling your parents?" Lizabeth asked. "Let's go tell them now."

"No, I want to wait until after dinner, when everyone's around the table. Papa will be proud that I could earn this much." Kat's smile became wider and wider. "I think he'll be so surprised and proud!"

That evening, as Kat helped shell the peas for dinner, Ma said, "Katherine, you look like the cat that's swallowed the canary."

Kat couldn't help it. She kept imagining Papa's amazement when she handed him all her money and then his big, happy smile.

thirteen

Ma passed the chicken stew around the table. Though it smelled wonderfully of sage and onions, Kat took only a tiny helping. She was much too excited to eat. She'd make her announcement right after dessert.

She listened with half an ear to the conversation flowing around her. Her hand was on the money stuffed in her dress pocket.

"May I go ice-skating after school tomorrow?" Todd asked. "The green flag's up on the pond."

"Are you sure?" Papa said. "Freezing water can . . ."

Kat wriggled in her chair. She couldn't sit still!

"The flag's up, I saw it yesterday and . . ."

Kat was bubbling over. She couldn't hold back for one more minute! "I did it, Papa!" she blurted out. "I did it!" She jumped up and gave him her wad of bills. "Look!" Everyone stared at her, startled. Papa looked at the money in his hand and put it on the table. "What is this?"

"It's half the tuition for the Bartholomew School!"

"Yippee!" Todd shouted.

"Twenty-five dollars, Papa! Half of my tuition!" Where was that big smile she'd expected to see on his face? He looked at Ma across the table.

Kat looked from one to the other. "Well . . . somebody say something! I did it! Aren't you proud? I earned it by—"

"Katherine." Papa's face was drawn. "I didn't think you had a chance in the world of making that much."

Maybe he was just too stunned and surprised, Kat thought; his smile would break out in a second.

"It seemed like a fantasy," Ma said.

"But it's not. It's right here, half the tuition!" Kat stood very straight and proud. "So now we can put it together with your half, Papa. We should mail it to Boston tomorrow."

"That's wonderful, Kat!" Todd said. Why was Todd the only one who looked happy? This wasn't the way it was supposed to be.

"What's happening?" James asked. "What's going on?"

"That's what I want to know." Kat looked at her parents. "What's going on?"

"Kat . . . I don't have my half," Papa said.

Kat blinked. "What? What do you mean?"

"I don't have it."

She stared at her father. "But where is it?"

"The roof," Papa said. "There weren't only broken shingles, there was a big hole and I had to . . . All the money had to go for materials."

"How could you?" Kat wailed.

"The roof was much worse than I thought," Papa said.

"You promised!"

"I don't have the money to give to you. There's nothing I can do."

"But you have to have *something*. The stipend?"

"This family still needs food on the table and the boys need new shoes for winter." Papa's voice sounded scratchy and defeated. He passed his hand over his forehead. "There is no extra money."

"I don't care about food and shoes! It's not right! It's not!" She saw James's and Todd's stunned expressions through a red haze of anger.

"Ma, Kat's not allowed to yell at Papa!" James said.

"I'm sorry, Kat," Papa said. "I wish I could—"

"Sorry? That's not good enough. I *trusted* you!" Kat

knew she was hurting the person she loved most, but she couldn't stop. "You promised!" Blood was pounding in her head. "I worked so hard!"

"I've never broken a promise to you before." Papa's face was ashen. "I never intended to."

"Except for this one! The most important one. The big opportunity of my life and you ruined it!"

"You will *not* speak to your father in that tone!" Ma said.

"The roof was an emergency," Papa's voice had become very low. "It would have leaked and become worse. You're old enough to understand priorities, Katherine."

"You don't know how hard I worked!" Kat's mouth was dry. She was beyond tears. "You just don't know." Her hand shook as she took the money from the table and stuffed it back into her pocket. She couldn't look at her father.

Todd's face was sorrowful. "I feel so bad for you."

Kat couldn't speak.

"Maybe it's all for the best," Ma said. "You belong here, with the people who love you. And what would we do without your help at the lighthouse? I know you're disappointed now, but—"

"Don't tell me it's all for the best!" Kat exploded. She whirled around and ran up the stairs. "Don't tell me that!"

In her room, Kat lay on her bed and stared at the ceiling. She didn't even pet Sunshine, who sniffed at her anxiously. She saw the last of daylight fading away. She could hear the murmur of voices downstairs. No one was calling her for her shift. Someone else could take it. She didn't care.

How could all her hopes suddenly disappear in one horrible moment? Her visions had seemed so real and so right! Walking among the crowds on Commonwealth Avenue, her skirt stirred by the breeze of automobiles passing by. Standing at an easel under skylights, tubes and tubes of paint stacked nearby—all those colors! At the tea in the dining hall, she was wearing Lizabeth's green dress. . . . Back Bay. Beacon Hill.

She couldn't give it up! She wouldn't! If her parents didn't care enough to help her, if her dreams meant so little to them, she'd do it on her own!

She'd talk to the headmaster. She'd offer to work at the school for the rest of the tuition. She could sweep up and wash dishes and make beds. When the headmaster saw how much she'd already earned, wouldn't he let her in anyway? He would! He had to be nice; he was a friend of the Carstairses, wasn't he? She had to go to Boston and talk to him.

The train, the ferry . . . She couldn't use up all her money to get there, she'd need it. By boat . . . That was the answer! By boat! A lot of the fishermen sailed from Cape Light to Boston on Thursdays with the fresh catch. Friday was fish-eating day in the city. She would stow away. On Thursday, the day after tomorrow. Plenty of time to get ready. It was too late to write to the Carstairses—they'd never get the letter in time. They'd said she was welcome. She'd see them when she arrived. She could do this!

After school on Wednesday, Kat told her friends about her plan. Amanda and Lizabeth sat on the front steps of the schoolhouse. Kat saw them exchange glances as they listened.

"Now remember, you promised. You crossed your hearts. You can't tell a soul about this." Kat was too excited to sit.

"We won't," Amanda said. "But Kat, why can't you just write a letter to the headmaster?"

"And see what he says," Lizabeth added. "Instead of going off and—"

"Because talking in person is altogether different," Kat said. "Anyway, I'll be in Boston!"

"You *can't* stow away," Amanda protested.

"Sure I can. Early in the morning, I'll sneak aboard and—"

"You'll be in so much trouble if you get caught!" Amanda said. "A lot of sailors think a woman aboard is bad luck."

"And I bet there are rats in the hold," Lizabeth said.

"Boston's a big city," Amanda said. "You'll get lost."

"No, I won't. I'll have the school's and the Carstairses' address and I can always ask for directions. That's not so hard."

"I heard there are dangerous streets that a girl shouldn't even walk on!" Lizabeth said.

Kat laughed. "Boston was still in the United States the last time I checked. I'm not exploring a foreign jungle."

"Amanda!" Hannah called from the swing in the schoolyard. "When are you walking me home?"

"In a minute!" Amanda turned back to Kat. "You have the nicest parents in the world. Not the least bit strict."

"I know, but they don't understand. They're not helping at all," Kat said. "So it's up to me to make my dreams come true."

"They'll be so upset," Amanda said. "Just because you're mad at them now—"

"I'm not that mad anymore. And I don't want them to worry. I wrote a letter." Kat handed it to Amanda. "Please give it to them on Thursday afternoon, when they expect me home from school. By then, I'll already be safe in Boston. Thursday afternoon, not a minute earlier, or you'll spoil everything. And not a word to anyone. Swear! On our friendship!"

Amanda and Lizabeth nodded unhappily.

"Say it out loud."

"All right, we swear," Lizabeth said slowly.

"On our friendship," Kat prompted.

"On our friendship," Amanda and Lizabeth repeated.

They read what Kat had written.

Dear Ma and Papa,
    When you read this, I'll already be in Boston. I'm going to talk to the headmaster of the Bartholomew School in person so that I can go to school there. And I have the Carstairses' address with me and they did write that I'd be welcome at their home. So you see, there's nothing at all to worry about. I love you both, and Todd and James. Please tell Todd to pay extra attention to Sunshine.

I hope the things I do in Boston will make you proud.

Love,
Kat

"Kat, this is scary!" Amanda said. "Please, Kat. Let's just go ice-skating after school tomorrow. Please?"

"No. I'm not staying." Kat waited every winter for Mill Pond to finally freeze solid. Everyone would be there, slipping and sliding over the rough ruts in the ice. . . . She shook her head fiercely. "No, I'm going to Boston."

"Well, I won't say good-bye to you, Katherine Williams!" Amanda stood up with her hands on her hips. "I won't! I'm going to pray for you to change your mind."

"My mind is made up," Kat said. "I'm leaving for Boston in the morning and nothing can stop me now!"

fourteen

That evening Kat found her father's duffel bag in the back of the hall closet. Papa used to take it with him when he went to sea. No one would miss it now.

Kat packed her Sunday dress and pinafore, and Lizabeth's green dress. She'd need her very best things for tea and the theater. She chose one shirtwaist and skirt for school. More of her things could be sent to her once she was settled. She packed a flannel nightgown. Kat put in one of her best seascapes, something to show the headmaster that she was talented.

It was hard to leave her art supplies behind, but if Ma or Papa noticed them missing from the tower during their watches tonight, they'd know something was wrong. And there wasn't enough room in the duffel. Anyway, the school would have plenty of supplies and probably better ones, too!

She put the school's brochure and address and the envelope with the Carstairses' address right on top, easy to reach. She tucked the bundle of money on the side. She was all packed up and suddenly she had to swallow hard to get rid of the lump in her throat. She slid the duffel bag under her bed.

Before she went up to the tower for her evening shift, she stopped in the kitchen.

"Ma, I can't walk to school with Todd and James tomorrow morning," Kat said. "I have to leave before they do."

"Oh?" Ma didn't look up from the pan she was scraping.

"I have to go extra early." The boats would leave at dawn.

"Why is that?"

"For a special project. A special school project I'm doing." Kat blushed. She wasn't used to lying and it didn't feel good.

"I'll tell the boys." Ma nodded, without turning around, without asking any questions. Ma didn't have the slightest suspicion and that made Kat feel even more guilty. Kat paused in the doorway for an extra moment, her eyes on Ma's back. She wanted to say something. It was hard to tear herself away but there was nothing she could say without giving away too much.

Kat stood watch for the last time and gazed out at the sea. "Good-bye, Durham Point," she whispered. "Good-bye, Cape Light."

That night, Kat kept waking up to check the clock. At this time tomorrow, she'd be in Boston and starting a new life!

At dawn, Kat pulled on a heavy sweater, a warm wool skirt, and a knit cap. The hold of a ship would be cold and she'd have to sit in it for hours. She had to decide right now: her heavy, warm everyday coat or the good navy blue princess-style coat she wore to church? The princess coat. She needed her best things for Boston! She added mittens and tied a woolly scarf around her neck.

She hoisted the duffel bag on her shoulder and tip-toed out of her room. Sunshine raised his head but thankfully didn't bark. Ma would have left the tower at first light; she would have dropped off to sleep as soon as she got back into bed. Kat waited, listening. All was quiet. She waited another moment, just to be sure. She went down the stairs, skipping the second one from the bottom that creaked. She opened the front door slowly and inched it shut behind her so it wouldn't slam.

Then she was running along Lighthouse Lane. She hardly felt the weight of the bag. Her excitement propelled her forward and made her fly!

It was good sailing weather, cold and windy but sunny; a cloudless blue sky, nothing at all to keep the boats from heading out. Perfect. The brisk wind reddened Kat's cheeks and shocked her wide awake. She made a right turn off Lighthouse Lane onto the short dirt path of Wharf Way. The docks were spread out in front of her.

Even at this early hour the noise and activity at the docks was amazing. Kat looked in all directions at once. Men and boys were moving back and forth among ships of all sizes. "Hoist it up, come on, this way . . ." There was the sound of grinding chains being pulled by thick ropes. A faint ringing as a buoy stirred in the water. "Let's go, easy does it!"

Pick a boat, Kat thought, quick, before anyone notices me.

Heavy footsteps pounded on the gnarled boards of the dock nearby. "On the starboard side!" someone called out. Several men were leaning back against huge wooden barrels banded with metal; their pipe smoke curled into the air.

Hurry, Kat thought, find a boat. The ones with empty lobster traps and nets being loaded on deck had to be going out for a day's fishing. Her eyes darted to the boats where crates of fish and blocks of ice were being carried below deck, along with squirming, clawing lobsters piled up in huge cages. "Hose them down, Buddy," someone shouted. The catch had to be kept cold and wet to stay fresh for a trip. The night's catch, for delivery to Boston. She'd have to share a dark hold with dead fish and scrabbling lobsters! She could handle it. She could! The trip wouldn't be *that* long.

Kat headed toward the *Mary Lee*, freshly painted and trim. She loitered on the dock next to it but there were too many people nearby. Sneaking aboard would be the hard part! Kat moved over to the *Second Chance*. It was a smaller vessel, but it looked almost new. And they had just finished loading cages of lobster. The men were on deck, adjusting the sails. They had their backs to her. Now, Kat thought. Move fast and be invisible. *Now!* She kept her eyes on the backs of the men, busy, no one turning around; she took a quick step and—

"Hey there, Katherine!"

Kat gasped and jumped a mile at the sound of the voice behind her. Mr. Fiering, a friend of Papa's! One more step and she would have been caught!

Her heart was thumping so hard, she was sure it showed through her coat! It took a moment before she could speak. "Hello, Mr. Fiering." She tried to sound normal.

"What are you up to so early?" he asked.

"A project. For school. About the harbor. A harbor project." That made no sense at all! Kat pressed her shaking lips together to keep them from more nervous babbling.

Luckily, Mr. Fiering was too busy to listen. He was already walking away as he spoke to Kat. "Tell your father hello from me," he said as he boarded the *Second Chance.*

Her heart was still hammering. She had to pull herself together! Kat drew in a long, shaky breath. All right. She needed to get away from the center of activity. And she had to get on board, quick, before they all set sail for Boston!

Kat hurried to the far end of the dock, where there were fewer people around. The *Evangeline.* The berths on both sides of it were empty. She could see the men taking full crates of fish below. All right. This was it . . . Go! Then she hesitated. The *Evangeline*'s paint was peeling, it looked old. But she wasn't buying it, just hitching a ride. She saw Mr. Gardner on deck giving orders. So he was the captain. She knew him by sight, a heavyset man with a grizzled beard, one of the regular Cape Light fishermen. Surely none of them would go out on a boat that wasn't shipshape. Anyway, good maintenance didn't always show on the outside. Here, at the end of the dock, was her best chance of getting aboard unseen. And she was running out of time.

Kat took a look behind her. No one. She checked the men on the deck of the *Evangeline*. They were busy, their backs to her, wrestling with a full lobster cage.

All right, now or never. *Go!* She clambered aboard and dove down the steps into the hold. Oh, no, they were still loading lobsters! The open hatch let in shafts of light. They'd see her. Footsteps thundered on the metal rungs down to the hold. Kat scrambled to a far, dark corner. She squeezed against a damp crate. In the dim light she could see men bent over in the cramped space and intent on the job. If they looked this way . . . A pulse in her forehead was drumming. No, they couldn't hear that! They couldn't! Kat didn't move a muscle. She held her breath and waited. Finally the men went up again. The hatch slammed shut, plunging the hold into darkness.

Kat exhaled and her body went limp. Everything around her was black. Slowly her eyes adjusted. She could just make out some vague shapes. She heard footsteps over her head. She heard awful scrabbling sounds. The lobsters in the cages. Right next to her! Well, she could move over. She started to stand up and banged her head. *Ow!* Her forehead throbbed and she sank down again and found another place to sit. She tried shifting into a comfortable position.

She felt the boat lurch as the anchor was pulled up. Then there was a rocking motion. The boat was just getting under way! It felt like she'd been down here for hours already. There was an awful smell. Fresh fish, Papa always said, had no odor at all. This was a pungent smell of rotting wood and decay. She'd never been seasick in her life . . . but that smell! Don't think of getting sick, think of something else, anything else!

Kat's body swayed with the boat but her arms and legs were tight and tense. She adjusted the duffel bag behind her back and leaned against it. She was trapped in a small, dark space, sailing miles away from her family and friends. What had she done? Stop, don't be a baby. It was only for a few hours. And then she'd be in Boston.

Time dragged by.

So far, excitement had carried Kat forward; she'd been in action. Now she had nothing to do but sit still and think. Was Boston's harbor right in the city or far away on the outskirts? How far was it from the Bartholomew School and the Carstairses' home? Where did you get trolleys and what was the fare? What if the school was closed by the time she arrived and the Carstairses weren't at home? Where would she spend the night? She should have written to the Carstairses and told them she was coming!

The awful smell filled her nose and clung to her clothing. Her legs were cramped. She started to stand up to stretch—no, not straight up! She tried half-stretching, bent over. Sitting again, she pushed her legs out in front of her. She flexed her toes and her feet.

Kat rocked with the boat and had no sense of how long they'd been under way. It seemed like hours. Maybe it *was* hours. She wanted to get up and escape this tight, dark space! She hoped they were at least halfway to Boston.

Maybe it was already afternoon. Amanda and Lizabeth might be skating on Mill Pond this very minute.

She missed them already. And her family—she could imagine their shocked faces when they read her letter. Oh, what had she done? . . . Cape Light, where she knew everyone, where you could always count on neighbors for a kind word or a barn raising . . . She'd never run into that boy Michael again, she'd never find out if he liked her or not. . . .

She listened to the swishing sounds of the waves against the sides. She'd have to wait it out.

Suddenly she heard a different noise, scratchy, coming from another direction. Chills raced up her back. Scratchy noises of little claws against the old wooden boards, coming closer to her. She couldn't see anything in the dark. It's nothing, she told herself, just the men working above me, sounds carrying down from the deck.

Something furry crossed her hand! Kat smothered her scream. A rat? Her whole body jumped in panic. She crawled away frantically, not knowing where she was going. She wanted to escape to the deck! Please, God, she prayed, give me courage.

Kat huddled into a small, miserable ball. Please, God, let us reach Boston soon. Or anywhere.

Her legs were aching and cramped. Her skin crawled. She'd die if something furry touched her again!

She was afraid to move. The scratchy sound had stopped—but was something sitting on its haunches with beady little eyes watching her? Kat shuddered.

She had to stretch again, she just *had* to! Cautiously, she shifted position and moved her legs out from under her. There, that was better. But—her ankles felt wet! She felt around with her hands. There was water at the bottom of the hold! Was that normal? It had been dry before. Stop. This awful trip was making her panic. It had to be normal for some seawater to seep through the boards during the journey. That sounded right. How would she know—she'd never sailed in a hold before.

Now the back of her coat was wet. Oh, her good coat! Water had soaked through to her skirt and petticoat, too! Bent over, she moved to find a dry place to sit. Would a rat be looking for a dry place, too? She didn't want to think about that. She couldn't find a dry place!

Wait! Stop and think. She couldn't see where the water was coming from. Maybe it was just leaking from the fish crates that had been hosed down. That was perfectly possible, wasn't it? She shifted uncertainly. She was damp and cold.

Soon she was sopping wet, up to her knees. Her skirt had become heavy, weighting her down. And her feet were now sloshing in water! Kat shivered. This wasn't from any fish crates. This wasn't normal. But maybe it was. Please, let it be normal. She had to stay put or else she'd be in big trouble. She *couldn't* let them know she was here—or should she?

The water was rising!

Kat heard the hull start creaking and then the terrible sound of water rushing in. . . .

fifteen

at crawled to the hatch. She couldn't fool herself any longer. The boat was in trouble! She banged and banged on the hatch until it opened. Dripping and frightened, she climbed onto the deck.

"Who— What are you—?" A sailor's jaw dropped with astonishment.

"There's water in the hold! Please! Do something!"

"Wait a minute. Captain Gardner!" he shouted. "Look what we've got here!"

"What is this? What's going on?" The captain came over. The other men gathered around Kat and stared. "Where in blazes did you come from?"

"There's no time to explain!" Kat said desperately. "There's water in the hold! I think something is awfully wrong."

"What are you doing on my boat?" Captain Gardner yelled. Kat shrank under his angry stare. "I don't take kindly to stowaways!"

"Please, sir, listen to me! *Water's rushing in!*"

Captain Gardner still looked furious. "All right. Bud, go down and see what she's talking about. Probably nonsense."

"Hurry, please!" Kat urged.

The man called Bud reappeared from the hatch. His face was drawn. "It's filling up!"

Kat was relieved to see the crew spring into action.

Some of the men rushed down to bail. They immediately returned to the deck. "No use, sir, the boards are giving way!"

"Everyone, life preservers!" Captain Gardner called. The men grabbed bright orange cushioned rings. Some sent up S.O.S. flares.

Kat looked out at the horizon. There were no other boats anywhere. No one to see the flares and no sign of land. Just sea and more sea.

Some of the men worked the sails, turning the boat around, guiding it back to port. "Dear God," one of them moaned. "Let the boards hold."

Let the boards hold, Kat's mind echoed. One thing she knew for sure, if they didn't, no one could last long in the icy sea. She stood alone and terrified, in the midst of the furious activity around her.

The captain beckoned to Kat. He took off his life preserver. "Put it on, fast!"

At first, Kat didn't understand. Then she realized there weren't any extras. One preserver per man, and the captain was handing his to her.

"But . . . it's yours."

"Hurry up, take it! You're young yet."

"I . . . I can't," Kat said.

"Take it! That's an order!" the captain barked.

Shamefaced, Kat put on the life preserver. If she hadn't stowed away, there would have been enough to go around.

"Not that it'll do much good if we have to abandon ship," the captain said.

Kat knew he was thinking of the freezing ocean.

The captain glanced at Kat's stricken face. His voice softened. "If we're lucky, we'll make shore."

But Kat was certain shore was hours away. They were trying to sail the boat back just to have *something* to do.

A man with a telescope shouted, "No ships any-where in sight, sir."

Suddenly the boat shuddered.

Kat grabbed the railing. "What's that?" she whispered.

Captain Gardner looked grim. The boat shook again. Everyone on the crew stopped moving. There was a long, agonizing moment of silence. Then a splintering sound filled the air. There was a horrible shriek as the wooden boards started coming apart. The boat listed to one side and water swamped the deck.

"Abandon ship!" the captain called.

Another wrenching move by the boat and Kat was flung into the sea. The icy water made her gasp. Though the life preserver was keeping her afloat, every instinct told her to grab onto something.

She kicked her legs. She reached out and hung on to a plank of wood. The boat was sinking fast. She saw some of the men swimming toward whatever parts of the boat were still floating. The captain hugged a piece of wood. Near her, men were calling to God and calling out their wives' names.

Kat watched as the mast, the very last part of the *Evangeline*, disappeared under the water.

The water was frigid. The cold sliced through her body like a million knives. All her life, Kat had heard about Cape Light sailors lost at sea. Now she knew. This terrible, terrible cold.

How long could a person last in cold water? She couldn't remember exactly, only that she'd been surprised by what a very short time Papa had said it was. Oh, Papa!

"Dear God," Kat prayed through chattering teeth. She could no longer feel her legs. "Please help me and all these men and the captain. Please help us come home again."

Her arms went from the pain of freezing to total numbness. She couldn't feel her hands clutching the plank.

"Dear God," Kat whispered. "I want to live. But if I can't, please grant me the strength to accept whatever happens. Please help my family find peace in spite of the grief I've brought them." She stifled a sob; she wanted to be brave.

The words of the Twenty-third Psalm came to Kat and as she recited them, she felt her courage expand and grow. "Though I walk through the valley of the shadow of death, I will fear no evil. . . ."

A sailor clinging to a board nearby heard Kat. He spoke the rest of the words with her. "For Thou art with me; Thy rod and Thy staff, they comfort me. . . ."

Their voices carried over the endless sea.

❧sixteen❧

"**S**urely goodness and mercy shall follow me all the days of my life; and I shall dwell in the house of the Lord for ever."

Kat felt comforted, though the sun that shone down so brilliantly could not warm her. She hoped the sailor who had prayed with her felt that comfort, too.

The sea had swallowed up the *Evangeline* as if she had never been. All that remained of her was scattered debris.

The vast silence that engulfed them was occasionally broken by a snatch of prayer or by hopeless last words.

Kat couldn't feel her body anymore. It wouldn't be long now.

Ma, Papa, Todd, James. All that love. Why hadn't she known, every single day, how lucky she was? Cape Light, Durham Point, Amanda and Lizbeth, barn dances, the tower. . . . She didn't want to say good-bye to it all.

Kat closed her eyes. Her time was coming to an end. She had to give thanks for all she'd been given. If only her parents didn't have to suffer . . .

"Sails!" a hoarse voice shouted.

The cry went up again. "Sails! Coming this way!"

Kat blinked. Her vision was blurry now. There, on the horizon! A boat seemed to be heading toward them as fast as the wind would allow!

Someone was coming for them! With her last bit of strength, Kat looked for the captain. Was that him hanging on to a plank, afloat even without a life preserver? Kat blinked again. The boat came closer, and closer.

Everything seemed to be happening so quickly in a whirlwind of confusion. Kat was in a daze. Voices shouting. So loud. Lines thrown into the water. Sailors hauled up. Arms touching her, tugging at her. It was Papa! Papa, on the *Heron*! She saw him through a fog. Papa's strong arms pulling her out of the sea, his strong arms around her on the deck!

"Papa." Kat's knees buckled under her. What was he doing here? Was she dreaming him while she drifted under the waves?

155

"My Kat. Thank God," Papa said. He held her up. He pulled off his sweater and put it on her. It came to her knees. Then his jacket, the sleeves dangling far beyond her hands. His knit cap was on her head. Somehow her shoes were gone. A sailor's huge, thick socks were pulled over her feet. She was wrapped tight in a blanket and Papa was rubbing her arms and legs. Rubbing hard. Slowly, the feeling came back into them. With it came sharp twinges of pain. Kat couldn't help whimpering. Tears ran down her cheeks and mixed with the salty taste in her mouth.

"Hold on, kitten," Papa said. "It'll stop hurting soon."

Kat nodded.

"Any better?"

Kat felt herself coming back into focus. Piece by piece, the world tilted back into place.

"You're all right, Kat," Papa said.

Kat fiercely wiped her eyes. "And the others? All the sailors?"

"We picked everyone up. We got them all."

Kat looked around. The rescued men on the *Heron* wore odd bits of spare, dry clothing. She was overjoyed to see Captain Gardner; if he had drowned because of her . . .

The crew of the *Heron* were passing around whatever they had: blankets, sweaters, caps, vests, brandy. The sun was beating down on the deck and the drenched sailors tilted their faces up, taking in its rays.

Kat, too, soaked up the sun's warmth.

The boat was heading back to Cape Light. How wonderful to be going home!

"How did you—how did they know we—"

"We didn't know," Papa said. "We had no idea the *Evangeline* was in trouble. We came to intercept you. As soon as I heard you'd stowed away—Kat, what a foolish thing to do!"

"I know. I'm sorry. Are you mad, Papa?"

"I sure was. Running off to Boston without a thought! What gets into you, Kat? If I'd found you at the docks, you'd have been in big trouble. But I'm too glad to have you back safe." He smiled at her; his eyes were wet. "Too glad to be mad at my favorite daughter."

Kat's lips trembled as she tried to smile. "Your *only* daughter."

"If I had ten others, you'd still be my favorite."

"But how did you know? And on the *Evangeline*?"

"Amanda and Lizabeth came by early this morning; they skipped school to tell us. Thank heaven for their good sense! I ran down to the docks and someone remembered seeing you hanging around the *Evangeline*. Captain Caldeira volunteered his boat—lost a day of fishing for it—and we raced to catch you. We tried to follow a logical course, not knowing if we'd find the *Evangeline*. You owe Captain Caldeira and his crew your apologies, and your thanks."

"I know, Papa." Kat took a deep breath. "I have something to say to Captain Gardner, too." He was standing near the railing. Kat walked toward him awkwardly. The blanket was tight around her ankles, forcing her to take tiny, hobbled steps.

Other men were gathered around Captain Gardner. "I knew she needed some work," he said mournfully. "But I was short on cash, and I thought just one more catch, one more delivery. The *Evangeline*'s withstood all kinds of weather . . . and now she's gone. I can't believe she's gone."

A sailor shook his head. "It's a shame. It tears a man up."

"My fault. I shouldn't have taken her out." Captain Gardner drew himself up. "Well, she was only a boat. The important thing is, every one of us is going home again." He looked out to sea, his face full of sadness.

Kat approached him hesitantly. "Captain Gardner? I

want to thank you . . . you gave me your life preserver. And I need to apologize. I'm so sorry I sneaked aboard— I'm so sorry for the trouble I caused. Maybe women on board *are* bad luck, the way they say."

"Nonsense," he said. "You brought us the best of luck."

"But how?" Kat was puzzled.

"You're Tom Williams's girl, are you?"

"Yes, sir. Katherine."

"Well, Katherine, if you hadn't stowed away—if they hadn't come looking for you—there wouldn't have been anyone here to rescue us, would there? But mind you, don't ever do anything like that again!"

"I won't! Never!"

He put out his rough, callused hand and shook hers. "All right, Katherine. Next time we meet, I hope it'll be under better circumstances."

Kat smiled. "I hope so, too, Captain Gardner."

Kat was feeling much better when she came back to Papa. And then she remembered.

"Papa! Your duffel bag! It went down with the boat!"

"You couldn't have fit that much into it—just a few clothes? It was an old bag, nothing to worry about."

"The money, Papa! Twenty-five dollars at the bottom

of the ocean!" She'd worked so hard for it. And that pretty green dress. . . . But I have my life! she thought. I'm going home. Nothing else matters.

At the cottage, Kat sank into the tub and inhaled the steam. Ma had boiled the biggest pots on the stove for lots of hot water. Kat soaked and soaked. Nothing had ever felt so good! She soaped her hair into a high tower of suds. She scrubbed the salt off her body. She scrubbed off the odor and grime of the hold until her skin was tingling and rosy. Then she put on a heavy sweater and a thick woolen skirt; it was miraculous to feel clean again and truly warm. She ran downstairs to the heartfelt embraces of her family.

Kat looked at them as if a cloudy film had been removed from her eyes. Ma's face, full of love and concern, was so beautiful! James with those soft little-boy cheeks. She wanted to hug and hug him. Her sweet, serious Todd. And Papa. Papa was her rock. They meant everything to her. How she would have missed them!

That evening, Kat insisted on taking her regular watch.

"You don't have to," Papa said. "Not tonight, kitten."

"You want me to take it for you?" Todd asked.

"Don't you need rest?" Ma asked. "If you'd like to go

to bed, I'll bring up cinnamon toast."

"I'm fine, really I am," Kat said. "I couldn't be better! I *want* to do my share at the lighthouse. Tonight and every night."

In the tower, Kat saw her art supplies on their shelf. She gently touched her tubes of paint and the watercolor pad. If she had packed them in the duffel . . . But they were here and not at the bottom of the ocean; they were safe and waiting for her.

I'll keep working on my art, she thought, right here in Cape Light. Someday, she'd get the training she wanted, someday she could still go to Boston or another big city. Later, when her family didn't need her so much at the lighthouse. When she was older and far more ready to leave everyone and everything she loved. In the meantime, she would paint and learn from her mistakes and paint some more. Maybe it's better to keep trying and experimenting on my own for a while, Kat thought, before I depend on someone else to show me how. Maybe I'll develop my own style and the critics will see a fresh new talent. She was dreaming again, Kat knew, but she was going to hold on to her dream. It had changed a little, that's all. It left room for all the good things in her life in Cape Light.

Kat followed her usual routine: climbing up the second ladder to the top of the tower, checking the glass around the light—it was spotless, thanks to Todd—and winding the spring that made the light revolve. Then she climbed down and shoveled coal into the stove. She lit the coals, trimmed the wick of the lantern, and pulled her chair to the window.

The sea glistened in the moonlight. A merciless sea, Kat knew, but she still loved it.

Kat heard footsteps on the lower ladder and then Amanda appeared in the tower.

"Kat?" Amanda said. "Your mother said you were up here." She looked very uncomfortable.

"Hi, Amanda! Wait till I tell you what happened to me!" Kat stopped short, puzzled. "Aren't you out awfully late tonight?"

"I had to come and talk, even if you're mad. Lizabeth was afraid to even face you." Amanda cleared her throat. "Kat, can we still be friends?" She seemed close to tears.

"Of course! Why wouldn't we be?"

"Because . . . I feel so bad, Kat. Lizabeth and I *swore* not to tell, but we were so worried. We didn't know what to do. We *had* to tell someone. We couldn't wait until after school, because if you were in trouble or . . . We were so scared. So we decided, even if you'd never forgive us, we still had to tell your parents right away. I'm sorry, Kat. So is Lizabeth."

"Don't be sorry! You saved my life, that's all! Mine and all the men on board! If you hadn't told . . . I mean, no one would have come after me. They found us just in time!"

"I hope you'll . . . Will you ever trust me again?"

"I'll *always* trust you. With *anything*! I was plain crazy and you did the right thing. When I was in that hold, I started to realize dreaming about Boston was one thing, but actually leaving, well, Cape Light is exactly where I want to be. At least for now. And you're the very best friend I'll ever have."

Amanda beamed. "I'm so glad, Kat!"

"Me, too."

"You worked so hard for that Boston money. What are you going to do with it now? Are you going to—"

"It's at the bottom of the ocean." Kat shrugged at Amanda's shocked look. "It's all right. I owe Todd, and I'll make Valentine's cards and things until I can pay him back. And I discovered that I *can* earn money. That's a good thing to know. I guess I'll keep making gift paper— well, not as much and not as fast—then I can buy more paints and brushes and—"

Kat heard more footsteps on the ladder and then Ma and Papa came into view.

"Your father has something for you," Ma said. Papa was holding a small package covered with her ribbon gift paper. Kat looked at him, puzzled.

"From the Pelican Street Bookshop. Nice paper." He grinned. "Mrs. Cornell told me." Awkwardly, he held out the package to Kat. "Here—open it."

Kat searched her father's face. She'd never seen him look so self-conscious and pleased with himself all at the same time. It felt very strange to be tearing open her own gift paper! Oh, a book. *Masters of Watercolor*! "Papa, thank you!"

"That's all Mrs. Cornell had in stock."

"It's wonderful, thank you!" Kat riffled through the colorful, glossy pages. So many paintings to look at!

"We didn't take your wish for art training that seriously," Papa said. "Not seriously enough."

"We should have listened better. It wasn't just a whim, was it?" Ma said.

"When I saw how much you'd earned," Papa said, "I felt terrible. So I went to the bookshop the next morning. Just a token, to show you that we do believe in your dream, even if we didn't have the money to give you."

"I'm sorry, Papa," Kat said. "I understand about the roof. I never meant to hurt—"

"Let me finish," Papa said. "We decided you should get all the art instruction books you need. *Good* ones. Order them from Mrs. Cornell and we'll pay out of household money somehow."

Ma nodded and smiled at her.

A big lump was suddenly in Kat's throat. "Oh, Ma! Papa!" She hugged them both.

"I bet you'll become a *great* artist!" Amanda said.

"Maybe start off by ordering just a few," Ma said. "Give us a chance to catch up, I don't know how much those books cost . . ."

Kat broke into a huge brilliant smile. "Thank you." Her parents were supporting her dreams now. They understood! That meant more than all the instruction books and tuition in the world.

Out the window, she saw the light sweeping around and around in the dark. To guide wayfarers home, Kat thought. Wayfarers like me. The scene before her was hypnotic and mysterious and Kat's eyes welled up. She had been guided home.

MARTIN CLASSICAL LECTURES

These lectures are delivered annually at

OBERLIN COLLEGE

on a Foundation established in honor of

CHARLES BEEBE MARTIN

LONDON : HUMPHREY MILFORD

OXFORD UNIVERSITY PRESS

EARLY GREEK ELEGISTS

MARTIN CLASSICAL LECTURES
VOLUME VII

BY

C. M. BOWRA
Fellow of Wadham College, Oxford

CAMBRIDGE : MASSACHUSETTS

HARVARD UNIVERSITY PRESS

1938

THE MARTIN CLASSICAL LECTURES

VOLUME VII

The Martin Foundation, on which these lectures
are delivered, was established by his many friends
in honor of Charles Beebe Martin, for forty-five
years a teacher of classical literature and
classical art in Oberlin College

PREFACE

IN THESE lectures I have attempted to give brief
sketches of the works and personalities of the early
Greek elegists, and to discuss some of the problems
connected with them. Limitations of space have pre-
vented me from giving full discussion to many dis-
puted points and compelled me sometimes to appear
more dogmatic than I am.

I am much indebted to the editions of H. Diehl and
T. Hudson-Williams, to books and articles by U. von
Wilamowitz-Moellendorff, W. Jaeger, E. Römisch and
A. Hauvette, and to the helpful and scholarly criticism
of A. Andrewes. I am grateful for leave to publish
versions to Sir William Marris, J. M. Edmonds, G. B.
Grundy, T. F. Higham, Gilbert Highet, W. C. Lawton,
F. L. Lucas, J. W. Mackail, and Gilbert Murray, and
to Messrs. Grant Richards, Gowans and Gray, and
Kegan Paul, Trench, Trübner and Co. for other versions of which they possess the copyright. Finally I
would like to thank my kind hosts of Oberlin College,
and especially Professor and Mrs. Louis E. Lord, for
the warm welcome which made the giving of lectures
a pleasure.

C. M. B.

OXFORD
March 16, 1938

CONTENTS

I

ORIGINS AND BEGINNINGS

FEW forms of verse can have had so long a history as the Greek elegiac couplet. It first appears, so far as we know, in the eighth century before Christ, and it was still vital in the tenth century after Christ. It is the aim of these lectures to give a sketch of this form and of its users in its early days and to mention some of its chief characteristics in a period when it was the vehicle not only for passing emotions but for considered ideas. In the centuries from the eighth to the fifth before Christ the elegiac existed by the side of lyric poetry and was to some extent an appanage of it, but it kept its own kind of language and subject and may well be studied by itself.

The elegiac couplet has been called "a variation upon the heroic hexameter in the direction of lyric poetry." [1] It consists of two lines which form, so to speak, a verse or stanza. The first line is the familiar hexameter of the epic and differs little from it in structure. But the second line is more peculiar; it is usually called a pentameter, but only mathematically can it be said to have five feet. For when we scan a so-called pentameter such as William Watson's

Man and his glory survive, lost in the greatness of God,

we find that we have not five successive dactyls but

[1] W. R. Hardie, *Res Metrica*, p. 49.

two and a half dactyls followed by another two and a half:

$$-\cup\cup\,|-\cup\cup\,|-\,\|-\cup\cup\,|-\cup\cup\,|-$$

So the alleged pentameter is really made out of two separate metrical units, which were in practice kept distinct from each other by the simple rule that a word could not be carried over from the first to the second. By attaching the so-called pentameter in this way to the hexameter the Greeks created a new metrical unit for poetry. The elegiac couplet differed on the one hand from the epic hexameter which was operated as a single line and never built into regular stanzas, and on the other from the varying stanzas of lyric verse in which different metrical units were formed into an endless variety of patterns. The couplet had the advantage of being both regular and melodious; it provided a set form for the poet to compose in, but inside this there were many possible harmonies, especially as the Greeks, unlike their Roman imitators, did not insist that a sentence should be confined to a single couplet but freely allowed it to flow over into the next. It is, then, not surprising that a form so free and musical was much used.

The origin of this form is a matter of some dispute. The word ἐλεγεῖον, from which the modern word "elegy" is ultimately derived, first occurs in a fragment of Critias, the friend of Socrates, written at the end of the fifth century.[2] The word must be connected

---

[2] Fr. 2, 3 Diehl.

with ἔλεγος, which is freely used by Euripides and later writers to mean "lament." Moreover, long before this Echembrotus won the contest for the flute at Delphi about 586 B.C. by singing ἔλεγοι, which must be elegiac verses. It is therefore not surprising that Hellenistic and Roman writers regarded the elegiac as a mournful measure — Ovid's "flebilis Elegeia." But to this view of the nature of the elegiac there is an insuperable objection, — that the oldest types of elegiac verse have little or nothing to do with lamentation.[3] They seem in the main to be either military or convivial, and such grief as they express is seldom concerned with the dead. Even the early and frequent use of the elegiac for inscriptions on tombs can hardly be described as a form of lamentation, since it seldom expresses grief and is usually put in the form of words spoken by the dead about themselves. It is, in fact, fairly certain that the use of the elegiac for laments was an old Peloponnesian custom practiced by Echembrotus, Sacadas and Clonas. It survives in the elegiac lament of Euripides' *Andromache* 103-116, and a late example may be seen in Callimachus' *Bath of Pallas*. But all earlier examples of such elegy are now lost, and this Peloponnesian use, whatever it once was, does not concern us. It was isolated and no doubt had its own characteristics. But it had little to do with early elegy as we know it.

In practice the elegiac couplet seems to have been

[3] The whole question is discussed with great ability and fullness by D. L. Page in *Greek Poetry and Life*, pp. 206–217.

a song sung to the accompaniment of the flute, just as lyric poetry was sung to the lyre. This conclusion emerges from a statement of Archilochus,[4] from a tradition that Mimnermus was a fluteplayer,[5] and from passages in the *Theognidea* where the poet says that he sings to the flute and refers to his elegiacs.[6] It was also known to ancient authorities such as Plutarch [7] and Pausanias.[8] Moreover it gets support from a simple fact. The earliest known elegiac pieces are either military like those of Callinus and Tyrtaeus or convivial like those of Mimnermus, and it happens that the flute was a favorite instrument for both soldiers and feasters. Homer illustrates both uses. He names "flutes and pipes" among the musical instruments heard by Agamemnon in the Trojan encampment at night,[9] and he makes flutes an important element of noise in the scene of feasting on the Shield of Achilles.[10] There seems, then, little reason to doubt the simple theory that the elegiac was originally a flute-song. The word may be of Asiatic origin, and some have recognized a collateral descendant in the Armenian root *elegn-*. The names of Greek musical instruments are usually of foreign origin, and since the first pieces of elegiac verse come from Asia Minor and the adjacent islands, an Asiatic influence, whether Phrygian or Lydian or the like, is easy to understand. In any case the flute was an in-

---

[4] Fr. 123 Bergk.
[5] Strab. xiv. 643.
[6] 241, 533, 825, 943, 1041.
[7] *Mus.* 8.
[8] x. 7, 5.
[9] *Il.* x. 13.
[10] *Il.* xviii. 495.

strument in ancient Babylon and was certainly not invented in Greece.

The elegiac, then, came into existence as a flute-song, and such it remained for some three or four centuries. Who first invented it is a mystery. The Greeks seem to have hesitated between Archilochus, Callinus, and Tyrtaeus,[11] but since these are the earliest known elegists, it looks as if the Alexandrian scholars knew no more than we do and assigned the invention to the first elegists known to them. Of these three Archilochus has perhaps the greatest claims, if not to the invention of the elegiac, at least to its improvement and adaptation to different uses. Blakeway showed that Archilochus lived between about 735 B.C. and 665 B.C.[12] A man of surpassing power and originality, he polished for Greek poetry some of its most enduring forms of verse and wrote poems of an astonishing directness and strength. His poetry was the reflection of his wandering, unsuccessful, and unhappy life. A bastard, poverty-stricken and crossed in love, he could not help bursting into words of bitter hate against his enemies, so that for later generations he was the type of the harsh-spoken man, and Pindar referred to him as "fattening his leanness with hate and heavy words."[13] But his hatreds are to be found more in his iambic than in his elegiac verses, and he shows a truly Greek

[11] Didymus, quoted by Orion, p. 58, 7 ff.
[12] *Greek Poetry and Life*, pp. 34-55.
[13] *Pyth.* ii. 54-6.

sense of appropriateness in keeping the subject matter
of the two kinds apart.

So far as we can tell from the scanty fragments,
Archilochus' elegiacs were often written in moments
of relaxation when he was leading an active life on
campaign. In Thasos, which he helped to colonize
about 708, he had trouble from Thracian barbarians,
and his war experiences were not confined to this. He
may have taken a part in the Lelantine War in which
Chalcis fought Eretria and strong powers were
ranged on either side; tradition tells that he died
fighting.[14] Against this background of active life we
may set his elegiac verses, which are, so to speak, his
own candid and disarming comments on it. He saw
himself as passing his life under arms and wrote:

ἐν δορὶ μέν μοι μάζα μεμαγμένη, ἐν δορὶ δ' οἶνος
'Ισμαρικός, πίνω δ' ἐν δορὶ κεκλιμένος.[15]

My spear wins bread, my spear wins Thracian wine:
To drink it, on my spear-head I recline.

But in spite of this he did not see himself as nothing
but a soldier. He was also a poet, and proud of it:

εἰμὶ δ' ἐγὼ θεράπων μὲν 'Ενυαλίοιο ἄνακτος
καὶ Μουσέων ἐρατὸν δῶρον ἐπιστάμενος.[16]

I am the servant of the Lord of War,
And I know too the Muses' lovely gift.

Such simple couplets were probably improvised and
sung in the intervals of fighting, when someone had a

---

[14] Plut. *de Ser. Num. Vind.* 17, Aelian fr. 80.
[15] Fr. 2 Diehl.   [16] Fr. 1.

flute and the poet was called upon for a song. They
are eminently topical, and yet they are so concentrated, so careful to state only the essential facts,
that this topical origin is left behind. They have become verses suitable to any soldier-poet. Crisply and
firmly they state some aspect of Archilochus' life,
and nothing can be added to their brief directness.

Archilochus knew many sides of war, and had many
different feelings and views on the subject. He did
not stage himself as a hero and had the true soldier's
dislike for any kind of heroics. He liked to show his
realistic attitude towards war by a lighthearted
cynicism and contempt for appearances. Twice at
least he wrote verses which would not please a ser-
geant-major. In one he is concerned with the bore-
dom of keeping watch, and his solution is to drink
wine:

ἀλλ' ἄγε σὺν κώθωνι θοῆς διὰ σέλματα νηὸς
  φοίτα καὶ κοίλων πώματ' ἄφελκε κάδων,
ἄγρει δ' οἶνον ἐρυθρὸν ἀπὸ τρυγός· οὐδὲ γὰρ ἡμεῖς
  νήφειν ἐν φυλακῆι τῆιδε δυνησόμεθα.[17]

Come, pass a cup along the swift ship's benches:
  Draw the drinks off from the hollow tuns.
Drain red wine to the lees. No more than others
  Can we keep sobriety on guard.

This is bad enough by all military rules, but what are
we to think of the following?

[17] Fr. 5.

ἀσπίδι μὲν Σαΐων τις ἀγάλλεται, ἣν παρὰ θάμνωι
  ἔντος ἀμώμητον κάλλιπον οὐκ ἐθέλων.
αὐτὸς δ' ἐξέφυγον θανάτου τέλος. ἀσπὶς ἐκείνη
  ἐρρέτω· ἐξαῦτις κτήσομαι οὐ κακίω.[18]

A perfect shield bedecks some Thracian now;
  I had no choice: I left it in a wood.
Ah, well, I saved my skin, so let it go!
  A new one's just as good.[19]

The delightful insouciance of these lines presents a
marked contrast to the way in which Homer makes
his heroes fight over armor, as if to lose a weapon were
an appalling dishonor. Archilochus, with years of
military experience, had no such illusions, and
started a fashion which was copied by Alcaeus,
Anacreon, and Horace,[20] as if Archilochus had made
the loss of a shield respectable, at least for a poet.

These poems come from the lighter side of war, and
if a soldier is to keep sane, he must see things as
Archilochus saw them. This does not mean that he
was dulled to war's horrors and sorrows: rather, he
steeled himself to endure them and not to complain
about the inevitable. In some verses to a friend,
Pericles, he shows a philosophic spirit about suffering
and loss, but it is based on genuine sympathy and
understanding:

κήδεα μὲν στονόεντα, Περίκλεες, οὔτε τις ἀστῶν
  μεμφόμενος θαλίηις τέρψεται οὐδὲ πόλις·

[18] Fr. 6b.
[19] Tr. Sir William Marris.
[20] Cf. *Greek Lyric Poetry*, p. 152.

τοίους γὰρ κατὰ κῦμα πολυφλοίσβοιο θαλάσσης
  ἔκλυσεν· οἰδαλέους δ' ἀμφ' ὀδύνηισ' ἔχομεν
πνεύμονας· ἀλλὰ θεοὶ γὰρ ἀνηκέστοισι κακοῖσιν,
  ὦ φίλ', ἐπὶ κρατερὴν τλημοσύνην ἔθεσαν
φάρμακον. ἄλλοτε τ' ἄλλος ἔχει τάδε· νῦν μὲν ἐς ἡμέας
  ἐτράπεθ', αἱματόεν δ' ἕλκος ἀναστένομεν,
ἐξαῦτις δ' ἑτέρους ἐπαμείψεται. ἀλλὰ τάχιστα
  τλῆτε γυναικεῖον πένθος ἀπωσάμενοι.[21]

Of lamentable miseries complaining
  Neither man nor town enjoys the feast:
These men, 'tis true, the sea's wave loud-resounding
  Overwhelmed, and our hearts swell with grief.
And yet for cureless ills in staunch endurance,
  Friend, the Gods have given us a drug.
To-day this man may suffer, that to-morrow:
  Now our turn to weep a bloody wound:
Soon will it pass to others. Lay aside, then,
  Quickly woman's sorrow and endure.

The circumstances in which these lines were sung are
fairly clear. The poet is at a feast, and his companion
cannot help weeping because of some friends who
have been lost in a disaster at sea. Archilochus
knows what Pericles suffers, but feels that it is better
to cheer and console him than to sympathize too
tenderly. He preaches the doctrine of "staunch
endurance," and calls such grief womanish. His
apparent sternness is due not to hardness of heart but
a lesson which he has learned from experience, to
face adversity without complaining and to accept
disaster with an almost Stoic calm.

[21] Fr. 7.

These small pieces of poetry throw some light on Archilochus' life and character, but they have also a technical interest. They are the earliest elegiacs we possess, and they may well have had an influence on later work. In any case they show at least one characteristic which was to persist in the elegiac until the Alexandrian poets changed its style. In these pieces Archilochus uses definitely Homeric language. We may note the familiar epithets, the "swift" ship, the "loudly-resounding" sea, the "red" wine, the "kneaded" bread, the traditional phrases like "the War-god's mellay" and "the end of death," the archaic genitive in -οιο which did not belong to Archilochus' own spoken tongue. Archilochus, it is clear, wrote elegiacs with his mind full of Homer and the epic vocabulary. And this is easily understood. The epic was preëminently the poetry of martial men, and it was only natural to use its phrases when writing about war. Moreover its vocabulary was too rich and too appropriate for an elegiac poet to neglect it; it lay there for his taking and fell at once into his dactylic couplets. But Archilochus showed his sense of form and style by excluding these epic phrases from his other forms of verse.[22] When he wrote in iambic and trochaic meters, he not only avoided them but used a more homely language which included words too colloquial for epic dignity. The distinction which he made is important; for others observed it. All the early elegists used the epic language, not,

[22] Cf. A. Hauvette, *Archiloque*, pp. 232–245.

indeed, slavishly, but with ease and discernment. But the iambic poets allowed themselves considerably more freedom and nearness to the speech of every day. The elegiac at its very beginning was dignified with the rich vocabulary of Homer.

The elegiacs of Archilochus belong to the camp. Hence their brightness and briskness, their touch with life and their absence of trimmings. This was the kind of poetry that soldiers liked. But in different circumstances, especially in Ionian cities where elegiac poems were sung over the wine in select company, there was a natural tendency to spread oneself, to make a poem of some length if the subject was important enough. The result was an art less concentrated than that of Archilochus, but still undeniably impressive. In the first half of the seventh century the whole of Asia Minor was ravaged by barbarian hordes of Cimmerians.[23] Among other places, they attacked Ephesus about 650 B.C. but failed to take it, though they burned the temple of Artemis outside the town. The crisis of this invasion inspired a poet of whom hardly anything else is known, the Ephesian Callinus. That he feared the invasion of the Cimmerians is shown by his splendid lone line:

νῦν δ' ἐπὶ Κιμμερίων στρατὸς ἔρχεται ὀβριμοεργῶν[24]

Now comes the murderous Cimmerian army.

[23] Cf. T. Hudson-Williams, *Early Greek Elegy*, pp. 12–19.
[24] Fr. 3 Diehl.

But perhaps we may see more clearly what his emotions were from the one long piece which survives under his name. In this the convivial and military types of elegiac are combined. It is addressed to men lying idly at a feast, not caring what is happening, as the opening lines show:

> μέχρις τεῦ κατάκεισθε; κότ' ἄλκιμον ἕξετε θῦμον,
>   ὦ νέοι; οὐδ' αἰδεῖσθ' ἀμφιπερικτίονας
> ὧδε λίην μεθιέντες; ἐν εἰρήνηι δὲ δοκεῖτε
>   ἦσθαι, ἀτὰρ πόλεμος γαῖαν ἄπασαν ἔχει.[25]

> How long, young men, unsoldiered, disregarding,
>   Laze you, scorned by neighbours round about?
> Slack to the bone, on peace resolved, supinely
>   Careless in a land where all is war? [26]

From this idle convivial scene Callinus turns to the threat of war, and mingles advice on how to fight with praise for the brave and gloomy forebodings of the future which awaits the cowardly. He claims that it is a fine thing to die for one's country, and he clinches his argument with the words:

> λαῶι γὰρ σύμπαντι πόθος κρατερόφρονος ἀνδρὸς
>   θνήισκοντος, ζώων δ' ἄξιος ἡμιθέων·
> ὥσπερ γὰρ μιν πύργον ἐν ὀφθαλμοῖσιν ὁρῶσιν·
>   ἔρδει γὰρ πολλῶν ἄξια μοῦνος ἐών.[27]

> The whole land mourns a man of heart heroic
>   dead: in life a demigod he seems.
> His strength is as a tower to all beholders —
>   work for many hands he does alone.[28]

[25] Fr. I, 1–4.
[26] Tr. T. F. Higham.

[27] Fr. I, 18–21.
[28] Tr. T. F. Higham.

This is truly noble verse, and the whole poem has a
singular force as if it had been inspired to a heroic
spirit by the awful emergency of the barbarian onset.
In it, as with Archilochus, the present becomes the
means of giving a universal lesson — the honor paid
to the brave man in life and in death. Callinus uses
very little decoration to secure his effect and relies on
the plain language of exhortation. His only metaphor
is when he compares the brave men to a tower, and
that may be seen in Homer [29] and was probably traditional. The force of the poem is greater because of
the extreme ease and naturalness of its composition.
The words follow the poet's feelings without hin-
drance, and they seem to be poured out; there is no
logical structure or development of thought, but
simply a series of emotional appeals.

This effect of simplicity is combined with a vocabulary which is almost entirely taken from the epic.
Only two of the words used are not to be found in
Homer, and one of these is built on a Homeric
model.[30] And not only words but whole phrases are
Homeric. Callinus likes to end a pentameter with a
Homeric phrase such as ἀλλά τις ἰθὺς ἴτω or κουριδίης
τ' ἀλόχου, and all his hexameters end with a word
which occurs at the end of a Homeric hexameter.
The explanation of these Homeric echoes is similar
to what we have seen in the case of Archilochus, but
here we see on a larger scale how the elegiac poet used

[29] *Od.* xi. 556.
[30] Cf. Hudson-Williams, *Early Greek Elegy*, p. 71.

the epic language. The borrowing is not due to the fact that Callinus was a mere imitator and did not know how to make a language of his own. It is rather the case that in his time almost any poet writing elegiac verse learned not to operate with a vocabulary of single, select words which were characteristically his own but with phrases and even with whole lines which belonged to his craft. He composed his verses in his head, and the task of composition was made easier, almost made possible, by the fact that for most situations and thoughts there was a phrase ready-made in the epic. The poet must often, too, have had to improvise as popular poets still do in the less literate parts of Europe, and for improvisation a stock vocabulary of this kind is almost indispensable. So the circumstances in which Callinus composed were different from any modern poet's. Nor was he expected to be remarkably original. He must say the right thing for the occasion, and he must say it in language sufficiently elevated. But he could use the ordinary language of poetry as he and his hearers knew it. Callinus indeed used it with ease and fluency. The epic phrases fall easily into his verse; there is no sense of strain or of obstacles overcome with difficulty.

This poem of Callinus is a stray fragment, washed up from an age of which we know almost nothing. In it the life of an Ionian city is in peril, and the Ionian poet responds with an almost heroic spirit to the emergency. Ionia survived the Cimmerian menace and maintained under Asiatic influence a delightfully

natural view of life. It is a great change to pass from
Homer's heroes or the militant Archilochus and
Callinus to Mimnermus of Colophon, who was writing about 630 B.C. He gives the other side of the elegiac, its convivial and amatory character. On the
whole his verses are full of a sweet melancholy, of
that delicious sadness which may come to a man after
he has eaten and drunk well. They recall those
marvelous Elizabethan songs which in a vigorous
full-blooded life of action lamented the futility of
living and the inevitability of the grave. To this task
Mimnermus brought a splendid assortment of gifts.
Of the early elegists he had the best ear. He manipu-
lated his meter with great confidence, and his swelling
emotions carried him beyond the narrow confines of a
couplet so that he built long passages which give in a
composite whole the ebb and flow of his thought.
Characteristic are some famous lines which stirred
the imagination of Horace and still remain a perfect
expression of a mood:

Τίς δὲ βίος, τί δὲ τερπνὸν ἄτερ χρυσῆς Ἀφροδίτης·
  τεθναίην, ὅτε μοι μηκέτι ταῦτα μέλοι,
κρυπταδίη φιλότης καὶ μείλιχα δῶρα καὶ εὐνή·
  οἷ' ἥβης ἄνθεα γίγνεται ἁρπαλέα
ἀνδράσιν ἠδὲ γυναιξίν· ἐπεὶ δ' ὀδυνηρὸν ἐπέλθηι
  γῆρας, ὅ τ' αἰσχρὸν ὁμῶς καὶ κακὸν ἄνδρα τιθεῖ,
αἰεί μιν φρένας ἀμφὶ κακαὶ τείρουσι μέριμναι,
  οὐ δ' αὐγὰς προσορῶν τέρπεται ἠελίου,
ἀλλ' ἐχθρὸς μὲν παισίν, ἀτίμαστος δὲ γυναιξίν·
  οὕτως ἀργαλέον γῆρας ἔθηκε θεός.[31]

Fr. 1 Diehl.

O golden love, what life, what joy but thine?
    Come death when thou art gone and make an end!
When gifts and tokens are no longer mine,
    Nor the sweet intimacies of a friend.
These are the flowers of youth. But painful age,
    The bane of beauty, following swiftly on,
Wearies the heart of man with sad presage
    And takes away his pleasure in the sun.
Hateful is he to maiden and to boy,
And fashioned by the gods for our annoy.[32]

The underlying thought of this poem is the familiar theme of *Carpe diem*, but though it makes its first appearance here, it is set out with great charm and skill. The pleasures of youth are put forward in the first three lines, and Mimnermus has no hesitation in speaking honestly about them. Love is his main subject, and he does not allow any competition with it. From it he turns to the horrors of old age when the handsome and the ugly man are in the same sad state. His thoughts are simple enough, though they need not necessarily be his whole philosophy of life. But what cannot fail to impress and delight is the art with which these thoughts are expressed. We may note the sure touch in his choice of adjectives, "golden" Aphrodite, "secret" love, "honey-sweet" gifts.[33] None of these adjectives is used for the first time in such a context; the first two appear in Homer,[34] the third in a Homeric Hymn,[35] but how exact and vivid each one is, how shortly the combinations in which

---

[32] Tr. G. Lowes Dickinson.
[33] I regret that these are not fully represented in the translation.
[34] *Il.* vi. 161, iii, 64.   [35] *Hom. Hymn* x. 2.

they are used conjure up the hidden delights of youth! We may notice too the few but forceful uses of imagery, the beautiful phrase about the flowers of youth which are ravished so soon, the bitter words about the evil cares which "wear out" the heart. And lastly we may notice the remarkable way in which the rhythm varies with the changes of thought and feeling. After the challenging, flaunting opening we are led through a swift account of youth, and then as we approach the horrors of old age, the verse becomes slower, the sentences shorter, the stops more emphatic, until the poet closes with a short, damning line of summary:

οὕτως ἀργαλέον γῆρας ἔθηκε θεός.

In every sentence the rhythm answers to the poet's feeling and may be said to make the poem.

Mimnermus indeed recurred to this theme, and another piece shows how well he could vary his treatment. We might think that once was enough, but Mimnermus attacks it twice and even three times, and each time he has something new to say. The second piece is a variation on a theme of Homer, the famous words of Glaucus to Diomedes:

οἵη περ φύλλων γενεή, τοίη δὲ καὶ ἀνδρῶν.[36]

even as the generation of leaves, so is that of men.

Homer, of course, referred to the speed with which one generation succeeds another, but Mimnermus

[36] *Il.* vi. 146.

takes his figure of the year's flowers and uses it as an
image for the single life which passes all too quickly:

ἡμεῖς δ' οἶά τε φύλλα φύει πολυάνθεμος ὥρη
  ἔαρος, ὅτ' αἶψ' αὐγῆισ' αὔξεται ἠελίου,
τοῖσ' ἴκελοι πήχυιον ἐπὶ χρόνον ἄνθεσιν ἥβης
  τερπόμεθα, πρὸς θεῶν εἰδότες οὔτε κακόν
οὔτ' ἀγαθόν· Κῆρες δὲ παρεστήκασι μέλαιναι,
  ἡ μὲν ἔχουσα τέλος γήραος ἀργαλέου,
ἡ δ' ἑτέρη θανάτοιο· μίνυνθα δὲ γίγνεται ἥβης
  καρπός, ὅσον τ' ἐπὶ γῆν κίδναται ἠέλιος.
αὐτὰρ ἐπὴν δὴ τοῦτο τέλος παραμείψεται ὥρης,
  αὐτίκα δὴ τεθνάναι βέλτιον ἢ βίοτος·
πολλὰ γὰρ ἐν θυμῶι κακὰ γίγνεται· ἄλλοτε οἶκος
  τρυχοῦται, πενίης δ' ἔργ' ὀδυνηρὰ πέλει·
ἄλλος δ' αὖ παίδων ἐπιδεύεται, ὧν τε μάλιστα
  ἱμείρων κατὰ γῆς ἔρχεται εἰς Ἀίδην·
ἄλλος νοῦσον ἔχει θυμοφθόρον· οὐ δέ τίς ἐστιν
  ἀνθρώπων, ὧι Ζεὺς μὴ κακὰ πολλὰ διδοῖ.[37]

We are as leaves in jewelled springtime growing
    That open to the sunlight's quickening rays;
So joy we in our span of youth, unknowing
    If Gods shall bring us good or evil days.
Two fates beside thee stand; the one hath sorrow
    Dull age's fruit, the other gives the boon
Of Death, for youth's fair fruit hath no to-morrow,
    And lives but as a sunlit afternoon.
And when thine hour is spent, and passeth by thee,
    Surely to die were better than to live,
Ere grief or evil fortune come anigh thee,
    And penury that hath but ill to give.
Who longs for children's love, for all his yearning
    Shall haply pass to death anhungered still;
Or pain shall come, his life to anguish turning,
    Zeus hath for all an endless store of ill.[38]

[37] Fr. 2.   [38] Tr. J. A. Pott.

Here too there is the same mastery of imagery and
rhythm, the same leading to a tense climax. But
here Mimnermus may be illustrated on two small
points which are significant for his art and view of
life. First, there is his conception of the two Fates, of
death and old age, which stand by a man. The word
used, Κῆρες, shows that he had in mind a famous
passage of the *Iliad*, where Achilles says that he has
two alternative fates: either he can die with glory at
Troy or he can return home unrenowned and live to
an old age.[39] It is clear that in either case the fate
means death, whether soon or late. But Mimnermus
takes the idea and makes a different antithesis. For
him the fate of old age is, if anything, worse than
death, since it despoils a man but does not annihilate
him. No doubt he was able to use the word in this
sense because in popular mythology it was connected
with monsters such as Gorgons, Sirens, Harpies, and
the Sphinx, all of whom brought death. But the fact
remains that in giving a man two fates which are not
alternative but successive he adds to the horrors of a
simple belief and shows that for him old age is itself a
form of living death. And so indeed he believed. For
in another fragment he laments that it destroys a
man's eyes and wits and makes him unrecognizable.[40]
So an idea, simple enough in Homer, is made to play
an almost sophisticated part in Mimnermus' philosophy.

Secondly, this poem contains perhaps the nearest
attempt made by Mimnermus to sum up his view of

[39] *Il.* ix. 411 ff.   [40] Fr. 5.

life and of man's place in it. The early Greek poets in
their different ways made such attempts, which
largely took the form of asking in what the Good for a
man lies. In this poem Mimnermus gives his answer
and finds the Good in those years of a man's life when
he can enjoy pleasures. After this a man is faced by
old age with its accompaniments of poverty, child-
lessness, and disease. To all Greeks these were un-
questionable evils, and there is no need to defend
Mimnermus' choice of them. But it is interesting that
another poet of this time, Semonides of Amorgos,
dealt with a similar topic in rather a different way.
In an elegiac poem he quoted Homer's words on
which Mimnermus had built his poem and drew a
lesson from them:

> ἓν δὲ τὸ κάλλιστον Χῖος ἔειπεν ἀνήρ·
> 'οἵη περ φύλλων γενεή, τοίη δὲ καὶ ἀνδρῶν.'
> παῦροι μὴν θνητῶν οὔασι δεξάμενοι
> στέρνοισ' ἐγκατέθεντο· πάρεστι γὰρ ἐλπὶς ἑκάστωι
> ἀνδρῶν, ἥ τε νέων στήθεσιν ἐμφύεται.
> θνητῶν δ' ὄφρα τις ἄνθος ἔχηι πολυήρατον ἥβης,
> κοῦφον ἔχων θυμὸν πόλλ' ἀτέλεστα νοεῖ·
> οὔτε γὰρ ἐλπίδ' ἔχει γηρασέμεν οὔτε θανεῖσθαι
> οὐδ', ὑγιὴς ὅταν ἦι, φροντίδ' ἔχει καμάτου.
> νήπιοι, οἷς ταύτηι κεῖται νόος, οὐ δὲ ἴσασιν,
> ὡς χρόνος ἔσθ' ἥβης καὶ βιότου ὀλίγος
> θνητοῖσ'. ἀλλὰ σὺ ταῦτα μαθὼν βιότου ποτὶ τέρμα
> ψυχῆι τῶν ἀγαθῶν τλῆθι χαριζόμενος.[41]

One best thing the Man of Chios said:
"Like that of leaves, so is men's generation."

[41] Fr. 29 Diehl. Cf. E. Römisch, *Studien zur älteren griechischen Elegie*,
pp. 48–60.

Yet but few have listened with their ears
And set it in their hearts. Each has for comrade
  Hope, who grows within a young man's breast.
So long as mortal man has youth's loved blossom,
  Light his heart is, vain his many dreams.
He has no thought of growing old or dying,
  Nor in health has any care for pain.
Poor fools, whose mind is such, who have no knowledge
  That for men the span of youth and life
Is short. Listen to this, and till life's closing
  Let your soul find pleasure in good things.

It looks on the whole as if Semonides wrote after
Mimnermus and carried the war into his own ground.
Semonides starts from the same quotation and
accepts the main facts as Mimnermus states them
about old age, sickness, and death. But he turns
these facts to a different conclusion. He does not
accept the view that youth is man's Good, but asserts
that it is a period of illusion and vain hopes. Mimnermus had complained that youth lasted only for a
short span, but Semonides corrected him by adding
that the whole of life is short. So he undermined the
consolation which Mimnermus had found and sub-
stituted for it a complete nihilism in which the only
pleasant things seem to be hopes which are doomed to
failure. And just as Mimnermus had found that the
worst evils were what a man suffered in his heart, so
Semonides makes his vain hopes grow inside a man,
taking the same subjective standpoint but showing
that it must be reckoned for in youth as well as in old
age. But in the end Semonides seems to have come to
a conclusion which resembled that of Mimnermus.

Because there is no sure good in life, we should enjoy the "good things." He does not say what they are; but surely this is a hedonistic argument, based not on the fugitive nature of youth but on the uncertainty and shortness of human life.

The philosophy which Mimnermus outlined in these poems is simple enough, and it appeals more to the imagination than to the intellect. He was unquestionably sincere in what he said, but it did not cover all his interests or take account of all his admirations. It looks rather as if Mimnermus wrote like this because at certain times he felt like this. At other times his imagination was engaged by other subjects than love and pleasure. So he used the elegiac as a medium also for narrative and historical or mythological subjects. That these too were sung to the flute need not surprise us; for in the seventh century the Greeks had no history in the modern sense, and its place was taken by narrative poetry. Just as Homer in his *Iliad* had told of the Siege of Troy, so Mimnermus wrote about the past, making, as we might expect, no distinction between myths of the heroic age and records of a time much nearer to his own. Of his mythological themes two bright examples survive. In one he speaks of Jason and the golden fleece, an age-old theme to which Homer had made a casual reference as if it were already a well-worn topic in his day.[42] In the few lines of Mimnermus which survive on the subject he seems to follow

[42] *Od.* xii. 70.

the main outlines of the story as we know it in later
poets like Pindar and Apollonius Rhodius. He told
of king Aeëtes dwelling in Colchis, of Jason being
sent on a long journey by Pelias, of the golden fleece,
and of the Argonauts' return by the stream of
Ocean. To the telling of this he seems to have
brought a characteristic economy and skill, as three
lines show:

Αἰήταο πόλιν, τόθι τ' ὠκέος Ἠελίοιο
  ἀκτῖνες χρυσέωι κείαται ἐν θαλάμωι
Ὠκεανοῦ παρὰ χεῖλος, ἵν' ὤιχετο θεῖος Ἰήσων.[43]

Aeëtes' city, where the fleeting Sun-God's
    Rays are laid up in a golden room,
By Ocean's lips. There godlike Jason journeyed.

Small though the quotation is, it shows how Mimnermus brought his own fancy to play on the old story.
He makes Aeëtes live at the edge of the world on the
shore of the circumambient Ocean, and he makes his
home strange and magical because in it the Sun has a
treasure room of his beams which are kept, as it were,
in an arsenal. Aeëtes was the child of the Sun and
was said to live in the East; so Mimnermus on the
strength of this created a wonderful home for him.

In another passage Mimnermus elaborated an
idea which seems to come more from popular belief
than from the epic. It was always a difficulty to the
Greeks to find how the Sun, having crossed from East
to West in his chariot, came back from West to East

[43] Fr. 11, 5-7.

for his next day's work. An old idea, based on a still
older belief that the Sun was actually a golden cup,
was that he was carried home every night in a magic
cup or boat. The idea appealed to many poets and
was used by Stesichorus in his account of Heracles'
adventures in the West,[44] but Mimnermus treated it
with a more delicate fancy, when he wrote:

> Ἥλιος μὲν γὰρ πόνον ἔλλαχεν ἤματα πάντα,
>   οὐ δέ κοτ' ἄμπαυσις γίγνεται οὐδεμία
> ἵπποισίν τε καὶ αὐτῶι, ἐπεὶ ῥοδοδάκτυλος Ἠώς
>   Ὠκεανὸν προλιποῦσ' οὐρανὸν εἰσαναβῆι·
> τὸν μὲν γὰρ διὰ κῦμα φέρει πολυήρατος εὐνὴ
>   κο⟨ι⟩ίλη Ἡφαίστου χερσὶν ἐληλαμένη
> χρυσοῦ τιμήεντος, ὑπόπτερος, ἄκρον ἐφ' ὕδωρ
>   εὕδονθ' ἁρπαλέως χώρου ἀφ' Ἑσπερίδων
> γαῖαν ἐς Αἰθιόπων, ἵνα δὴ θοὸν ἅρμα καὶ ἵπποι
>   ἑστᾶσ', ὄφρ' Ἠὼς ἠριγένεια μόληι.[45]

Surely the Sun has labour all his days
    And never any respite, teams, nor god,
Since Eos first, whose hands are rosy rays,
    Ocean forsook and Heaven's high pathway trod:
At night across the sea that wondrous bed
    Shell-hollow, beaten by Hephaestus' hand,
Of winged gold and gorgeous, bears his head
    Half-waking on the wave, from eve's red strand
To the Ethiop shore, where steeds and chariot are,
Keen-mettled, waiting for the morning star.[46]

The old myth is seen with clear eyes, and each detail
has just that additional touch which makes it intimate and significant. The magic vessel which carries

---

[44] Cf. *Greek Lyric Poetry*, pp. 86–88.   [45] Fr. 10.
[46] Tr. Gilbert Murray.

the Sun is gold and winged, true product of Hephaestus' workshop, and in it the god sleeps until he
reaches his home where he must begin his labors over
again. And in the very notion of the unwearying
Sun, Mimnermus lets his own philosophy peep out.
Not even a great god like this is free from toil and
trouble.

Both these mythological pieces come from a poem
which was known in antiquity as the *Nanno*, called, it
seems, after a girl whom Mimnermus loved. The precise character of this poem is still rather a mystery,
but it seems to have been composed on rather a large
scale and to have interwoven episodes of mythology
with its amatory matter. Callimachus indeed seems
to have thought it inferior to Mimnermus' shorter
pieces,[47] but he was grinding a private axe against
Apollonius and the advocates of long poems, and
need not be taken too seriously. But his description
of it as ἡ μεγάλη γυνή, "the tall lady," certainly shows
that it was built to some size. Into it episodes must
have been woven which illustrated Mimnermus'
views on life and love. Perhaps the unwearying
Sun belonged to the first class; the second seems to
have contained the story of Jason. We have only the
one half of an unfulfilled conditional sentence, but it
looks as if the other half had said something like "if
he had not been helped by Medea who loved him":

οὐδέ κοτ' ἂν μέγα κῶας ἀνήγαγεν αὐτὸς Ἰήσων
    ἐξ Αἴης τελέσας ἀλγινόεσσαν ὁδόν,

[47] *Ox. Pap.* 2079. 11–12.

ὑβριστῆι Πελίηι τελέων χαλεπῆρες ἄεθλον,
οὐδ' ἂν ἐπ' Ὠκεανοῦ καλὸν ἵκοντο ῥόον.[48]

Nor would have Jason made his painful journey,
    Nor have brought from Aea the great fleece,
Achieving for proud Pelias a grim labor,
    Nor would they have found fair Ocean's stream.

The story of Jason was suitable enough for a love poem, but there were other episodes in the *Nanno*, whose relevance is not so easy to see. Among them are some lines important for the historian in which Mimnermus touched on the history of the Ionian colonization of the Asiatic seaboard and told of the early wars for the site of Smyrna.[49] This seems to have been a careful, almost dry, piece of narrative, and it is hard to see how it fitted into a poem which also lamented the passing of youth[50] or the sad fate of Tithonus who was allowed to grow old but not to die.[51]

This intermingling of themes in the *Nanno* might be explained by the twofold character of the elegiac which allowed both convivial and military themes. But it might equally be explained by Mimnermus' own tastes. He was a man of pleasure, but he was also an admirer of warlike prowess, and he may well have put both sides of himself into a long poem. A recent discovery throws some light on another poem of his which seems to have been purely historical. A papyrus commentary on Antimachus says that Mimnermus wrote a *Smyrneis*,[52] and this must be the poem

[48] Fr. 11, 1-4.   [49] Fr. 12.   [50] Fr. 5.   [51] Fr. 4.
[52] *Antimachi Colophonii Reliquiae*, ed. B. Wyss, p. 83.

to which Pausanias refers when he says that Mimnermus wrote elegiac lines on the battle between the
Smyrneans and the Lydians under Gyges.[53] That
Mimnermus should write about Smyrna need occasion no surprise. Smyrna and Colophon were closely
connected by traditions of a common origin, and
Smyrna was said to have been founded from Colophon, while according to some authorities Mimnermus himself came from Smyrna.[54] The *Smyrneis*
must have dealt with what was for Mimnermus quite
recent history. For Gyges must have attacked
Smyrna about 680 B.C., and Mimnermus met sur-
vivors from the war. In the same war Miletus was
attacked and Colophon was taken, and Mimnermus
was acquainted with the living tradition of the
events. The lines quoted by the papyrus from the
Smyrneis show that it was a record of facts like
Mimnermus' account of the Ionian colonization:

ὡς οἱ πὰρ βασιλῆος, ἐπε[ὶ ῥ'] ἐνεδέξατο μῦθο[ν,]
ἤ[ϊξα]ν κοίληι[σ' ἀ]σπίσι φραξάμενοι

So from the King, when he made known his order,
   Darted they, fenced in their hollow shields.

But it seems to have reached a higher level than this.
For some other lines seem to belong to it and show
Mimnermus in an unexpectedly heroic temper:

οὐ μὲν δὴ κείνου γε μένος καὶ ἀγήνορα θυμὸν
   τοῖον ἐμεῦ προτέρων πεύθομαι, οἵ μιν ἴδον

[53] Paus. ix. 29, 4.
[54] Suidas *s.v.* Μίμνερμος. Cf. Hudson-Williams, *Early Greek Elegy*,
p. 18.

Λυδῶν ἱππομάχων πυκινὰς κλονέοντα φάλαγγας
  Ἕρμιον ἂμ πεδίον, φῶτα φερεμμελίην·
τοῦ μὲν ἄρ' οὔκοτε πάμπαν ἐμέμψατο Παλλὰς Ἀθήνη
  δριμὺ μένος κραδίης, εὖθ' ὅ γ' ἀνὰ προμάχους
σεύαιθ' αἱματόεν⟨τος ἐν⟩ ὑσμίνηι πολέμοιο
  πικρὰ βιαζόμενος δυσμενέων βέλεα·
οὐ γάρ τις κείνου ληῶν ἔπ' ἀμεινότερος φώς
  ἔσκεν ἐποίχεσθαι φυλόπιδος κρατερῆς
ἔργον, ὅτ' αὐγῆισιν φέρετ' ὠκέος ἠελίοιο.[55]

Not his such puny strength and flinching temper,
  So my fathers told me: him they saw
Routing the serried ranks of Lydian horsemen
  In the plain of Hermus with his spear.
Pallas Athene never once upbraided
  His keen strength of spirit, as he ran
Vanwards amid the bloody press of battle,
  And defied his foemen's bitter shafts.
No man has ever fought his enemies better
  Nor done more in battle's fearful crash,
Than he when he ran forward like a sunbeam.

This poem shows another side to Mimnermus' nature
and shows that in him the heroic spirit, of which
Homer had sung, was still alive. And the events
which it records were still recent, in fact recent
enough to have made a deep mark on Mimnermus.
Smyrna resisted Gyges, but Colophon submitted to
him, and passed at once into a proverb for the
punishment of insolent pride. It was thought to have
been punished for wanting too much from life, and
Theognis clinched the matter when he said:

[55] Fr. 13.

"Ὕβρις καὶ Μάγνητας ἀπώλεσε καὶ Κολοφῶνα
καὶ Σμύρνην. πάντως, Κύρνε, καί ὕμμ' ἀπολεῖ.[56]

Pride it was that laid Magnesia low,
And Colophon and Smyrna. Well I know,
Cyrnus, the way that you and yours will go.[57]

And another critic of morals, Xenophanes, himself a
Colophonian, described in vivid language the careless
effrontery of his countrymen before they were enslaved to "hateful tyranny." [58] No doubt Mimnermus knew this reputation and the moral which was
drawn from it, but he protested against it in this case.
The man of whom he writes is a real fighter, and
Mimnermus speaks of him with knowledge. This is
no academic praise of fighting; it comes from a man
who knew where the enemy's strength lay and how a
brave man set out to overcome it. And Mimnermus
felt, as the first words show, that in his own age there
were few men like this. No doubt the Lydian conquest and the ensuing tyranny had deeply wounded
the self-esteem of Colophon and made its citizens feel
inferior to their fighting forebears.

Mimnermus' attitude to acts of force and courage is
not quite what we might expect. He admires them,
but he is curiously outspoken about them. He betrays an admiration for successful acts of violence
and for the qualities that produce them. When he
speaks of his fighter as "defying his foemen's bitter
shafts," he uses the word βιαζόμενος, which means

[56] 1103-4.   [57] Tr. T. F. Higham.   [58] Fr. 3.

literally "doing violence to," and recalls the words
which Athene uses to Hector about the violent
onslaught of Achilles; [59] it is certainly more than
the usual word for "withstanding." Curious too is
the phrase δριμὺ μένος κραδίης, "sharp strength of
spirit," which recalls the δριμὺς θυμός, the sharp
anger which the Chorus of the *Choephoroi* feels for
Clytaemestra and Aegisthus. [60] Here they stand for
the fierce temper of the soldier who is carried away
by the excitement of battle. In both these phrases
Mimnermus shows a real knowledge of the qualities
which carry a brave man into battle; he has no ro-
mantic illusions about fighting. Even more significant are the lines in the *Nanno* on the early wars of
Smyrna, where Mimnermus' way of speaking would
have shocked many Greeks:

> ἐς δ' ἐρατὴν Κολοφῶνα βίην ὑπέροπλον ἔχοντες
> ἐζόμεθ' ἀργαλέης ὕβριος ἡγεμόνες· [61]

Fair Colophon in pride of strength we settled,
Leading on our armies harsh and proud.

Here two points may be noted. Mimnermus uses
of his compatriots the words βίην ὑπέροπλον ἔχοντες
which Hesiod had used of the Titans, [62] the traditional
example of that presumption which is punished.
Then not content with this he says that they were
ἀργαλέης ὕβριος ἡγεμόνες, and though he makes the
ὕβρις worse by giving it such an adjective, he still

[59] *Il.* xxii. 229.
[60] *Cho.* 391-2.
[61] Fr. 12, 4-5.
[62] *Theog.* 670.

seems to claim it is a virtue, or at least not to be
ashamed of it. His words are almost an acceptance
of the claim that Colophon suffered from presumption
and look like a glorying in the charge. Mimnermus
seems to have been a proud man and to have felt that
at least in war it was well to be quite ruthless.

We may, then, see in Mimnermus an aristocrat who
loved the pleasures of life but was also a keen admirer
of fighting qualities. He had in him a certain proud
exclusiveness, as befitted a Colophonian, and it was
this which made him not care too much what other
men might say:

> τὴν σαυτοῦ φρένα τέρπε· δυσηλεγέων δὲ πολιτέων
> ἄλλος τίς σε κακῶς, ἄλλος ἄμεινον ἐρεῖ.[63]

Make glad your own heart. Of your pitiless townsmen
   One will speak with ill words, one with good.

We may contrast this independence with Pindar's
horror of slander or with Solon's prayer to have a
good report. Noble too are the words which Mimnermus speaks about the truth:

> ἀληθείη δὲ παρέστω
> σοὶ καὶ ἐμοί, πάντων χρῆμα δικαιότατον.[64]

   For you and me let there be present
   Truth, the rightest of all things that are.

He seems to have felt no desire to compromise or to
adapt himself to circumstances. He felt secure in his
own opinions, and the society in which he lived must

[63] Fr. 7.   [64] Fr. 8.

have allowed considerable rein to individuality. Such anxieties as assailed him were not, like those of Theognis, from social revolution but from decay of faculties and old age. He seems not to have been haunted, as many Greeks were, with the notion that the gods were jealous of human success, and such pleasures as life could offer he proposed to enjoy.

Mimnermus turned his feelings into melodious verse. Of the early elegists he is the most accomplished and the most musical, and though he has not the sinewy strength of Archilochus, he has a finer grace and a more lyrical charm. Compared with him Solon and Tyrtaeus are amateurs who sometimes find the technique of verse making difficult and write with a curious clumsiness. He was a master of his own kind of poetry, and we can understand why Propertius, himself no mean poet of love, could say:

> plus in amore valet Mimnermi versus Homero.[65]

It was as a poet of love that Mimnermus won renown, and yet in his remains love is not the only nor the most important theme. His interest is wider, and what really awakes his inspiration is not love but pleasure. And this he turns into high poetry because he sees it in a special light as something soon lost and uniquely desirable. He is less a hedonist than an artist, who makes his subject a matter of universal importance and almost literally a question of life and death. We may suspect too that Mimnermus, like

[65] Prop. I. 9, 11.

Pindar, found something in poetry and the exaltation of making it which he could not easily define but symbolized by the image of light. In the seventy-one verses of his which survive, six mention the Sun. If we omit the lines on the Sun's journey, the rest are instructive enough. He regrets the time when a man finds no pleasure in looking on the Sun; it is the Sun which swells the leaves in spring; youth comes as quickly as the Sun rises; the Sun's beams are laid up in the house of Aeetes; the fighter against the Lydians went into battle like the Sun's rays. It may be an accident that the Sun appears so often in his verse, but it is easier to believe that this was a favorite symbol with him because in the Sun's light and strength he found something which touched him deeply and resembled the glory which he found in the fleeting joys of youth.

II
TYRTAEUS

ELEGY was born in Ionian lands, and its first practitioners were Ionians, even though, like Archilochus, they wandered far from home. But one of the most notable homes of early elegy was Dorian Sparta. In the seventh century Sparta was not what it was in the fifth. It had its indigenous arts of pottery, ivory carving, and gold work, and it had too a literature well suited to its taste for music and its many festivals. This literature was in the main the work of men who came from other cities, but the fragments of Alcman show how well they habituated themselves to the spirit of Spartan institutions. Spartan poetry was in the main lyrical and choral. But other forms were introduced from outside and made their mark. Terpander of Lesbos seems to have started recitations of Homer and to have composed Preludes to them in epic hexameters. And closely after the epic came the Ionian elegiac. This is connected with the name of Tyrtaeus, whose works were still popular in the fourth century and who was always regarded as the characteristic poet of Sparta and the Spartan spirit. But even in antiquity there was some mystery about Tyrtaeus, and modern critics have found difficulties both in his origin and in his works. It has been debated where he came from, when he lived, and what he wrote. Before attempting more detailed criticism of his fragments, we may pause for a moment on this dusty battleground.

Plato asserted,[1] and many followed him, that Tyrtaeus was by origin an Athenian who was given Spartan citizenship; and later writers such as Pausanias [2] had a more elaborate story that he was a lame Athenian schoolmaster who was brought to Sparta by an oracle. Variations of this kind need not detain us: they belong to legend. But it is just conceivable that Tyrtaeus was an Athenian — not likely, but conceivable. In the seventh century most of the poets who were active at Sparta — Terpander, Thaletas, Alcman, Polymnestus — came from elsewhere, and except for Tyrtaeus no poet who worked in Sparta has claims to be called a Spartan. Perhaps the true Spartan felt that poetry was below his dignity and preferred to employ professionals. But Tyrtaeus does not seem to be quite in the same case as these others, and there are good reasons for believing that he was born and bred a Spartan. First, he undoubtedly held an important position in the Spartan state. Diodorus [3] and Athenaeus [4] both say that he was a general, and the statement is borne out by a passage in Strabo [5] which asserts that on his own statement Tyrtaeus led the Spartans in the second Messenian War, and by at least two of his surviving fragments,[6] of which one is concerned with details of military organization and the other tells his followers how to conduct themselves in battle. It is surely inconceiv-

---

[1] *Laws* i, 629 a.
[2] Paus. iv. 15, 6.
[3] Diod. viii. 36.

[4] Ath. xiv. 630e.
[5] Strab. viii. 362.
[6] Frs. 1 and 8.

able that a post of such importance could be held by one who was not a Spartan at a time when the whole Spartan polity was in grave danger of destruction. Secondly, the other poets who worked in Sparta in Tyrtaeus' time were writers of choral songs and had nothing to do with the almost sacred military activities of the Spartan ruling class. But Tyrtaeus is the very voice of this class, the interpreter of its ideals, and its instructor on the art of war. He speaks with authority and is not afraid of saying harsh words to shirkers. This too is surely improbable in a foreigner. Whatever they might feel about their lack of skill in poetry, the Spartans can have felt no such lack where war was concerned and would not have taken orders from a stranger, no matter how distinguished.

It looks in fact as if Plato's story and its later variations were mythical. Plato may well have invented it in his deep desire to find an ancient connection between Athens and Sparta and so secure a historical justification for his belief that the ideal state would be a mixture of the two. In the Alexandrian age the early history of Sparta became a subject for poetical romance. Rhianus wrote an epic poem about the Messenian Wars which was treated as a record of fact by Pausanias but was almost a pure work of fiction, and it is perhaps to him that some of the more picturesque elements in the legend of Tyrtaeus are due. The only authentic sources for his life are his poems, and these show that he was a man of authority in Sparta, an administrator and a general. He lived, beyond question, at the time of the Second Messenian War, when the non-Dorian inhabitants of the southern Peloponnesus made a desperate attempt to regain their liberty. The struggle was bitter and ended with the complete triumph of Sparta and the real consolidation of the Spartan system of government. Its date can be fixed in the second half of the seventh century, and that must be when Tyrtaeus lived. One of his fragments [7] mentions the three tribes which formed the Dorian system of organization until they were superseded by the five tribes of the Lycurgan reform, and in another [8] he says that he lived two generations after King Theopompus, who may be placed shortly before 700 B.C. Dates and details cohere into a single picture. Tyrtaeus was the poet of Sparta at a time of great danger. He held an important position, and the spirit of discipline which he preached was what won the war. So he was remembered as the incarnation of Spartan character, and his songs were sung for centuries after his death.

The elegiac was, as we have seen, sung to the flute. The Spartans marched into battle to the sound of the flute, and we may assume that the poems of Tyrtaeus were composed to be sung on the march. At all events Athenaeus says that the Spartans recited them in war and even moved in time to them.[9] Unlike the elegy of Callinus, which was sung to sluggards lying at a feast, the elegies of Tyrtaeus were sung when action was afoot and exhortation and advice were

[7] Fr. 1, 12.   [8] Fr. 4.   [9] Ath. xiv, 630e.

useful. They were in consequence longer than the
elegies which Archilochus sang to his friends; for the
march leaves plenty of time for singing. Of the complete specimens which survive one has thirty-two
and the other forty-four lines; only Solon can show
pieces so long. In composing elegies for Spartans
Tyrtaeus was probably a pioneer, and he had to look
abroad for his models. He found them in Ionian war
elegies like that of Callinus. Here was a type of poem
well suited to his need, and he modeled his own on it.
That is why, though a Spartan, he wrote in the
Ionian dialect, which must have been difficult for his
countrymen to understand. At times, it is true, his
own dialect breaks through, and he uses forms of the
Spartan vernacular alien to Ionic, such as the short
accusative plural in -as [10] and the future form
ἀλοιησεῦμεν.[11] But these are exceptions and in the
main he followed Ionian models. In this there was at
least one advantage. For a poet who was not a professional but modeled his art on that of others the
Ionian dialect was of great use because it possessed in
the Homeric poems an extensive assortment of words
and phrases which dealt with military matters and
fell automatically into the elegiac meter. Tyrtaeus
uses few words which are not to be found in Homer,
and of these nearly half are to be found in Hesiod and
the Homeric Hymns and belonged to the traditional
epic style.

[10] Fr. 1, 39 χαίτᾰς, 3, 5 δημότᾰς, 5, 4 δεσπότᾰς.
[11] Fr. 1, 16.

At a first glance the poems of Tyrtaeus seem to fall into two classes: in one he told of the Spartan past, in the other he gave advice for the present. But this distinction is probably illusory. He certainly told about the past, but he used it to illustrate lessons for the present. Thus he is the earliest authority for the legend that the Spartan state was founded when the sons of Heracles came from Doris to the Peloponnesus. His words survive:

αὐτὸς γὰρ Κρονίων, καλλιστεφάνου πόσις Ἥρης,
    Ζεὺς Ἡρακλείδαις τήνδε δέδωκε πόλιν·
οἷσιν ἅμα προλιπόντες Ἐρινεὸν ἠνεμόεντα
    εὐρεῖαν Πέλοπος νῆσον ἀφικόμεθα.[12]

Zeus, Cronus' son, the lord of bright-crowned Hera,
    Gave this town to sons of Heracles;
With them we left wind-swept Erineüs, coming
    Here to Pelops' spreading island-realm.

Whatever the actual facts may have been, this was the tradition as Tyrtaeus told it and after generations accepted it. The Dorians had come, they believed, from the North and occupied the valley of the Eurotas which had belonged to the Achaean Pelops some generations before. These lines come from a poem called Εὐνομίη or "Good Order." The name may not be so old as Tyrtaeus, but it shows that the poem was concerned with the new Spartan régime which was introduced after the Second Messenian War and attributed to Lycurgus. In it Tyrtaeus must have laid down some principles for this new system, and

[12] Fr. 2.

he seems to have strengthened its case with examples from the past. Here he shows the divinely ordained origin of Sparta and the heroic ancestry of its kings. But he did not confine himself to such generalities. In the same poem he told that the Delphic Oracle had given advice to the builders of the Spartan state, and this advice he quotes in detail:

'ἄρχειν μὲν βουλῆς θεοτιμήτους βασιλῆας,
  οἷσι μέλει Σπάρτης ἱμερόεσσα πόλις,
πρεσβύτας τε γέροντας, ἔπειτα δὲ δημότας ἄνδρας
  εὐθείαις ῥήτραις ἀνταπαμειβομένους·
μυθεῖσθαί τε τὰ καλὰ καὶ ἔρδειν πάντα δίκαια
  μηδέ τι βουλεύειν τῆιδε πόλει ⟨σκολιόν⟩·
δήμου δὲ πλήθει νίκην καὶ κάρτος ἔπεσθαι.'
  Φοῖβος γὰρ περὶ τῶν ὧδ' ἀνέφηνε πόλει.[13]

"The Kings, honoured by God, shall start all counsel,
    — Their's the care of Sparta's lovely town:
Next the Elders, after them the Commons
    Answering to forthright ordinance;
Say what is fair and do all things in justice,
    Nor give crooked counsel to the land.
So shall the multitude have strength and triumph."
    So did Phoebus show us his commands.

This cannot be taken as a correct statement of historical fact. The constitution, attributed by Tyrtaeus to Theopompus in the eighth century, is that which was brought into existence by the so-called reforms of Lycurgus. The Kings kept the power of leadership in war, but they were assisted and controlled by a Council of twenty-eight Elders. The rest of the citizens

[13] Fr. 3, 3-10.

were formed into the Apella, which was supposed to have sovereign powers but in fact could be dismissed by the Elders, who alone had the power of initiating legislation. The position of the people was well defined by a sentence which survives from the Lycurgan law: αἰ δὲ σκολίαν ὁ δᾶμος αἱρέοιτο, τοὺς πρεσβυγενέας καὶ ἀρχαγέτας ἀποστατῆρας ἦμεν — "If the people choose wrongly, the elders and rulers shall have power to dissolve." This law was probably made in the lifetime of Tyrtaeus and was of Spartan origin. But to give it dignity Tyrtaeus ascribed it to Apollo.

In another fragment Tyrtaeus tells of an important chapter of recent history. Two generations before him, in the last years of the eighth century, the Spartans under their King Theopompus had fought the First Messenian War. It lasted for twenty years, and the center of Messenian resistance was Mount Ithome, the key to the rich plain of Stenyclarus. The Spartans won, and the Messenians disappeared from history as a free people. Hitherto they had sent victors to the Olympic Games, but the change of affairs is shown by the absence of any Messenian victor after 736 B.C. and the appearance of the first Spartan victor in 716 B.C. Tyrtaeus describes the war with knowledge; for the tradition of it must have been still young in his day:

ἡμετέρωι βασιλῆϊ, θεοῖσι φίλωι Θεοπόμπωι,
    ὃν διὰ Μεσσήνην εἵλομεν εὐρύχορον,
Μεσσήνην ἀγαθὸν μὲν ἀροῦν, ἀγαθὸν δὲ φυτεύειν·
    ἀμφ' αὐτὴν δ' ἐμάχοντ' ἐννεακαίδεκ' ἔτη

νωλεμέως αἰεί, ταλασίφρονα θυμὸν ἔχοντες,
αἰχμηταὶ πατέρων ἡμετέρων πατέρες
εἰκοστῶι δ' οἳ μὲν κατὰ πίονα ἔργα λιπόντες
φεῦγον Ἰθωμαίων ἐκ μεγάλων ὀρέων.[14]

. . . Unto our king, the Gods' friend Theopompus;
  By his aid was broad Messene ours,
Messene good for tilth and good for planting;
  Nineteen years they fought to conquer it,
Without respite, and keeping hearts unfailing,
  Spearmen, fathers of our fathers they.
In twentieth year the foe left his fat acres,
  Fleeing from Ithome's mountain lands.

After this victory the Spartans reduced the Messenians to serfdom, and Tyrtaeus describes their plight
in a picturesque simile:

ὥσπερ ὄνοι μεγάλοισ' ἄχθεσι τειρόμενοι,
δεσποσύνοισι φέροντες ἀναγκαίης ὑπὸ λυγρῆς
ἥμισυ πᾶν ὅσσων καρπὸν ἄρουρα φέρει.[15]

Galled like asses, carrying great loads,
  Bringing in painful despite to their masters
  Half of all the fruit their ploughlands bore.

The conquest, however, was not final. In Tyrtaeus'
own day the Messenians revolted, and in their reduction he took an important part. So here too we may
suspect that the past is not entirely recalled for its
own sake but is a lesson for the present. The example
of the twenty years' endurance of an earlier generation was surely held out as a lesson to Tyrtaeus'
contemporaries, and the severe punishment of the

[14] Fr. 4.   [15] Fr. 5.

Messenians a cry for a punishment no less severe
after their revolt was crushed. There is no reason to
believe that Tyrtaeus advocated clemency to the
conquered.

It seems, then, that when Tyrtaeus dealt with the
past, he had the present firmly fixed in his mind; and
it is with it that his other fragments deal. An illumi-
nating example is contained in a papyrus of the third
century B.C. in the Berlin Museum. Unfortunately it
is very fragmentary and leaves more questions asked
than answered. In it Tyrtaeus gives excellent practi-
cal advice. He tells soldiers that they are to advance
"fenced behind hollow shields," [16] and this is a hint of
a type of warfare which was superseding the old
heroic method of single combat. It is the use of the
phalanx which came to be characteristic of Spartan
fighting and was well suited to their disciplined
armies. Tyrtaeus then issues orders and gives advice,
first to the three Spartan tribes, then, it seems, to his
own command:

χωρὶς Πάμφυλοί τε καὶ Ὑλλεῖς ἠδ[ὲ Δυμᾶνες]
  ἀνδροφόνους μελίας χερσὶν ἀν[ασχόμενοι].
[ἡμεῖς] δ᾽ ἀθανάτοισι θεοῖσ᾽ ἐπὶ πάντ[α τρέποντες]
  [ὄκνου] ἄτερ μονίηι πεισόμεθ᾽ ἡγεμ[όσιν].
ἀλλ᾽ εὐθὺς σύμπαντες ἀλοιησεῦ[μεν ἁμαρτῆι]
  [ἀ]νδράσιν αἰχμηταῖσ᾽ ἐγγύθεν ἱσ[τάμενοι].
δεινὸς δ᾽ ἀμφοτέρων ἔσται κτύπος [ὁρμηθέντων]
  ἀσπίδας εὐκύκλους ἀσπίσι τυπτ[έμεναι].[17]

Apart Pamphyli, Hylleis and Dymanes,
  Raise manslaying spears in hand.

[16] Fr. 1, 11.   [17] Fr. 1, 12–19.

We shall put all our trust in gods undying,
And obey our leaders unafraid.
And straightway all of us shall stand together,
Posted near to where the spearmen are.
Dread shall the din be when both charge together,
Striking rounded shield on rounded shield.

From this Tyrtaeus went on to a realistic account of
the actual fighting which would follow, with its falling
men and stones clattering on brazen helmets. The
details seem to show that he was writing for an actual
battle. It is hard to make out precisely what the organization is that he describes, but it seems clear that
each of the three tribes will advance separately and
that Tyrtaeus' command, whatever it was, will take
its place by the spearmen. Mention of a wall at 63
and 67 and of a tower at 72 seem to indicate that a
siege is in question, and that is more than likely if the
Messenians had entrenched themselves in the fortress
of Hira. It is interesting, too, to note that Tyrtaeus
here normally uses not the imperative but the future
indicative: we find at 15 πεισόμεθα, 16 ἀλοιησεῦμεν,
18 ἔσται κτύπος, 22 ἐρωήσουσιν, 24 καναχὴν ἔξουσι,
40 συνοίσομεν, 42 λογήσει, 73 λείψουσι. This is con-
trary to the practice of his other poems, where
general rules of fighting are more the matter than a
definite engagement, and they seem to support the
conclusion that these lines were written almost in
the trenches before an attack. After these details the
poem seems to have moved to first principles, to have
appealed to the Spartan gods, especially of course to

the Dioscuri but also to the more recently introduced Dionysus and Semele.

This topical and temporary interest is not to be seen so clearly in three other poems of Tyrtaeus, which are well preserved and probably complete and deal with the general aspects of war. These poems are of different lengths. No. 6–7 has 32 lines, No. 8 has 38, and No. 9 has 44; but all are built on a similar pattern.[18] In No. 6–7 Tyrtaeus devotes the first half to a general praise of dying for one's country, and in the second half he addresses the young men in particular. In No. 8 he begins by another general praise of courage and ends by specific advice about the conduct of fighting in an attack. In No. 9 he devotes the first half to a consideration of various types of ἀρετή, and the second half to a special study of the ἀρετή of the brave man. This method of construction is of some literary interest. It was observed by other elegists, and it seems to have been part of the elegiac art. Xenophanes follows it in his instructions to wine-drinkers, and "Theognis" in his poem on the proper use of wealth.[19] It survived into the Hellenistic age and may be detected in Catullus' translation of Callimachus' *Lock of Berenice*. There is, however, no satisfactory explanation of it. It was traditional to this form of composition, and by its observance Tyrtaeus shows that he had learned his art in a strict school.

[18] Cf. R. Reitzenstein, *Epigramm und Skolion*, pp. 46–48.
[19] 903–930.

All three poems are written in a similar language. In fact there are many verbal similarities between them, which have been misinterpreted as evidence for some of them being later than others. No. 9 has some five phrases which appear in the same or a very similar form in No. 8 and six which appear in No. 6–7. This shows no more than that Tyrtaeus composed, like Callinus, with epic phrases and words, and since the subjects of the three poems are similar, he fell naturally into repeating himself. He wrote for his own time and people, rather as Homer had made his princes address their followers in imaginary battles. There was indeed no other style open to him. The Choral Ode was concerned with quite different circumstances from soldiers on the march, and the only existing alternatives were the iambic and trochaic measures of Archilochus, which Solon was to use for public purposes. But these were too colloquial for Tyrtaeus' high task. They were also too intimate. What he needed was a literary form which had a certain dignity and impersonal quality suited to public use, and the elegiac was the only form that existed with these qualities. In practice he was not uninventive. He varied his stock phrases, and though the variations may be slight, they show some care for the technique of his craft. For the standard formula of "young and old" he has three different expressions: 9, 27 ὁμῶς νέοι ἠδὲ γέροντες, id. 37 ὁμῶς νέοι ἠδὲ παλαιοί, id. 41 ὁμῶς νέοι οἵ τε κατ' αὐτόν . . . οἵ τε παλαιότεροι. The variation is small, but not actually necessary. Tyrtaeus lacked Homer's great adaptability and resource, but he felt that he must do something to differentiate one line from another.

In No. 6–7 Tyrtaeus shows his twofold method of construction in so simple a form that many have thought it to be two poems.[20] But the orator Lycurgus quotes it as a single poem, and such undoubtedly it is. It is almost a recruiting poem, in which the poet first lays down the general principles of patriotic enlistment and then goes on to encourage the young men who are shirking their duty. The whole is bound together by the opening couplet which lays down the rule that it is good to die for one's country, because in so doing a man proves himself an ἀνὴρ ἀγαθός. The precise meaning of this will be considered later. For the moment it is interesting to see what arguments Tyrtaeus uses. He says nothing about the joy of battle or of what his country stands for. He simply develops the theme that it is appalling to be a beggar and an exile. He is evidently, though he does not say so, forecasting what will happen to the Spartans if they are defeated. In that case they will be robbed of their lands and sent to beg from unwilling givers. He draws his picture with some knowledge and power as if he knew what his threat meant, and its climax is that in such conditions a man loses all honor and respect:

> ἐχθρὸς μὲν γὰρ τοῖσι μετέσσεται, οὕς κεν ἵκηται
> χρησμοσύνηι τ᾽ εἴκων καὶ στυγερῆι πενίηι,

[20] Wilamowitz, *Textgeschichte der griechischen Lyriker*, p. 111.

αἰσχύνει τε γένος, κατὰ δ' ἀγλαὸν εἶδος ἐλέγχει,
πᾶσα δ' ἀτιμίη καὶ κακότης ἕπεται.[21]

Unwelcome he shall be, wherever turning,
    press'd by want and hateful penury;
he shames his folk and cheats his glorious manhood;
    all disgrace attends him, all despite.[22]

It was easy to use this as an argument to fight for
one's country, and Tyrtaeus did.

The second half appeals personally to the young
men and makes a point which is only applicable to
them — that it is disgraceful to leave all the fighting
to the old. After some general remarks on not
running away, Tyrtaeus produces a more special
argument, and makes a point which is not that made
by Spenser:

For age to die is right, but youth is wrong.

Tyrtaeus felt that the opposite was true. He first describes the horrors of an old man's death and then
says how fine it is for a young men to die. Here too he
makes his appeal through a realistic picture intended
to stir a sense of shame:

αἰσχρὸν γὰρ δὴ τοῦτο μετὰ προμάχοισι πεσόντα
    κεῖσθαι πρόσθε νέων ἄνδρα παλαιότερον
ἤδη λευκὸν ἔχοντα κάρη πολιόν τε γένειον
    θυμὸν ἀποπνείοντ' ἄλκιμον ἐν κονίηι,
αἱματόεντ' αἰδοῖα φίλαισ' ἐν χερσὶν ἔχοντα —
    αἰσχρὰ τά γ' ὀφθαλμοῖς καὶ νεμεσητὸν ἰδεῖν —
καὶ χρόα γυμνωθέντα· νέοισι δὲ πάντ' ἐπέοικεν,
    ὄφρ' ἐρατῆς ἥβης ἀγλαὸν ἄνθος ἔχηι· [23]

[21] Fr. 6–7, 7–10.   [22] Tr. T. F. Higham.   [23] Fr. 6–7, 21–28.

O foul reproach, when fallen with the foremost
    lies an elder, hindermost the young —
a man whose head is white, whose beard is hoary,
    breathing out his strong soul in the dust,
with blood-wet hands his naked members clutching —
    foul reproach, a sight no gods condone —
naked he lies where youth were better lying —
    sweet-flow'r'd youth, that nothing misbecomes.[24]

This might well bring a blush to a youthful Spartan
cheek. It would appeal to that respect for the old
which was inculcated by Spartan discipline and embodied in the position of the Elders in the Spartan
state. To make his effect Tyrtaeus has used a famous
passage of Homer, and a comparison between the
two is instructive. He has in mind the words which
Priam says to Hector when he anticipates his owns
death:

> νέωι δέ τε πάντ' ἐπέοικεν
> ἀρηϊκταμένωι, δεδαϊγμένωι ὀξέϊ χαλκῶι,
> κεῖσθαι· πάντα δὲ καλὰ θανόντι περ, ὅττι φανήηι.
> ἀλλ' ὅτε δὴ πολιόν τε κάρη πολιόν τε γένειον
> αἰδῶ τ' αἰσχύνωσι κύνες κταμένοιο γέροντος,
> τοῦτο δὴ οἴκτιστον πέλεται δειλοῖσι βροτοῖσιν.[25]

It well becomes a young man killed in war
To lie with all his battle-gashes on him;
All that is seen doth honour to his corpse.
But when dogs desecrate the hoary head
And beard and vitals of an old man slain,
That is the height of human tragedy.[26]

[24] Tr. T. F. Higham.
[25] Il. xxii. 71–6.
[26] Tr. Sir William Marris.

Tyrtaeus' debt to Homer, both in words and in matter, is clear enough. And since he follows his original closely, he is open to some criticism. Homer's lines are perfectly appropriate to an old man imagining the gruesome circumstances of his own death, but Tyrtaeus is concerned with old men as such, and the details, however impressive, are not absolutely relevant — there are other ways of being wounded than this. Moreover, to fit Homer's ideas into his elegiacs he has to resort to devices which are a little awkward. Thus he uses ἔχοντα in two different senses in the space of three lines, and his choice of two words to mean "hoary" is not so successful as Homer's repetition of the same word in πολιόν τε κάρη πολιόν τε γένειον. No doubt we could argue that all Tyrtaeus wants is a single scene of horror, and this he has. But the fact remains that he is after all not so skillful a poet as Homer whom he imitates.

No. 8 also begins with general reflections on courage, and here too the argument is unusual: Spartans must be brave because the dishonor of flight is not to be endured. To this point Tyrtaeus moves by an appeal to the Spartans as the descendants of Heracles, and tells them that Zeus is still on their side:

'Αλλ' — Ἡρακλῆος γὰρ ἀνικήτου γένος ἐστέ —
θαρσεῖτ' — οὔ πω Ζεὺς αὐχένα λοξὸν ἔχει — [27]

Sons of unconquered Heracles, show courage!
Zeus has not yet turned his head away.

[27] Fr. 8, 1–2.

It looks from this as if the Spartans had been defeated
and imagined that the gods were against them.
Tyrtaeus proclaims the friendliness of the gods, and
calls on the Spartans to show the spirit of their ances-
tor. Heracles was the ideal of Spartan manhood,
the hero who spent his life doing difficult tasks at the
bidding of another. In his endurance even when the
outlook seemed hopeless Tyrtaeus finds an example
for his soldiers. From this he elaborates to them his
case against flight. His argument is that they have
experience of both pursuit and of flight and can find
no real choice between them:

οἳ μὲν γὰρ τολμῶσι παρ' ἀλλήλοισι μένοντες
  ἔς τ' αὐτοσχεδίην καὶ προμάχους ἰέναι,
παυρότεροι θνήισκουσι, σαοῦσι δὲ λαὸν ὀπίσσω·
  τρεσσάντων δ' ἀνδρῶν πᾶσ' ἀπόλωλ' ἀρετή.
οὐδεὶς ἄν ποτε ταῦτα λέγων ἀνύσειεν ἕκαστα,
  ὅσσ', ἢν αἰσχρὰ πάθηι, γίγνεται ἀνδρὶ κακά·
ἀρ⟨π⟩αλέον γὰρ ὄπισθε μετάφρενόν ἐστι δαΐζειν
  ἀνδρὸς φεύγοντος δηΐωι ἐν πολέμωι·
αἰσχρὸς δ' ἐστὶ νέκυς κακκείμενος ἐν κονίηισι
  νῶτον ὄπισθ' αἰχμῆι δουρὸς ἐληλαμένος.[28]

Who have the courage, shoulder next to shoulder,
    Daring to advance to fray and van,
Of these are fewer slain; they save the people:
    But for cowards is all manhood lost.
And none can tell in speech of all the evils
    Which befall a man who finds disgrace.
Nay, sweet it is to pierce one's back behind him
    When he runs away in fearful war;
But shameful is the corpse in the dust lying,
    Stricken with a spear-point in the back.

[28] Fr. 8, 11–20.

The argument here, that it is safer to pursue than to
retire, is perhaps a case of special pleading. Tyrtaeus
had to vary his appeals, and he was here concerned
with preventing his troops from running away. So
he put forward an ingenious, if not altogether convincing, argument, and backed it with a simpler
appeal to the sense of shame.

The second half of No. 8 is again concerned with
details, and especially with advice on hand-to-hand
fighting. The soldier must take a firm stand and
follow his instructions:

ἀλλά τις ἐγγὺς ἰὼν αὐτοσχεδὸν ἔγχεϊ μακρῶι
   ἢ ξίφει οὐτάζων δήιον ἄνδρ' ἐλέτω·
καὶ πόδα πὰρ ποδὶ θεὶς καὶ ἐπ' ἀσπίδος ἀσπίδ' ἐρείσας,
   ἐν δὲ λόφον τε λόφωι καὶ κυνέην κυνέηι
καὶ στέρνον στέρνωι πεπλημένος ἀνδρὶ μαχέσθω,
   ἢ ξίφεος κώπην ἢ δόρυ μακρὸν ἑλών.[29]

Let each man close the foe and with long spear-shaft
   Or with sword attack and kill his man;
Foot set by foot and shield on shield supporting,
   Touching crest with crest and helm with helm,
And drawing breast to breast let him start fighting,
   Taking hilted sword or straight long spear.

Over these lines there has been some misunderstanding. It has been claimed that they are an interpolation because they indicate the phalanx type of
fighting which, it is also claimed, did not exist in the
time of Tyrtaeus.[30] But, as the Berlin papyrus shows,
something like the phalanx did exist in the seventh

---

[29] Fr. 8, 29–34.
[30] Wilamowitz, *Textgeschichte*, p. 113, criticized by W. Jaeger, *Tyrtaios
Über die wahre ἀρετή*, pp. 8–9.

century, and, what is more important, Tyrtaeus is here not concerned with the phalanx. He is concerned with issuing orders to each man on how to engage his opponent, and he advises him to get to close grips. The misunderstanding is due to Tyrtaeus' again borrowing from Homer and turning his loan to a new purpose. He had in mind a passage in the *Iliad* which gives the earliest known case of advancing in close formation:

ἀσπὶς ἄρ' ἀσπίδ' ἔρειδε, κόρυς κόρυν, ἀνέρα δ' ἀνήρ,
ψαῦον δ' ἱπποκόμοι κόρυθες λαμπροῖσι φάλοισι
νευόντων, ὡς πυκνοὶ ἐφέστασαν ἀλλήλοισιν.[31]

Shield pressed
On shield, and helm on helm, and man on man:
Their horse-hair crests on glinting helmet-peaks
Touched as they nodded, in such close array
They stood together.[32]

Tyrtaeus had to describe a situation which Homer had omitted, and he was forced to use the language appropriate to a different kind of action. This was not necessarily due to poverty of invention. It is possible that Tyrtaeus felt it right to give his views in traditional language, and this was the best that he could find. In any case it shows the close dependence of an early elegist on the heroic epic.

These two poems, No. 6–7 and No. 8, are complete and show how elegy was constructed in the early days of its career. In addition to their bipartite construc-

[31] *Il.* xvi. 215–17.
[32] Tr. Sir William Marris.

tion they show other signs of careful workmanship
and of a feeling for the structure of the whole which is
not noticeable in the poem of Callinus. In both a
general proposition is enunciated, and then followed
by a striking example of its application. In both the
first half is paralleled by the second, not merely in
being of the same length but in having a beginning, a
special piece of pleading, and a summary close. Both
are concerned with general aspects of warfare and
both seem to have been inspired by national failure,
the first in recruiting, the second in defeat. There
was, it seems, some unwillingness among Spartans
to fight in the Second Messenian War; tradition [33]
records that the ranks were beaten by their officers if
they gave ground. To this recalcitrance Tyrtaeus
addressed himself in general terms, using the present
imperative as a sign that his advice was always useful. But at least in No. 8 the single word οὔπω at the
beginning seems to show that he wrote for a single
occasion when things were not going too well.

Both these poems have also an underlying philosophy of life which was to play a considerable part in
Greek thought and makes its first appearance here.
Tyrtaeus is concerned with two closely related conceptions, the ἀνὴρ ἀγαθός or good man and his ἀρετή
or excellence. The first appears at the beginning of
No. 6–7 and sets its tone in the couplet:

τεθνάμεναι γὰρ καλὸν ἐνὶ προμάχοισι πεσόντα
ἄνδρ' ἀγαθὸν περὶ ἧι πατρίδι μαρνάμενον.[34]

---

[33] Aristot. *Nic. Eth.* iii. 8. 1116a, 36 with scholia.   [34] Fr. 6–7, 1–2.

Noble is he who falls in front of battle
bravely fighting for his native land,[35]

and the second appears in the account of the coward
in No. 8, 14

τρεσσάντων δ' ἀνδρῶν πᾶσ' ἀπόλωλ' ἀρετή.[36]

But for cowards is all manhood lost.

When a man does what he should, it is καλόν, and
when he does the opposite, it is αἰσχρόν. These two
words are repeated and give a strongly ethical character to both poems. In No. 6–7 it is καλόν to die in
battle, but flight and the death of old men are αἰσχρά.
In No. 8 the fate which meets the coward and the
corpse struck in the back are both αἰσχρά. The
adjectives are simple and imply not much more than
approval and disapproval, or what makes a man
proud and what makes him ashamed. But they are
closely related to the conceptions of the ἀνὴρ ἀγαθός
and his ἀρετή. And the whole moral system implied is
vital to Tyrtaeus' doctrine.

In this we find the first Greek attempt to define
ideas which came to have great importance for them.
To reach a clear idea of a good man, an ἀνὴρ ἀγαθός,
demanded a considerable degree of abstraction. Before a man can be called "good" there must first be an
idea of what a man as such is.[37] In Homer there is
hardly any mention of the good man as such. We

[35] Tr. T. F. Higham.   [36] Fr. 8, 14.
[37] On the question generally cf. J. Gerlach, ΑΝΗΡ ΑΓΑΘΟΣ, esp.
pp. 14–21.

find of course men who are good at this or at that. A
man may be like Menelaus βοὴν ἀγαθός,[38] "good at
the war-cry," that is, a stout comrade in need; he can
be βίην ἀγαθός,[39] good in physical strength as Hector
wishes his son to be, or πὺξ ἀγαθός,[40] good at boxing
like Polydeuces; he can be a good king like Agamemnon [41] or a good doctor like the sons of Asclepius,[42]
or a good servant like the servant of Achilles.[43]
But the fact remains that not one of Homer's heroes
is called ἀνὴρ ἀγαθός. There is no hint that Homer
praised this or that hero as a type of what a man
ought to be. But he does sometimes use ἀγαθός alone
as an epithet for a person without specifying at what
its possessor is good. And when he does this for the
father of Achilles [44] or the son of Alcinous,[45] he seems
to hint at some such meaning as "noble" and to
imply that the man is well bred and comes of a good
stock. But such hints are few and on the whole it is
clear that for Homer the idea of ἀνὴρ ἀγαθός hardly
existed. It was quite different with Tyrtaeus, for
whom it formed a cardinal point in his philosophy.

The abstract quality of the good man was ἀρετή,
which was the manifestation of his qualities in action.
Homer recognizes the word and applies it to various
forms of activity, but it does not cover for him the
whole duty of man. Tyrtaeus, however, was clear

[38] *Il*. ii. 408, etc.
[39] *Il*. vi. 478.
[40] *Il*. iii. 237.
[41] *Il*. iii. 179.

[42] *Il*. ii. 732.
[43] *Il*. xvi. 165.
[44] *Il*. xxi. 109.
[45] *Od*. viii. 143.

what he meant by it, and his exposition is made in his longest extant poem, No. 9. This, in fact, amounts to a disquisition on the nature of the ἀνὴρ ἀγαθός and a detailed discussion of his ἀρετή. The poem is the most literary, the most original, and the best constructed of the surviving works of Tyrtaeus, but in spite of this, or perhaps because of this, it has been denied to him and attributed to an Athenian poet of the fifth or fourth century.[46] The arguments for such an attribution are fortunately delusive. The mythology displayed in the opening lines is far better suited to Sparta than to Athens; Athens was not concerned with kingly qualities as displayed in Pelops, and Adrastus was essentially a Peloponnesian hero. The mention of the phalanx at 21 and of the round shield at 25 are as appropriate to the seventh as to the fifth century, as the Berlin papyrus shows. The close similarities of language to Nos. 6–7 and 8 are at least as good an argument for authenticity as they are against it. On the other hand, both the construction of the poem and its lesson are strong arguments for its having been written by Tyrtaeus. In it he shows the same craft and the same principles that we have noted elsewhere.

No. 9 falls into two halves. The first half consists of an enunciation of the thesis that the "good man" is proved in war and is thus a development of the opening thesis of No. 6–7. The method adopted is by comparison and exclusion of alternatives. Other

[46] Wilamowitz, *Textgeschichte*, p. 111, answered by Jaeger, *Tyrtaios*, pp. 4–10.

claimants to the title of good man are mentioned and
dismissed, and the impression made is that Tyrtaeus
is considering current ideas with which he is not in
sympathy. So the poem begins with a list of alternatives, stated with some art:

Οὔτ' ἂν μνησαίμην οὔτ' ἐν λόγωι ἄνδρα τιθείην
  οὔτε ποδῶν ἀρετῆς οὔτε παλαιμοσύνης,
οὐδ' εἰ Κυκλώπων μὲν ἔχοι μέγεθός τε βίην τε,
  νικώιη δὲ θέων Θρηίκιον Βορέην,
οὐδ' εἰ Τιθωνοῖο φυὴν χαριέστερος εἴη,
  πλουτοίη δὲ Μίδεω καὶ Κινύρεω μάλιον,
οὐδ' εἰ Τανταλίδεω Πέλοπος βασιλεύτερος εἴη,
  γλῶσσαν δ' Ἀδρήστου μειλιχόγηρυν ἔχοι,
οὐδ' εἰ πᾶσαν ἔχοι δόξαν πλὴν θούριδος ἀλκῆς·
  οὐ γὰρ ἀνὴρ ἀγαθὸς γίγνεται ἐν πολέμωι,
εἰ μὴ τετλαίη μὲν ὁρῶν φόνον αἱματόεντα
  καὶ δήιων ὀρέγοιτ' ἐγγύθεν ἱστάμενος.
ἥδ' ἀρετή, τόδ' ἄεθλον ἐν ἀνθρώποισιν ἄριστον
  κάλλιστόν τε φέρειν γίγνεται ἀνδρὶ νέωι.
ξυνὸν δ' ἐσθλὸν τοῦτο πόληί τε παντί τε δήμωι,
  ὅστις ἀνὴρ διαβὰς ἐν προμάχοισι μένηι
νωλεμέως, αἰσχρῆς δὲ φυγῆς ἐπὶ πάγχυ λάθηται
  ψυχὴν καὶ θυμὸν τλήμονα παρθέμενος,
θαρσύνηι δ' ἔπεσιν τὸν πλησίον ἄνδρα παρεστώς·
  οὗτος ἀνὴρ ἀγαθὸς γίγνεται ἐν πολέμωι.[47]

I would not call to mind nor tell in story
    Prowess in the race or wrestling-ground,
Not though a man had strength and size of Cyclops,
    Were he swifter than North Wind from Thrace,
Not though he were more lovely than Tithonus,
    Wealthier than Cinyras or Midas,

[47] Fr. 9, 1-20.

Though kinglier than Tantalus' son Pelops,
　　Than Adrastus were he sweeter-tongued,
Not though with every fame, — save soldier's valour;
　　No man proves that he is good in war,
Unless he bravely face the bloody carnage,
　　Standing by the foe to strike him down.
This is man's excellence and finest guerdon,
　　Fairest glory for the young to win.
A good for all the city, all the people,
　　When a man stands up in battle's front
And flinches not, nor thinks of base withdrawal,
　　But sets heart and spirit to endure,
And with his words makes brave the man beside him:
　　So the good man is revealed in war.

The form of the poem with its choice of alternatives is probably traditional. At least it may be paralleled by "Theognis" 699–718, which adopts the same procedure and considers the modesty of Rhadamanthus, the wisdom of Sisyphus, the eloquence of Nestor, and the swiftness of the sons of Boreas, only to come to the conclusion that ἀρετή lies in none of these. It seems to have been a custom in such songs to debate between existing ideas of what a man ought to be, and that is what Tyrtaeus does here. Moreover, the alternatives which he proposes are probably real. There must have been men, even in Sparta, who felt that these types of excellence were supreme, and it is with them that Tyrtaeus deals.

Such a conclusion is warranted by the history of aristocratic Greece. Tyrtaeus names athletic success

first, and for that he had reason; for not merely
Simonides, Pindar, and Bacchylides, but Xenophanes
also, bears witness to the high renown of Greek
athletes; and the fact that in the preceding century
Spartans had begun to win at Olympia may have
carried weight with Tyrtaeus. The claims of beauty,
as instanced in Tithonus, may be illustrated by the
inscriptions of Attic vases in honor of young men re-
nowned for their good looks, and by the place which
Simonides gives to beauty in his quatrain on the
Four Best Things. To be a royal king like Pelops
recalls Pindar's *Olympian* I, where the actual example
of Pelops is used as the real type of royalty, and the
honey tongue of Adrastus recalls Xenophanes' complaint that poetry deserves more honor than ath-
letics. Against these ideals Tyrtaeus sets up the ideal
of the brave soldier. For him the "good man" is he
who stands up to the enemy, and in this his excellence,
his ἀρετή, lies. This is the first time that this idea is to
be found in Greece, and it may be characteristic of
Sparta.

Tyrtaeus does not confine himself to this; he makes
his ἀρετή something of general good to the city, and
thus he shows how the ideals of the city-state had
superseded those of the heroic individual as Homer
displayed them. Achilles, Diomedes, and the rest
fought not for their city but for their own glory, and
there are none of the Achaean heroes who can be
claimed as "good men" in Tyrtaeus' sense. But

Homer had in the character of Hector created a man nearer to Tyrtaeus' ideal. The man who said

εἷς οἰωνὸς ἄριστος ἀμύνεσθαι περὶ πάτρης [48]

Our one best omen is our country's cause

and whose son was called Astyanax, "for Hector alone protected Troy," [49] had something in common with the Spartan ideal. Indeed Homer makes him rebuke Paris on the ground that his abduction of Helen brought shame on the whole of Troy:

πατρί τε σῶι μέγα πῆμα πόληί τε παντί τε δήμωι.[50]

A woe to sire and city and thy people.

In Hector, Homer certainly created a man like Tyrtaeus' ideal, but he is only one character among many, and we cannot be sure that he was Homer's own ideal of what a man ought to be. Tyrtaeus is far more drastic than this. He has only one ideal, and such a man must give his life for his city and people. It is in their cause that he may realize his possibilities of becoming a "good man." Outside the city there seems to be no such chance.

In the second half of the poem Tyrtaeus describes the rewards which await such a man, first in death and then in life. The order need not worry us, and is adopted presumably because Tyrtaeus thinks that death is more likely and more satisfactory in such a case than life. When a good man dies in battle, his reward is clear:

[48] *Il.* xii. 243.   [49] *Ibid.* vi. 403.   [50] *Il.* iii. 50.

τόνδ' ὀλοφύρονται μὲν ὁμῶς νέοι ἠδὲ γέροντες
    ἀργαλέωι τε πόθωι πᾶσα κέκηδε πόλις,
καὶ τύμβος καὶ παῖδες ἐν ἀνθρώποισ' ἀρίσημοι
    καὶ παίδων παῖδες καὶ γένος ἐξοπίσω·
οὐ δέ ποτε κλέος ἐσθλὸν ἀπόλλυται οὐδ' ὄνομ' αὐτοῦ,
    ἀλλ' ὑπὸ γῆς περ ἐὼν γίγνεται ἀθάνατος,[51]

For him young men and old make lamentation,
    All the city weeps with sad regret;
Well known to men his grave is, and his children,
    Children's children and those after them.
His good name dies not nor his noble glory:
    Under earth he liveth evermore.

In this remarkable doctrine we may notice two points.
First, the dead man's renown is in his own city and his
own people. In life, as in death, he belongs to them,
and it is they who mourn and remember him. Homer's heroes expected to be told of in song but had no
notion that their fame would be greatest in, or confined to, their own cities. Indeed they might have re-
sented such an idea, since they hoped for a vaguer and
vaster fame on the lips of men. But for Tyrtaeus the
city is all in all, and its remembrance is the highest
reward that a man can desire. Secondly, the kind of
immortality which he promises is no mere literary
fancy. The dead man would in some sense live on in
the memory of others. This was not difficult to believe in a community where men lived in so close
touch that individuality was hardly a real thing to
them. A man's life seemed to be interpenetrated by
that of his fellows, and if they lived and remembered

[51] Fr. 9, 27-32.

him, he too was somehow alive. Tyrtaeus gives the
first hint of a belief which was developed, also for
Spartans, by Simonides. For him the men who fell at
Thermopylae had become ἀνδρὲς ἀγαθοί and were
alive though dead, honored by everlasting renown.

The last lines of the poem describe the honor which
such a man has while he is still alive. Then Tyrtaeus
clinches the matter with a final couplet:

> ταύτης νῦν τις ἀνὴρ ἀρετῆς εἰς ἄκρον ἱκέσθαι
> πειράσθω θυμῶι μὴ μεθιεὶς πολέμου.[52]

> Let a man try to reach the height of prowess
> With his heart, and never slack in war.

That was the end of his doctrine, and there is no
doubt about its meaning. It recalls, indeed, a famous
passage of Hesiod and shows how Tyrtaeus with his
new teaching implicitly contradicted an old belief.
Hesiod had also concerned himself with ἀρετή and
had said that it was hard to reach ἄκρον ἀρετῆς, the
peak of excellence.[53] He had referred simply to hard
work and the success which it brings. Tyrtaeus came
to a very different conclusion and initiated a new
view of man's duty and end. Naturally enough he
did not agree with Hesiod. The Spartan ruling class
did not have to work for its living as the poor Boeo-
tian farmers did. So Tyrtaeus had to make his own
definition, and in this he was surely guided by the
political events of his time. He had lived through the
dangers of the Second Messenian War and come to

[52] Fr. 9, 43–44.   [53] *Op.* 291.

the conclusion that the most valuable quality in man was ability to fight well without fear of death. This he praised, and for this he promised rewards. History justified him. He was regarded by posterity as the true poet of the Spartan spirit, and the Spartan organization of the sixth and fifth centuries was the embodiment of his ideas. From Sparta they spread elsewhere, and by the fifth century they were accepted even at Athens. Herodotus [54] and Thucydides [55] use the adjective ἀγαθός of a man who has shown his worth in battle, and Athenian epitaphs refer to the dead in battle as ἀνδρὲς ἀγαθοί. But this was perhaps a specialized use, and the full implications of Tyrtaeus' teaching were on the whole confined to Sparta. He was the poet of the Lycurgan reforms and of the spirit which had made them possible and insisted on them. It was this spirit which caused him to be remembered, when Thaletas and Polymnestus and the rest were forgotten.

The Spartan view of life was unquestionably severe, and Tyrtaeus interpreted it without mercy. At first sight it might seem to have something in common with the Homeric view in its respect for warlike prowess. But it is rather a fruit of the change from the heroic world to the city-state. Tyrtaeus' soldier fights not for himself but for his city; he fights not alone but in regiments; his honor comes not from an anonymous posterity but from his countrymen. He is a citizen before he is a hero, and he only becomes a

[54] Hdt. i. 169, vi. 14, vii. 53.   [55] Thuc. iv. 40, v. 9.

hero by being a good citizen. Nor has Tyrtaeus any sense of the delight of battle, as Homer, as even Mimnermus, understood it. His attitude is grim and self-denying. The pain must be endured because of the reward which it brings and of the shame which cowardice means. At times indeed he makes us wonder whether he was a fighting man himself, and not simply a superior officer at headquarters who had a gift for encouraging the troops. And yet we cannot deny that he was a poet, who gave sincere utterance to beliefs which meant almost all to him and who in his own way tried to find out a coherent explanation of man's place in the world. Other Greeks found systems more attractive than his, but it is something to have found a system at all.

III

SOLON

IN SPITE of his leading position and his influential opinions Tyrtaeus can hardly be called a personality. His authority comes from the fact that he interpreted Spartan ideals to other Spartans and that in him the military caste found a voice. He presents a remarkable contrast with the next great figure in the development of elegiac poetry, Solon. Indeed, in the differences between these two men we can see figured on a small scale the differences which were later to turn Sparta and Athens into implacable enemies. Solon played a large part in Athenian history. As conqueror of Salamis, legislator, and arbitrator between rich and poor, he had a unique position in his own time and became a legend for later ages. Man of action though he was, he was also a poet, who gave in verse his opinions on life and politics. He is the only early lawgiver of Greece who is a human being for us. From his own words we know his motives and his emotions, his reasons for what he did, and his feelings after he had done it. Nor is this his only claim. He has, too, his place in the history of poetry. Before him poetry did not exist in Athens, and even after him it took the greater part of a century to find its full strength. But Solon paved the way, and the Athenian verses included in the *Theognidea* show that one of his favorite forms had successors in Athens. Like Archilochus he used three forms of verse, elegiac, iambic

and trochaic, but unlike Archilochus he used all three
for almost identical purposes. And we can see why
he did this. He wished to reach an audience wider
than a circle round a campfire or over the wine. He
wished to touch with his verse the Athenian people
and tried different ways of doing it. His attempt was
something new. Tyrtaeus had no doubt stirred multi-
tudes, but they were drilled and disciplined. Solon
fought his way by his own efforts and relied on his
skill in words to convince men of his case. With him the
elegiac became an instrument of high politics.

Solon came of an important Athenian family. Born
about 640 B.C., he seems to have spent his early manhood in trade, gathering an experience of life and
lands which was to stand him in good stead. In his
own circle he had acquired a taste for aristocratic ease
and pleasure which he never quite lost. It formed the
background of his later activities and saved him from
becoming a rancorous revolutionary. That he kept
the tastes of his class may be seen from lines like

> ὄλβιος, ὦι παῖδές τε φίλοι καὶ μώνυχες ἵπποι
> καὶ κύνες ἀγρευταὶ καὶ ξένος ἀλλοδαπός.[1]

Blest who has loving sons and hooved horses,
   Hounds to hunt, a friend in foreign lands.

and

> ἔργα δὲ Κυπρογενοῦς νῦν μοι φίλα καὶ Διονύσου
> καὶ Μουσέων, ἃ τίθησ᾽ ἀνδράσιν εὐφροσύνας.[2]

I love what Cypris does, and Dionysus,
   And the Muses — these give joy to men.

[1] Fr. 13 Diehl.   [2] Fr. 20.

In such pleasures he might have passed his days, seeking nothing better and seeing nothing wrong in his life. But he was not content. He saw injustice being done around him, and he wished to stop it. He had a conscience, a sense of *noblesse oblige*. His innate philosophy may be deduced from some lines which he wrote to Mimnermus, who was his senior and had written:

αἴ γὰρ ἄτερ νούσων τε καὶ ἀργαλέων μελεδωνέων
  ἑξηκονταέτη μοῖρα κίχοι θανάτου.[3]

Untouched by sickness and heart-breaking sorrows,
  May my death come in my sixtieth year.

That was the doctrine of the hedonist. Solon rejected it and saw another end for life than pleasure. So he corrected Mimnermus and said:

ἀλλ' εἴ μοι κἄν νῦν ἔτι πείσεαι, ἔξελε τοῦτον,
  μὴ δὲ μέγαιρ', ὅτι σεῦ λῶιον ἐπεφρασάμην,
καὶ μεταποίησον, λιγυαιστάδη, ὧδε δ' ἄειδε·
  'ὀγδωκονταέτη μοῖρα κίχοι θανάτου.'[4]

If you will listen more to me, erase this,
  Nor be angry with my better plan,
And to this tune, sweet singer, change your matter:
  "May my death come in my eightieth year."

It would be hard to think of anything that Mimnermus was less likely to wish, believing as he did in the unique pleasantness of youth and the horror of old age. But Solon did not share his beliefs, and his cor-

[3] Fr. 6.   [4] Fr. 22, 1–4.

rection reflected his different philosophy. He wanted
not to enjoy himself but to do good and to win a good
name, as he said in the same poem:

> μηδέ μοι ἄκλαυστος θάνατος μόλοι, ἀλλὰ φίλοισι
> καλλείποιμι θανὼν ἄλγεα καὶ στοναχάς.[5]

May death come not unwept to me, but dying
May I leave sorrow and tears to friends.

He wished to be missed for his good works, and for
good works the longer life is, the better.

Solon's choice of verse as a means for awakening
political interest was natural enough in an age when
prose was not an art and poetry was the usual means
of expression for any matter of permanent importance. Solon shows this in an elegiac poem which he is
said to have recited in the market place at Athens as a
summons to the conquest of Salamis. It was a hundred lines long and admired by Plutarch. The few
fragments left throw some light on Solon's view of his
art. He began it with the words:

> Αὐτὸς κῆρυξ ἦλθον ἀφ᾽ ἱμερτῆς Σαλαμῖνος
> κόσμον ἐπέων ᾠδὴν ἀντ᾽ ἀγορῆς θέμενος.[6]

From lovely Salamis I come a herald,
With a well-made song instead of talk.

In his desire to persuade the Athenians to conquer
Salamis Solon was determined to find the largest
possible audience, and that is why he called himself a
herald. He intimated that he had news of public importance to which all must listen. And in delivering

[5] Fr. 22, 5–6.   [6] Fr. 2, 1–2.

his message he appealed to those patriotic feelings
which he had strong in himself and expected in others.
The abandonment of Salamis was for him a question
of national honor, and he said that it made him wish
to live in any small and unimportant island rather
than in Athens, so great was the disgrace:

εἴην δὴ τότ' ἐγὼ Φολεγάνδριος ἢ Σικινίτης
ἀντὶ γ' Ἀθηναίου πατρίδ' ἀμειψάμενος·
αἶψα γὰρ ἂν φάτις ἥδε μετ' ἀνθρώποισι γένοιτο·
"'Ἀττικὸς οὗτος ἀνὴρ τῶν Σαλαμιναφετῶν.' [7]

I'd liefer be a man of Pholegandrus,
  Or Sicinos, — not Athenian born;
For quickly men shall say: "He comes from Athens,
  From the letters-go of Salamis."

His elegy was public and patriotic. It appealed not
to the individual but to the national conscience, and
the shame which he felt belonged to all. His art
is that of the city-state and reflects issues which
touched the whole community.

It is from Tyrtaeus that Solon seems to have learned
his craft. This may be seen not merely in the use of the
elegy like a great political speech for public ends, but
even in some verbal reminiscences which are too close
to be accidental and too peculiar to be derived from
a common stock. His φειδωλὴν ψυχῆς οὐδεμίαν θέμενος,
at Fr. 1, 46, recalls Tyrtaeus' ψυχέων μηκέτι φειδόμενοι, at
Fr. 6, 14; his ἢ παῖδες τούτων ἢ γένος ἐξοπίσω, at Fr. 1, 32,
Tyrtaeus' καὶ παίδων παῖδες καὶ γένος ἐξοπίσω, at Fr. 9,
30; his πείσεται ἡγεμόνι, at Fr. 18, 2, Tyrtaeus', πεισόμεθ'

[7] Fr. 2, 3–6.

ἠγε[μόσιν, at Fr. 1, 15; and his οἳ πολλῶν ἀγαθῶν ἐς κόρον ἠλάσατε, at Fr. 4, 6, Tyrtaeus' ἀμφοτέρων δ' ἐς κόρον ἠλάσατε, at Fr. 8, 10. But Tyrtaeus was not his only literary forebear. He seems, indeed, not to have made much use of Homer, except in one important instance, and perhaps this was because war was not his usual theme. But he had certainly studied Hesiod with care and owed to him some formalities, and, what is more important, some ideas which he developed in his own way to a new conclusion.[8] This influence is particularly clear in the great elegy, quoted by Demosthenes, on political strife in Athens.

Hesiod provided a precedent for the poetry of advice. He told his brother Perses what to do and claimed the support of the Muses for his words. Solon also gave advice, but he attributed it not to the Muses but to his own heart, and when he said

ταῦτα διδάξαι θυμὸς 'Αθηναιούς με κελεύει[9]

My heart commands me to tell this to Athens,

he showed the difference. He felt that he could himself speak with authority and that his heart's commands were justification enough. In this he was influenced by an ancient belief. He saw that Athens was in a state of great moral danger and wished to warn it of the inevitable penalties to come, and to give this warning he claimed a special position which recalls a famous passage of Homer. In the *Odyssey*,

[8] Cf. W. Jaeger, *Solons Eunomie*, pp. 73–79.
[9] Fr. 3, 30.

when the Gods discuss the murder of Agamemnon by
Aegisthus, Zeus says:

ὡς καὶ νῦν Αἴγισθος ὑπὲρ μόρον ᾿Ατρεΐδαο
γῆμ' ἄλοχον μνηστήν, τὸν δ' ἔκτανε νοστήσαντα,
εἰδὼς αἰπὺν ὄλεθρον, ἐπεὶ πρό οἱ εἴπομεν ἡμεῖς,
῾Ερμείαν πέμψαντες ἐΰσκοπον ἀργεϊφόντην,
μήτ' αὐτὸν κτείνειν μήτε μνάασθαι ἄκοιτιν.
ἐκ γὰρ ᾿Ορέσταο τίσις ἔσσεται ᾿Ατρεΐδαο,
ὁππότ' ἂν ἡβήσηι καὶ ἧς ἱμείρεται αἴης.
ὡς ἔφαθ' ῾Ερμείας, ἀλλ' οὐ φρένας Αἰγίσθοιο
πεῖθ' ἀγαθὰ φρονέων· νῦν δ' ἀθρόα πάντ' ἀπέτισεν.[10]

As now, by no decree predestinate,
Aegisthus took to wife the wedded mate
Of Atreus' son, and him returning home
Slew, knowing sheer destruction for his fate;

As we foretold him, ere the deed was done,
By Hermes' mouth, the keen-eyed Shining One;
Bidding him neither kill nor take to wife;
Since from Orestes' hand for Atreus' son

Vengeance shall come when grown to man once more
His realm he claims: that message Hermes bore,
But his good counsel on Aegisthus fell
Fruitless: and now he has paid out the score.[11]

Just as Hermes was sent to warn Aegisthus, so Solon
felt that he must warn Athens of the wrath to come.
Nor was Homer his only precedent. Hesiod had
spoken to Perses in a like manner when he both
warned and advised him. Indeed the twofold structure of *The Works and Days*, with its warnings

[10] *Od.* i. 35–43.
[11] Tr. J. W. Mackail.

against unjust actions and its advice on good, recalls
the structure of Solon's Elegy and may well have
provided a model for it.

The Elegy begins with an introductory quatrain
which proclaims the indestructibility of Athens and
the protection of Athene. This served both to quit
Solon of any charge of unpatriotic feelings and to
introduce the important notion that the gods watched
over the city. Then the poem falls into two parts, the
first of which describes the existing evils while the
second prescribes a cure for them. The first part is
concerned chiefly with the leaders of the people, the
governing class, whom Solon regarded as mainly responsible for the trouble, and uses traditional language to describe their wrongdoing:

> αὐτοὶ δὲ φθείρειν μεγάλην πόλιν ἀφραδίηισιν
> ἀστοὶ βούλονται χρήμασι πειθόμενοι,
> δήμου θ' ἡγεμόνων ἄδικος νόος, οἷσιν ἑτοῖμον
> ὕβριος ἐκ μεγάλης ἄλγεα πολλὰ παθεῖν·
> οὐ γὰρ ἐπίστανται κατέχειν κόρον οὐδὲ παρούσας
> εὐφροσύνας κοσμεῖν δαιτὸς ἐν ἡσυχίηι.[12]

The townsmen wish to break our mighty city
    In mad folly listening to gain;
The leaders have unrighteous hearts, and certain
    In their pride are many woes for them.
They cannot curb excess nor keep in order
    Pleasures which are theirs in peaceful feasts.

The leaders, in fact, are accused of the traditional
vices incidental to pride. They suffer from insolence,

[12] Fr. 3, 5-10.

ὕβρις, and from surfeit, κόρος, and they act in mad
folly, ἀφραδίαι.

Solon had spoken to this tune before. He felt that
the ruling class wanted too much, and he had told
them so:

> ὑμεῖς δ' ἡσυχάσαντες ἐνὶ φρεσὶ καρτερὸν ἦτορ,
>   οἳ πολλῶν ἀγαθῶν ἐς κόρον [ἠ]λάσατε,
> ἐν μετρίοισι τ[ίθεσθ]ε μέγαν νόον· οὔτε γὰρ ἡμεῖς
>   πεισόμεθ', οὔθ' ὑμῖν ἄρτια πά[ντ'] ἔσεται.[13]

Do you calm in your breasts the heart's strong passion,
    Who have found excess of all good things:
Keep your high thoughts in bounds. For we shall never
    Yield, nor shall you find it good for you.

He was convinced that if the rich persisted in their
line of conduct it would do them nothing but harm,
and he counseled them to be moderate. In their
greed and insolence he saw the evil of excess, and he
wished to reëstablish the Mean. But according to his
lights he was scrupulously fair. He did not think that
the poor were entirely blameless, and he believed that
good order would save them too from the sin of presumption:

> δῆμος δ' ὧδ' ἂν ἄριστα σὺν ἡγεμόνεσσιν ἕποιτο,
>   μήτε λίαν ἀνεθεὶς μήτε βιαζόμενος·
> τίκτει γὰρ κόρος ὕβριν, ὅταν πολὺς ὄλβος ἔπηται
>   ἀνθρώποισιν ὅσοις μὴ νόος ἄρτιος ᾖι.[14]

So will the people follow best its leaders,
    Not too free nor overmuch constrained.

[13] Fr. 4, 5–8.
[14] Fr. 5, 7–10.

Surfeit breeds pride, when great prosperity follows
Those whose minds are not well made to judge.

The doctrine here stated is the same as that which he
proclaimed to the rich as the source of all woes.
When he says that Surfeit, κόρος, breeds Pride,
ὕβρις, he means simply that men get surfeited and
ask for too much when they have already more than
they ought to have. The idea may have been, and
probably was, traditional. Later writers, like Theognis, Pindar, and Aeschylus gave new versions of it to
suit their own theories, but Solon presented it in a
virgin form because he believed this version to be
true.

From this statement of ethical theory Solon advanced to describe the wrong actions of the rich,
their love of gain and reckless misappropriation of
public money, and warned them that Justice would
come to them. His conception of Δίκη as a punish-
ing Right has a historical and social significance. It is
addressed not to an individual but to a class or a city,
and in it Solon shows himself as the statesman and
the sage. In it he makes the Athenians responsible for
their own doom and assumes the important view that
not the gods but men are to blame for human ills.
Here too he recalls the speech of Zeus in the *Odyssey*,
where the general principles are laid down:

ὦ πόποι, οἶον δή νυ θεοὺς βροτοὶ αἰτιόωνται·
ἐξ ἡμέων γὰρ φασὶ κάκ' ἔμμεναι· οἳ δὲ καὶ αὐτοὶ
σφῇσιν ἀτασθαλίῃσιν ὑπὲρ μόρον ἄλγε' ἔχουσιν.[15]

[15] *Od.* i. 32–34.

Alas, how idly do these mortals blame
The Gods, as though by our devising came
The evil, that beyond what was ordained,
By their own folly for themselves they frame![16]

Between Solon's view and this there is much in common. Both say that men are the cause of their own ills, and in both cases they have been warned: Aegisthus by Hermes, the Athenians by Solon. And it looks as if the Athenians, like Aegisthus, may disregard the warning. Each may go to his own doom in full knowledge of what it means. But there are also differences between the two cases. Homer was concerned only with the individual. There is no case against anyone but Aegisthus; he will be punished, but the punishment will probably end there. But Solon did not live in the age of the individual hero. He lived in a city-state, and to it belonged the evil which he diagnosed. Therefore it is the city which will be punished, and he makes this clear:

τοῦτ' ἤδη πάσηι πόλει ἔρχεται ἕλκος ἄφυκτον,
    ἐς δὲ κακὴν ταχέως ἤλυθε δουλοσύνην,
ἣ στάσιν ἔμφυλον πόλεμόν θ' εὕδοντ' ἐπεγείρει,
    ὃς πολλῶν ἐρατὴν ὤλεσεν ἡλικίην·[17]

This wound unfailing comes on all the city;
    Quickly falls she to foul servitude,
Which wakes up civil strife and slumbering battle
    That destroys for many well-loved youth.

The words "all the city" show exactly how Solon

[16] Tr. J. W. Mackail.
[17] Fr. 3, 17-20.

saw it. Not merely the guilty rich but everyone else
would be punished.

Secondly, although Solon is using a traditional idea
of the punishment of wickedness by Right, he treats
it in a highly individual way. Hesiod had treated the
same idea and given a vivid picture of what may
happen if right is neglected:

> τοῖσιν δ᾽ οὐρανόθεν μέγ᾽ ἐπήγαγε πῆμα Κρονίων
> λιμὸν ὁμοῦ καὶ λοιμόν· ἀποφθινύθουσι δὲ λαοί.
> οὐδὲ γυναῖκες τίκτουσιν, μινύθουσι δὲ οἶκοι
> Ζηνὸς φραδμοσύνῃσιν Ὀλυμπίου.[18]

A great woe comes to them from God in heaven,
Hunger and pestilence. The peoples perish;
Women bring not to birth, and households waste
By counsels of Olympian Zeus.

But the woes foreseen by Solon are not of this kind.
They are political, and especially civil war and
slavery under a tyrant. Right is for him a divine
power, who knows what happens and is to come; but
she works through the ordinary machinery of human
life. She does not interfere by sudden catastrophes
but makes men find the punishment of their evil
deeds in the results of those deeds. Hesiod's Right is a
creature of theology, but Solon's belongs to political
philosophy. His conception of her was based on an
understanding of the logic of events.

The last part of the poem is taken up with Solon's
cure for his country's ills, and it lies simply in sub-

[18] *Op.* 242–245.

stituting Good Order, Εὐνομίη, for the prevailing,
Disorder, Δυσνομίη. On this subject Solon rises to
a considerable eloquence, and by metaphor and skil-
fully placed antithesis gives a convincing picture:

ταῦτα διδάξαι θυμὸς ᾿Αθηναίους με κελεύει,
  ὡς κακὰ πλεῖστα πόλει Δυσνομίη παρέχει,
Εὐνομίη δ᾿ εὔκοσμα καὶ ἄρτια πάντ᾿ ἀποφαίνει
  καὶ θαμὰ τοῖς ἀδίκοισ᾿ ἀμφιτίθησι πέδας·
τραχέα λειαίνει, παύει κόρον, ὕβριν ἀμαυροῖ,
  αὐαίνει δ᾿ ἄτης ἄνθεα φυόμενα,
εὐθύνει δὲ δίκας σκολιὰς ὑπερήφανά τ᾿ ἔργα
  πραΰνει, παύει δ᾿ ἔργα διχοστασίης,
παύει δ᾿ ἀργαλέης ἔριδος χόλον, ἔστι δ᾿ ὑπ᾿ αὐτῆς
  πάντα κατ᾿ ἀνθρώπους ἄρτια καὶ πινυτά.[19]

My heart commands me to tell this to Athens:
  Many woes Disorder brings our town,
But all is shaped in harmony by Order:
  It puts fetters on the wicked man,
Makes smooth the rough, stops pride, confuses outrage,
  Withers up mad folly's sprouting weeds,
Sets crooked judgments straight, makes proud deeds
      gentle,
  Stops the evil things which faction does,
Stops the wrath of deadly strife, and all things
  Are made wise and ordered among men.

Here almost for the first time Good Order, Εὐνομίη,
makes its appearance in Greek political thought.
Later it was to be the catchword of oligarchies just as
᾿Ισονομίη was of democracies, and so Pindar regarded
it as a characteristic of Corinth and Aegina, and

[19] Fr. 3, 30–38.

Herodotus used it of the Lycurgan régime in Sparta.
But Solon did not use it in this partisan sense. Before
him the idea had been used by Homer, whose
Odysseus tells Antinous that the gods go round cities

ἀνθρώπων ὕβριν τε καὶ εὐνομίην ἐφορῶντες[20]

Regarding every good and evil deed,

and by Hesiod, who had made it, with Justice and
Peace, a child of Themis.[21] In this earlier sense
Εὐνομίη was not a political principle but a frame
of mind, the opposite, as Homer shows, of Pride,
ὕβρις. So in the end the cure propounded by Solon is
not political, but a state of mind. It is almost the
same as σωφροσύνη or Moderation, and he assumes
that if both sides in the intestine struggle have this,
all will be well. His reforms were of course a fact and
he could not be accused of mere abstract moralizing.
But he felt that reforms were not enough and what
was needed was a change of heart.

Solon felt that in making his reforms he had been
completely impartial, that in spite of the evil doings
of the rich he had not legislated against them. In his
own words

Δήμωι μὲν γὰρ ἔδωκα τόσον κράτος, ὅσσον ἀπαρκεῖ,
   τιμῆς οὔτ' ἀφελὼν οὔτ' ἐπορεξάμενος·
οἳ δ' εἶχον δύναμιν καὶ χρήμασιν ἦσαν ἀγητοί,
   καὶ τοῖς ἐφρασάμην μηδὲν ἀεικὲς ἔχειν·
ἔστην δ' ἀμφιβαλὼν κρατερὸν σάκος ἀμφοτέροισιν,
   νικᾶν δ' οὐκ εἴασ' οὐδετέρους ἀδίκως.[22]

[20] Od. xvii. 486.   [21] Theog. 902.   [22] Fr. 5, 1-6.

I gave the commons their sufficient need
of strength, nor let them lack, nor yet exceed.
Those who were mighty and magnificent,
I bade them have their due and be content.
My strong shield guarded both sides equally
and gave to neither unjust victory.[23]

But Solon found, as other impartial men have found,
that neither side was satisfied. The rich thought that
they had been robbed of many rights, the poor still
clamored for land. But he kept to his opinions, and
especially to the philosophy which underlay his politics. Later in life, when he was an old man, Peisistratus overturned the Solonian system by making
himself tyrant. Against tyranny Solon had always set
his face, and when he saw it coming, he said so. When
the supporters of Peisistratus said that he was mad,
he answered in the fine lines:

> δείξει δὴ μανίην μὲν ἐμὴν βαιὸς χρόνος ἀστοῖς,
> δείξει ἀληθείης ἐς μέσον ἐρχομένης.[24]

A little time will show the town my madness,
    Yes, will show, when truth comes in our midst.

He spoke to warn as he had before, and again he
placed his trust on the facts proving him right. Like
Pindar, he felt that time sorts the false from the true
and that "the wisest witnesses of all are the days to
come." He still felt that he was entitled to warn the
city of the sorrows which must grow out of its faults,
and based his opinion on a sound political prescience.

[23] Tr. G. A. Highet.   [24] Fr. 9.

Nor, when he saw tyranny coming, were his essential principles changed. He stated first the phenomena which he observed and then his interpretation of them:

ἐκ νεφέλης πέλεται χιόνος μένος ἠδὲ χαλάζης,
  βροντὴ δ' ἐκ λαμπρᾶς γίγνεται ἀστεροπῆς·
ἀνδρῶν δ' ἐκ μεγάλων πόλις ὄλλυται, ἐς δὲ μονάρχου
  δῆμος ἀιδρείηι δουλοσύνην ἔπεσεν·
λίη ⟨ν⟩ δ' ἐξ ⟨ἁ⟩ραντ' οὐ ῥάιδιόν ἐστι κατασχεῖν
  ὕστερον, ἀλλ' ἤδη χρὴ ⟨περὶ⟩ πάντα νοεῖν.[25]

The strength of snow and hail comes from the storm-cloud:
  Thunder comes from out the lightning flame.
Great men destroy the city, and the people
  Are the tyrant's slaves from ignorance.
'Tis hard to bring back one too far from harbour:
  Now's the time to think of all these things.

These are his habitual ideas. The danger of great men becoming tyrants is part of his doctrine of ὕβρις, and his attribution of the people's subservience to ignorance is the other side of his insistence on sound wits. Nor are the impressive parallels from nature mere decoration. It was part of his philosophy that political events were natural events; in modern language he would have said that they were governed by laws. He saw the signs of coming tyranny and drew his conclusions. So in another passage he reversed the process and applied the language of politics to nature, when he wrote:

ἐξ ἀνέμων δὲ θάλασσα ταράσσεται· ἢν δέ τις αὐτήν
  μὴ κινῆι, πάντων ἐστὶ δικαιοτάτη.[26]

[25] Fr. 10.   [26] Fr. 11.

The winds disturb the sea, but if one move it
  Not, it is the justest of all things

and meant that when there were no disturbing
elements, the calm of the sea was like that of a well-
ordered city. In the case of Peisistratus the disturbing element was the baseness of men who had flattered
and helped the would-be tyrant, and were for that
reason enslaved:

εἰ δὲ πεπόνθατε λυγρὰ δι' ὑμετέρην κακότητα,
  μὴ θεοῖσιν τούτων μοῖραν ἐπαμφέρετε·
αὐτοὶ γὰρ τούτους ηὐξήσατε ῥύματα δόντες
  καὶ διὰ ταῦτα κακὴν ἔσχετε δουλοσύνην.[27]

If you have suffered sadly through your baseness,
  Do not lay the blame for this on gods.
For these men you protected and exalted,
  And for this you have foul servitude.

Again he makes it clear that men are to blame for
their own sorrows, and their baseness is the cause.

These poems, written as occasion called for them,
show how Solon applied his views to the problems of
politics. But he has left a poem of seventy-six lines,
in which he gives his general principles and what is
almost a philosophy of life. We do not know when in
his long life he wrote it. It seems too fully considered
to be a work of youth, while a reference to serfdom in
it seems to show that he cannot have written it after
his archonship when serfdom was abolished. It may
then be a work of his early middle age and belong to

[27] Fr. 8, 1-4.

the years before his reforms. Since he deals with ideas which were more or less familiar to his hearers, he does not make himself explicit on every point, and his sequence of thought is not easy to follow. In this poem Solon is not concerned with any crisis, and he gives no warning or advice. He abandons his didactic for a meditative manner and considers general principles. In some ways the poem may be compared with Tyrtaeus No. 9, but it is not so neatly composed, and it puts forward quite different views. Solon plainly thought it important and lavished on it the resources of his art in neat phrases and appropriate similes. If we follow its course carefully, its meaning and importance emerge.[28]

The poem opens with a prayer to the Muses:

> Μνημοσύνης καὶ Ζηνὸς Ὀλυμπίου ἀγλαὰ τέκνα,
>   Μοῦσαι Πιερίδες, κλῦτέ μοι εὐχομένωι·
> ὄλβον μοι πρὸς θεῶν μακάρων δότε καὶ πρὸς ἁπάντων
>   ἀνθρώπων αἰεὶ δόξαν ἔχειν ἀγαθήν·
> εἶναι δὲ γλυκὺν ὧδε φίλοισ', ἐχθροῖσι δὲ πικρόν,
>   τοῖσι μὲν αἰδοῖον, τοῖσι δὲ δεινὸν ἰδεῖν.[29]

Memory's and Olympian Zeus' bright children,
   Muses of Pieria, hear my prayer.
Grant to me from the blessèd Gods good fortune,
   And from all men always good report.
May I bring joy to friends, to enemies sorrow,
   Held by these in honour, those in fear.

It is remarkable that Solon should ask as much as he does from the Muses, who hardly had it in their power

---

[28] Cf. Wilamowitz, *Sappho und Simonides*, pp. 257–268; E. Römisch, *Studien zur älteren griechischen Elegie*, pp. 1–37.   [29] Fr. 1, 1–6.

to grant all this. But he uses them as intermediaries with the Gods in the sense that he wishes his verses to get his prayers answered for him. And these prayers demand a composite but intelligible kind of success. If the Gods give him good fortune, and the word ὄλβος certainly includes wealth, the rest follows. Men will honor him and he will have a good name. Then he will bring joy to his friends and grief to his ene-mies, and this combination is simply a test of his prosperity. When Odysseus speaks to Nausicaa of man and wife living in harmony, he says that it brings

> πόλλ' ἄλγεα δυσμενέεσσι
> χάρματα δ' εὐμενέτῃσι.[30]

Great grief to foes, but joy to well-wishers.[31]

and when Sappho prays for a good return for her brother, she wishes that he may be a "joy to his friends and a sorrow to his enemies." If a man got what he wanted, he was by Greek ideas rightly honored by his friends and envied by his foes. So this couplet simply clinches the wish of the preceding lines by providing a test through which this god-given happiness can be recognized when it comes.

The conception of happiness so outlined is reason-ably traditional. At the end of *Pythian I* Pindar puts forward a similar ideal to Hieron, when he says:

> τὸ δὲ παθεῖν εὖ πρῶτον ἀέθλων·
> εὖ δ' ἀκούειν δευτέρα μοῖρ'. ἀμφοτέροισι δ' ἀνὴρ
> ὃς ἂν ἐγκύρσῃι καὶ ἕλῃι,
> στέφανον ὕψιστον δέδεκται.

[30] *Od.* vi. 184-185.   [31] Tr. J. W. Mackail.

> Good fortune is first and best of prizes,
> A good name the second possession.
> The man who has found both and keeps them,
> Has won the highest crown.

But this is only a prelude. What follows is more complicated and more personal. In all the rest of the poem Solon says very little about the content of this happiness which he wishes for himself. He begins by a discussion of wealth, which is of course part of good fortune, and from this he moves on to the metaphysics of unjust gain. What Solon has to say on these matters is characteristic of his philosophy. The distinction between just and unjust gain was for him quite sensible. The just comes from the Gods and is like corn which fills a sack from top to bottom, and what is more, it is safe and stays; it is ἔμπεδος. Here again Solon uses the proverbial philosophy of Hesiod, who made a similar distinction when he said:

> χρήματα δ' οὐχ ἁρπακτά, θεόσδοτα πολλὸν ἀμείνω[32]

> Rob not your wealth; what the Gods give is better.

So we need not trouble to define very exactly what Solon meant by the distinction. He felt that there were right and wrong ways of making money, and most people would have agreed with him. The only hint of a special approach to the subject which he gives is when he says

> χρήματα δ' ἱμείρω μὲν ἔχειν, ἀδίκως δὲ πεπᾶσθαι
> οὐκ ἐθέλω.[33]

[32] Op. 320.   [33] Fr. 1, 7-8.

> I wish to keep my wealth; to gain unjustly
>   I desire not.

He seems to assume that the best thing is to be content
with what he has, and such is probably his meaning.
But he was not concerned to elaborate this point. He
wanted to get on to the question of unjust gain, and
its results.

The question was in itself important for him, and
much of his reforming activity was concerned with
different aspects of it. Here he sees it as a part of a
universal problem, of wrongdoing, and especially of
what prompts men to wrongdoing, blind infatuation
or ἄτη. Unjust wealth, he says, is sought out of pride,
ὑφ' ὕβριος; it comes in an irregular way, οὐ κατὰ
κόσμον, as the result of unjust actions; and more strikingly, it comes unwillingly, οὐκ ἐθέλων, which seems to
mean simply that it comes uncertainly because against
its real nature. Its acquisition, then, is associated
by Solon with those activities due to ὕβρις which he
censured in his political poems. It is another kind of
wanting too much. So far he adds little to what he
has said before. But this time he gives an explanation. This proud frame of mind is associated with a
kind of blind folly, ἄτη. Here again he uses an old idea.
Agamemnon tells Achilles that he has been the
victim of ἄτη and he assumes that this is the work of
Zeus.[34] Solon treats the question very much in his
own way and makes two corrections of the traditional
view. First, in a splendid simile of a wind which

[34] *Il.* xix. 136–137.

ravages land and sea and leaves a clear sky, he describes the wrath of Zeus against those who have ἄτη.
Then he explains what he means:

> τοιαύτη Ζηνὸς πέλεται τίσις, οὐ δ᾽ ἐφ᾽ ἑκάστωι
> ὥσπερ θνητὸς ἀνὴρ γίγνεται ὀξύχολος,
> αἰεὶ δ᾽ οὔ ἑ λέληθε διαμπερές, ὅστις ἀλιτρόν
> θυμὸν ἔχηι, πάντως δ᾽ ἐς τέλος ἐξεφάνη·
> ἀλλ᾽ ὃ μὲν αὐτίκ᾽ ἔτεισεν, ὃ δ᾽ ὕστερον· οἳ δὲ φύγωσιν
> αὐτοί, μὴ δὲ θεῶν μοῖρ᾽ ἐπιοῦσα κίχηι,
> ἤλυθε πάντως αὖτις· ἀναίτιοι ἔργα τίνουσιν
> ἢ παῖδες τούτων ἢ γένος ἐξοπίσω.[35]

So Zeus avenges. And, unlike a mortal,
  Is not swift to wrath at each thing done.
Never does one with sinning heart escape him:
  In the end he's utterly made plain.
One may pay now, another after. Vengeance
  Comes to those who flee the wrath of God
Full surely after. Innocent are punished,
  Children and their children after them.

For Solon the wrath of Zeus is not like the wrath of
man. He is not swift to anger at each thing done, as
Hesiod had made him, but he waits his time and in
due course inflicts punishment. Solon in his way
makes God less like man and retires a step further
from the anthropocentric conception to a more
grandiose conception in which God, who has all time
before him, can afford to wait. Secondly, Hesiod in
his account of the punishment of the wicked had made
this punishment an external act which did not rise

[35] Fr. 1, 25–32.

naturally out of the crimes committed. Solon sees it
as an inevitable consequence rising out of the very
nature of the case. If a man is the victim of ὕβρις
and ἄτη, he will sooner or later involve himself in ruin.
And what is more, his children too may be involved.
For there is no knowing where the consequences of a
wrong act will cease. Solon was thinking of the
trouble which unjust money-making brews for its
victims. Naturally enough this may turn against the
inheritors of an estate who have to pay for the mistakes and cruelties of earlier owners, as every social
revolution shows.

This closes what may be regarded as the first part
of the poem. In it Solon has explained to his satisfaction the nature of wrongdoing by the hypothesis that
it is due to ἄτη, and has related this idea to his general
system. The next section, 33–62, seems at first sight
not very well connected with what has gone before.
It is a description of different human activities and is
almost an account of Greek life in Solon's time. The
opening words might be thought to give a clue to this
list and to indicate that after discussing the folly of
unjust money-making Solon proceeded to discuss
other human illusions as instanced by the different
activities of man:

> θνητοὶ δ' ὧδε νοεῦμεν ὁμῶς ἀγαθός τε κακός τε,
>   ἐ⟨ῢ⟩ δ⟨ει⟩νὴν αὐτὸς δόξαν ἕκαστος ἔχει,
> πρίν τι παθεῖν· τότε δ' αὖτις ὀδύρεται· ἄχρι δὲ τούτου
>   χάσκοντες κούφαισ' ἐλπίσι τερπόμεθα.[36]

[36] Fr. 1, 33–36.

Thus are we mortals, good and bad, like minded:
　To his strange opinion each man keeps,
Until he suffers. Then he weeps. Before this,
　Gaping we enjoy our empty hopes.

This certainly is the clue to much that follows: to the
sick man who thinks that he will be sound, the
coward who thinks he is brave, the ugly who thinks he
is beautiful. It is the clue, too, to the professions
which come after, to the merchant and the farmer
who labor in the hope of gain. But after this a difficulty arises. Solon names some professions which do
not seem or are not said to be the victims of vain
hopes. The craftsman is said to make a livelihood, the
poet knows his art, the seer can foretell evil coming,
even the doctor sometimes heals his patient. These
are not said to be the victims of hopes, and indeed the
opposite is implied. What, then, does Solon mean?

It looks as if he had left out some necessary connecting links and explanations of his sequence of
thought. And so he has, though he may well have felt
that men who knew him and his opinions would
easily understand him. Nor are these connections
difficult to find. The class of the craftsman, poet,
seer, and doctor is distinguished from that of the merchant and the farmer by two things. First, nothing is
said of it indulging in hopes which may not be at-
tained, or of its love of gain. Secondly, each member
of the second class has a divine patron who is named.
The craftsman has Athene and Hephaestus; the poet
has the Muses, the seer Apollo; the doctor has Paeon.

These two distinctions speak for themselves. The professions so patronized are not anxious to get money and they are not absolutely uncertain what will happen to them. In fact, Solon is careful to stress their knowledge in the words δαείς in 50, ἐπιστάμενος in 52, and ἔγνω in 54, and in his statement that the doctor sometimes heals his patient. So he makes a distinction in human activities between those over which the Gods preside and which have a certain degree of assurance and those the motive of which is gain and which are completely a prey of uncertainty. This latter class are in their way related to the victims of ἄτη. It is true that their actions are not wrong and that they are not punished. But in their blindness they show how ἄτη grows and to what part of the human spirit it belongs. In other words they provide some psychological backing for Solon's moral theory by helping to explain the wayward desires of man.

In the emphasis which he lays on vain hopes, Solon recalls the elegy of Semonides with its devastating doctrine of human illusions, and he recalls Hesiod's drastic treatment of Hope which is shut into Pandora's box as a sign that man's life is quite hopeless. But he does not really agree with either. Semonides had reduced all desires to vain hopes, and Hesiod had felt that really life was better without such a consolation. But Solon gets round the difficulty by reducing hopes to desires for what is really uncertain, and so activities based on knowledge are no examples of hope. Moreover, he makes a moral distinction on the point of gain. He saw, truly enough, that where money is concerned men will have wild fancies, and of this he disapproved. So he called such fancies "empty hopes" and was able to keep them as the attributes of an inferior kind of life. If men have hopes, they are sure to be disappointed, and to this degree they resemble the victims of ἄτη. But if they pursue the learned professions, there are no such expectations and no such disillusionments.

He felt a difficulty, however. After all, the final decision rested not with man but with the Gods. It is the Gods who give man power in the arts, as he himself makes clear, and if they hold this back, what then? He faces this difficulty quite honestly, and his answer occupies the rest of the poem. He admits that in the last resort we are at the mercy of Fate. It is Fate who brings us good and evil fortune, and there is no escaping what she brings. Therefore there is always an element of uncertainty in life. We do not know how any action will turn out, and it is quite true that the good sometimes go wrong and the wicked prosper. All this he admits. But he sticks to his main point that, if we pursue gain, there is no knowing where to stop. This is a lust which cannot be satisfied, and out of it comes ἄτη, which indubitably Zeus will punish. So the poem ends on a highly ethical note.

It must be admitted that this elegy is not a closely knit work of art. It gives the impression that Solon's thoughts were put into verse as they came to him. And yet it proclaims what is after all a unified and on

the whole consistent outlook. It is concerned with his
deepest thoughts about life, and, as we might expect,
it is full not only of religious feelings but of religious
ideas. It considers man's place in nature and therefore before the Gods. Solon, like all Greeks, felt that
the will of the Gods was inscrutable, and once he said
so:

πάντηι δ' ἀθανάτων ἀφανὴς νόος ἀνθρώποισιν·[37]

None can discern the mind of the Immortals.

The same thought is in his mind here, but, instead of
acquiescing in absolute ignorance, he tries to state,
and to state coherently, the limits of his ignorance, to
know how much he does not know. So the subject of
the poem is simply human error, which is seen in
three forms: in the absolute moral blindness of the
proud, in the gain-ridden but more reputable ignorance of those who trust their living to chance, in the
moderate and occasionally redeemed ignorance of the
learned professions. The three types naturally have
each a theological importance. The first is the product of man's own baseness, the second of his own illusions, the third owes its occasional illuminations to the
help of the Gods. At the end, however, Solon has to
admit that in spite of everything there remains a great
uncertainty in all human activities. But even so it is
not therefore right to fall into the blind folly of the
wicked. The end, in fact, is the counterpart of the beginning. He had asked the Muses for the good life as

[37] Fr. 17.

he understood it, knowing that much of it was beyond his own power to get. He closes by stressing the moral that all such happiness is not found by man for himself but is the gift of the Gods.

It was not only in politics and ethics that Solon tried to discern an immanent order. He applied his method to more natural phenomena, and a curious poem of his survives in which he sees a pattern in the different stages of a man's life. The basis of this poem is the ancient belief that there was a special significance in the number seven. So Solon sees life as divided into periods of seven years, each of which has its own quality and adds something new to human experience. With what he has to say few will disagree, and we may actually find some scientific parallel to his theory in the view that every seven years the human body is renewed. In the first five of these periods Solon is concerned entirely with the physical side of life. In the first of them a child changes his teeth; he is as yet ἄνηβος and he is also νήπιος, which means that he is not yet an intelligent being. In the second he shows signs of growing youth: that is puberty. In the third his limbs grow stronger and hair appears on his face. In the fourth he is at the height of his strength, and that is the time for athletic prowess. In the fifth he is in the prime of life, and it is time for him to get married, and in this Solon follows Hesiod [38] and was followed by Plato,[39] both of whom fix thirty as the right age to get a wife. Then

[38] Op. 695.   [39] Rep. 460e; Laws, 772e.

Solon, evidently feeling that the physical growth is now complete, turns his attention to mental growth. In the sixth period, from thirty-five to forty-two, his man is grown up and his mind is fit for all things. In the seventh and eighth periods he is at his best in mind and tongue, and then decay begins to show. For in the ninth period, from fifty-six to sixty-three, his tongue and skill are weaker; and if he reaches seventy, he will not have an untimely death.

It is a strange poem, simple and a little prosaic. But that is no argument against its authenticity. Solon was concerned with what he believed to be true and stated his case with unaffected candor. It is no argument that he here accepts seventy as a suitable time for death, although he had told Mimnermus that he should wish to be eighty years old. With Mimnermus he was pressing a special point and allowed himself some pardonable exaggeration. The best argument for authenticity is not the good evidence which says that the poem is Solon's, but precisely this attempt to see an ordered pattern in life. Solon finds in it an ordered development, first physical, then mental; and it is characteristic of him that in each part there is a special excellence or ἀρετή. So in the fourth period this excellence is in the body:

> τῆι δὲ τετάρτηι πᾶς τις ἐν ἑβδομάδι μέγ' ἄριστος
> ἰσχύν, ἥν τ' ἄνδρες σήματ' ἔχουσ' ἀρετῆς.[40]

In his fourth seven every man is finest
   In his strength, men's sign of excellence.

[40] Fr. 19, 7–8.

But in the ninth period, the excellence, now on the wane, is mental:

τῆι δ' ἐνάτηι ἔτι μὲν δύναται, μαλακώτερα δ' αὐτοῦ
πρὸς μεγάλην ἀρετὴν γλῶσσά τε καὶ σοφίη.[41]

In his ninth age he still has power, but softer
Tongue and skill are for great excellence.

Here he is thinking of the poet and politician, whose excellence is found in words and other kinds of skill. So his conception of ἀρετή is much wider than that of Tyrtaeus, and he does not seem to have found a single ἀρετή for man but to have believed that with his different gifts and activities man was capable of excelling in more than one way.

Such a view is characteristic of Solon's mellow, tolerant wisdom. He enjoyed good things and had a wide view of what a man ought to be. Indeed his views were probably formed in an ancient tradition of cultivated and courteous life in which respect for the Gods played a large part. He had no wish to destroy this life, and the men he attacked were those of his own class who, in his view, were untrue to their proper standards and invited disaster by their selfish insolence. He might almost be said to look back from his own time to a simpler, more modest age, and he certainly felt that the best goods were the simple goods of the old landed gentry — enough money, lands and horses, food, clothes and shoes.[42] But he did not put all his trust in money, much though its

[41] Fr. 19, 15–16.   [42] Fr. 14.

problems occupied his mind. He saw that many bad
men were rich and many good poor, and he regarded
ἀρετή as more important than wealth, because it
lasts, while money changes hands and sometimes
leaves a rich man in want.[43] It was ἀρετή that
mattered for him, and though he did not define it, we
can see what he meant by it. It was above all a
matter of being just, of avoiding pride and mad folly.
Let a man be content with what he has and try to
make the best of himself in his station. In that case
he would be a good man.

Solon is a typical Athenian. In himself he combined, as the great Athenians did, a strong belief in
individuality with a belief no less strong in duty to
the community. In the first he differed from the
Spartan ideal which Tyrtaeus expressed, in the
second from the unfettered Ionian individualism of
Archilochus with its strong hates and paramount
sense of personal importance. But deeper and more
important was his resolute attempt to see the universe as something intelligible, to define laws in what
might seem irrational processes, and to interpret old
beliefs in the light of new experience. His rationalism
was not in the smallest degree destructive. It was
based on deep religious feeling, and it found strength
in a sensitive conscience. So his ideas passed into the
common consciousness of Athens, and it is no mere
fancy to discern his influence in the speculations of
Aeschylus on pride and guilt, in Sophocles' deep de-

[43] Fr. 4, 9-12.

votion to the Mean, in Pericles' vision of an Athens
where a man was both a complete individual and an
active member of the body of citizens. Among the
many good fortunes of Athens not the least was that
in the early years of its history it produced a man so
honest, so fair, so scrupulous, so public-minded as
Solon.

IV

XENOPHANES

SOLON was not unique in applying intelligence to natural phenomena like the growth of a man. A spirit more skeptical and more searching than his was already at work in Ionia, and the first physicists were trying to discover what was the primary substance of things. With them prose was born, and they lie for this reason outside our survey until their passionate curiosity touched a man who combined a ruthless intelligence with a gift for poetry. In Xenophanes of Colophon the Ionian intellectual movement found its poet, a man who put into verse a serious criticism of predominant beliefs and institutions and approached his subject with a fine appreciation of the human issues at stake. He seems indeed not to have used the elegiac for his boldest speculations; for these he used the hexameter, as Hesiod had used it to display the hierarchy of the Gods or the true ethics of agriculture. The elegiacs of Xenophanes are more personal than his hexameters and seem to have been concerned more with his feelings than with his views, more with the application of principles to particular issues than with the principles themselves. His audiences were in all probability much smaller than those of Tyrtaeus or Solon. He addressed not armies or crowds but select gatherings of friends, to whom he spoke in intimacy as an equal. In this he resembles Mimnermus and Theognis, but his matter is quite

different from theirs. His company was more specu-
lative; he himself was far more original. He stands at
the opposite pole to Tyrtaeus and gives not the senti-
ments proper to a community but his own highly
individual thoughts.

Xenophanes was born in Colophon about 565 B.C.
When he was twenty-five years old, in 540 B.C., the
city was captured by the Medes under Harpagus, and
Xenophanes began a long life of wandering. Of this
we know very little except that he was at some time
in the West at Zancle and Catana and was said to
have taken part in the foundation of Elea.[1] He lived
to a great age, and in 473 B.C., when he was ninety-
two, he summed up his life in four lines:

> ἤδη δ' ἑπτά τ' ἔασι καὶ ἑξήκοντ' ἐνιαυτοὶ
> βληστρίζοντες ἐμὴν φροντίδ' ἀν' Ἑλλάδα γῆν·
> ἐκ γενετῆς δὲ τότ' ἦσαν ἐείκοσι πέντε τε πρὸς τοῖς,
> εἴπερ ἐγὼ περὶ τῶνδ' οἶδα λέγειν ἐτύμως.[2]

> Already now have sixty years and seven
>   Tossed my thoughts about Hellenic land;
> Ere that were twenty-five years from my birthday,
>   If I know to speak the truth on this.

This is evidence for a long life, but it is ambiguous on
the details of that life; for the word φροντίδα in the
second line has reasonably been much discussed. It
has been taken to mean "art," a meaning which
might get some support from Pindar but hardly suits
βληστρίζοντες, which is a medical word for the tossings

[1] Diog. Laert. ix. 18 and 20.   [2] Fr. 7 Diehl.

of a sick man. So perhaps Xenophanes used φροντίς to speak of himself and his "brooding mind," [3] as another poet might perhaps speak of his θυμός or his ψυχή. So Xenophanes, proud of being a thinker, speaks of his φροντίς as a synonym for himself. If so, he must have passed a wandering life of exile, and if we press the meaning of βλῃστρίζοντες, he cannot have been very happy in it. But there was another side to the picture. He certainly had his moments of pleasure, even if the pleasure was simple. For in some hexameters he describes a scene where a full belly and old memories show him in a contented mood:

πὰρ πυρὶ χρὴ τοιαῦτα λέγειν χειμῶνος ἐν ὥρηι
ἐν κλίνηι μαλακῆι κατακείμενον, ἔμπλεον ὄντα,
πίνοντα γλυκὺν οἶνον, ὑποτρώγοντ' ἐρεβίνθους·
'τίς πόθεν εἶς ἀνδρῶν; πόσα τοι ἔτε' ἐστί, φέριστε;
πηλίκος ἦσθ', ὅθ' ὁ Μῆδος ἀφίκετο;' [4]

Say such words by the fire in winter-time,
Full-fed and lying on a downy couch,
Drinking sweet wine and masticating chick-pease:
"Whence do you come? what are your years, good sir?
And how old were you when the Mede first came?"

At this distance the capture of Colophon by Harpagus had passed into ancient history, and the memory of it might make an evening's entertainment.

Colophon had some tradition of elegiac poetry. In the seventh century it had produced not only Mimnermus but Polymnestus, who had migrated to Sparta and was remembered as "a very cheerful

---

[3] Cf. Hudson-Williams, *Early Greek Elegy*, p. 105.   [4] Fr. 18.

fellow." [5]   Life in Colophon had indubitably been
pleasant, and severe moralists saw in this a reason
for its fall.   But Xenophanes did not write in the
way of Mimnermus and Polymnestus. He wrote not
of love but of themes more serious and more ethical.
If he owed anything to earlier Colophonian poets, it
must be found not in his subjects but in his accomplished technique and in a certain gaiety, almost
amounting to wit, which he sometimes displays. That
he remembered Colophon is proved by the fact that
he wrote a poem called *The Foundation of Colophon*,[6]
which must have resembled, and may indeed have
been inspired by, such poems as Mimnermus' *Smyrneis* and the passages in the *Nanno* on the Ionian
migrations. But Xenophanes does not seem to have
shared Mimnermus' pride in the bold doings of their
forebears. His temper is more critical and recalls
Theognis in citing Colophon as an example of that
pride which is inevitably punished. Some lines of his
survive in which he speaks of the gay old days at
Colophon, when Asiatic influences had created a taste
for rich clothes and jewelry:

> ἀβροσύνας δὲ μαθόντες ἀνωφελέας παρὰ Λυδῶν,
>   ὄφρα τυραννίης ἦσαν ἄνευ στυγερῆς,
> ἤισαν εἰς ἀγορὴν παναλουργέα φάρε' ἔχοντες,
>   οὐ μείους ὥσπερ χείλιοι εἰς ἐπίπαν,
> αὐχαλέοι, χαίτηισιν ἀγαλλόμεν' εὐπρεπέεσσιν,
>   ἀσκητοῖσ' ὀδμὴν χρίμασι δευόμενοι.[7]

5 Hesychius s.v. Πολυμνήστειον ἀιδειν.
6 Diog. Laert. ix. 20.
7 Fr. 3.

They learned from Lydians dainty ways and useless,
    When still free from hateful tyranny,
Went to the market place in purple dresses,
    Quite a thousand of them commonly,
Proud and rejoicing in their hair's fine dressing,
    Drenched with perfume of elaborate scents.

It is not quite clear to what period Xenophanes refers. Colophon was taken by Gyges about 680 B.C. and again by Harpagus in 540 B.C. In either case Xenophanes disapproved of the pristine gaiety of Colophonian life; for he went on to say that some of its inhabitants were so drunk that they never saw the sun either rise or set.[8] The lines certainly contain a moral. The Colophonians were proud, αὐχαλέοι, and flaunted their wealth in public. This was ὕβρις, and was punished by servitude to "hateful tyranny." In drawing this moral Xenophanes resembles Solon and shows that he belonged to a more responsible generation than that of Mimnermus. He had lived through hard times, and from them he drew his own theory of history.

It would be wrong to draw any conclusion from these lines about Xenophanes' social position or political leanings. They simply show that whatever his views may have been on theology or physics, on politics he saw at least once eye to eye with Theognis and believed simply in the punishment of pride. A criticism of this kind was as likely to come from a die-hard aristocrat as from a revolutionary philosopher.

[8] Athen. xii. 526a.

A noble who sees the collapse of his own class is fully entitled to criticize his fellows and to find reasons for their downfall. Nor indeed is there any reason to believe that Xenophanes was a democrat in the later Athenian sense or even a man of the people. No doubt, like all exiles, he had sometimes to eat the bread of poverty, but it is certainly wrong to assume with some scholars that he was a professional poet who won a meager livelihood by reciting his verses. It has been claimed that he was a rhapsode who wandered about reciting Homer and prefixing to his recitations preludes of his own composition. This view is based on nothing but a statement of Diogenes Laertius, αὐτὸς ἐρραψῴδει τὰ ἑαυτοῦ,[9] which means no more than "he himself recited his own verses." Indeed it seems impossible that any man who held Xenophanes' views on Homer should have made a living by reciting the *Iliad* and the *Odyssey*, and it may well be doubted whether in these early centuries elegiac verses were composed by professional poets. There is no evidence that Archilochus or Solon or Tyrtaeus or Mimnermus or Theognis sang for money, and it is reasonable to assume that Xenophanes was like them.[10]

It seems on the whole more probable that Xenophanes belonged to the same class as men like Solon and Theognis. But unlike Solon he was an exile, and unlike Theognis he was a man of strikingly original

[9] ix. 18.
[10] For a different view, cf. K. Reinhardt, *Parmenides*, p. 134.

ideas. So he lacks the social background of the one, and the traditional aristocratic outlook of the other. But in the society in which he lived it seems that a conventional way of life was combined with great freedom in speculation and speech. It was in fact far more tolerant in religious matters than the Athenian democracy, which exiled Anaxagoras and sentenced Diagoras to death. Not all aristocrats were like Alcaeus and Theognis. For many the system of the Olympian gods, as Homer and Hesiod had framed it, was unsatisfactory. Heraclitus said that "Homer should be turned out of the lists and whipped," [11] and he was no democrat. Others, like Pythagoras, had deserted the Homeric theology for older and even less rational beliefs which proclaimed a way of salvation through the observance of certain formal abstinences. It was an age of religious turmoil, but religious divisions were no indication of political opinions, and there was a large variety of belief within the established frame of the old aristocracies.

In these intellectual and moral conflicts Xenophanes held a peculiar position. He seems to have sniped at most of the positions held in his day. He is said to have "opposed the views of Thales and Pythagoras and even to have assailed Epimenides." [12]   In opposing Thales he set himself against one who was not a religious thinker but a scientist, and his criticism was directed, it seems, against Thales' indubitable ability to foretell eclipses,[13] which implied a

[11] Fr. 119 Bywater.   [12] Diog. Laert. ix. 18.   [13] Id. i. 23.

theory of the sun's nature which was certainly different from Xenophanes' own. In opposing Epimenides
he was dealing with someone more like a witch-doctor
or a medicine-man, who claimed to have direct deal-
ings with the Gods through dreams and other miraculous experiences, and Xenophanes seems plainly to
have called his followers liars by casting doubts on the
story that he lived to be a hundred and twenty-four
years old.[14] In Pythagoras he was concerned with a
much more remarkable man, a mathematician and a
mystic, who both sought an explanation of life in
numbers and propounded curious rules of abstinence.
Of Xenophanes' treatment of him an excellent
specimen survives. Pythagoras believed in the trans-
migration of souls, and this belief was intimately
connected with his belief in the fundamental kinship
of man with the beasts.   Of this Xenophanes simply
made fun when he wrote:

> καί ποτέ μιν στυφελιζομένου σκύλακος παριόντα
> φασὶν ἐποικτῖραι καὶ τόδε φάσθαι ἔπος·
> 'παῦσαι, μὴ δὲ ῥάπιζ', ἐπεὶ ἦ φίλου ἀνέρος ἐστίν
> ψυχή, τὴν ἔγνων φθεγξαμένης ἀίων.'[15]

Once he was passing by an ill-used pup,
    And pitied it, and said (or so they tell)
"Stop, do not thrash it! 'tis a dear friend's soul:
    I recognized it when I heard it yell." [16]

There is considerable art in these malicious verses.
Xenophanes makes the Pythagorean theory of trans-
migration ridiculous by pretending to treat it seri-

[14] Id. i. 111.   [15] Fr. 6, 2-5.   [16] Tr. Sir William Marris.

ously and by showing what it looks like when related
to ordinary life. The word he chooses for being ill-
used, στυφελιζομένου, is used by Homer of the mal-
treatment of strangers [17] and has an emotional appeal
which Xenophanes uses ironically, while the word for
the dog's yelling, φθεγξαμένης, is more usually used
of the human voice. So each detail is put forward
with an apparent seriousness; there is no word of
abuse or of criticism. Pythagoras is condemned out
of his own doctrines, which look absurd when placed
in the light of common day and common sense.

But Xenophanes' chief target was the theology
of Homer and Hesiod. He seems to have regarded
Homer especially as the source of most existing beliefs about the Gods, for he wrote:

ἐξ ἀρχῆς καθ' Ὅμηρον, ἐπεὶ μεμαθήκασι πάντες . . . [18]

Since from the start all men have learned from
    Homer . . .

and what they learned he exposed in three damning
lines:

πάντα θεοῖσ' ἀνέθηκαν Ὅμηρός θ' Ἡσίοδός τε,
ὅσσα παρ' ἀνθρώποισιν ὀνείδεα καὶ ψόγος ἐστίν,
κλέπτειν μοιχεύειν τε καὶ ἀλλήλους ἀπατεύειν. [19]

Homer and Hesiod said that the Gods
Do all things that bring shame and blame to men,
Commit adultery, and thieve, and cheat.

[17] *Od.* xvi. 108, xviii. 416, xx. 318, 324.
[18] Fr. 9.
[19] Fr. 10.

It is plain from this that Xenophanes' disapproval of
the traditional theology is ethical. He objects to the
low view of the Gods' morals as Homer and Hesiod
displayed it. In this he may have had some following
even in his own day. Solon had said πολλὰ ψεύδονται
ἀοιδοί,[20] "poets tell many lies," and may have referred to myths of this kind, and in the next century
the traditionally minded Pindar was to reject some,
and correct many, stories which seemed to put the
Gods in an unfavorable light. The growth of moral
experience would naturally find it hard to accept such
legends as Hesiod's account of Uranus and Gaea in the
Theogony or Homer's *Deceiving of Zeus*. But of
course Xenophanes went much further than Pindar
ever went. Pindar may have rejected as impious
stories which made Demeter eat Pelops' shoulder [21]
or Heracles fight against the Gods,[22] but he gloried in
many stories of divine love affairs. Xenophanes rejected the whole pack of them as below the dignity of
divine beings. It was an enormous advance to have
made, and though we know nothing of Xenophanes'
antecedents in the matter, we may surely give him
some credit for one of the most far-reaching revolu-
tions which have ever taken place in human thought.

But this was not Xenophanes' only attack on
current theology. He delivered another from a different angle, which was not moral but scientific. He
had looked about him, and he saw that because there
were different types of men, gods were made differ-

[20] Fr. 21.   [21] *Ol.* i. 52.   [22] *Ol.* ix. 35–40.

ently in man's image. He phrased his conclusion
with his usual felicity and pertinence when he said
that the Ethiopian's gods were snub-nosed and black,
while the Thracian's were red-haired and blue-eyed,[23]
and he took his argument a step further by declar-
ing [24] that if horses and oxen had hands, they would
make images of gods like themselves. This is a devastating criticism of any anthropomorphic theology,
and there is no answer to it. In it Xenophanes was
again far ahead of his time. Heraclitus, who was
much younger, did not go nearly so far when he said:
"Man is called a baby by God, even as a child by
man," [25] or, "The wisest man is an ape compared to
God, just as the most beautiful ape is ugly compared
to man."[26] There the anthropomorphic conception
persists, though it is purified and idealized. But
Xenophanes aimed a blow at its root by making the
whole current conception of God subjective.

Xenophanes was particularly concerned to displace
some theological notions about physical nature. He
was enough of a scientist to feel that the old gods of
natural phenomena were an inadequate explanation
of facts. He took, for instance, the belief in the
fuoco di Sant' Elmo, the electric lights which appear
on ships at the end of a storm, and argued that they
were not the Dioscuri,[27] as Alcaeus had said in a
charming poem,[28] but simply "little clouds made
luminous by motion." When others thought that the

---

[23] Fr. 14.   [25] Fr. 97 Bywater.   [27] Aetius ii. 18, 1.
[24] Fr. 13.   [26] Frs. 98–99.   [28] Fr. 17 Lobel.

rainbow was the goddess Iris, he had another explanation:

> ἥν τ' Ἶριν καλέουσι, νέφος καὶ τοῦτο πέφυκε,
> πορφύρεον καὶ φοινίκεον καὶ χλωρὸν ἰδέσθαι.[29]

> Whom they call Iris, also is a cloud,
> Purple and green and scarlet to our eyes.

He is even said to have applied this method to the
sun, moon, and stars, and to have claimed that they
were "clouds ignited by motion."[30] His scientific
impulses, no less than his moral feelings, drove him to
destroy old beliefs. But his two kinds of attack came
from different origins and were not easily harmonized.
As a moralist he demanded that the Gods should be
far more righteous than Homer and Hesiod made
them, but as a scientist he almost expelled them altogether from their position in the world by substituting
natural laws for their personal guidance. Indeed, so
far as we can see, Xenophanes pushed his naturalistic
explanations so far that his Gods can have had little,
if any, place in nature. Thus in some famous lines he
says

> εἷς θεὸς ἔν τε θεοῖσι καὶ ἀνθρώποισι μέγιστος,
> οὔ τι δέμας θνητοῖσιν ὁμοίιος οὐδὲ νόημα.[31]

> One God there is, of Gods and men the greatest,
> Not like to them in body or in mind.

This might be, and indeed has been, acclaimed as
the first appearance of a thoroughgoing monotheism.

[29] Fr. 28.   [30] Aetius ii. 20.   [31] Fr. 19.

But it is nothing of the sort; for we know from Aristotle that this God is nothing more or less than the sky. In ascribing such preëminence to it Xenophanes simply asserts that the greatest of natural phenomena, which men usually call gods, is the sky. Nor was he content to leave the matter at this. He tried to see the universe as a whole, and he succeeded. He saw it as a sentient thing, and said of it:

οὖλος ὁρᾷ, οὖλος δὲ νοεῖ, οὖλος δέ τ' ἀκούει·[32]

It sees all over, thinks all over, hears all over.

But this single being was not a transcendental power influencing existence from without, but the whole totality of things. So in the end his scientific and philosophic enquiries led him to a conclusion which logically excluded any conception of the Gods which would have had a meaning for his contemporaries. If the chief, or only, God was the sum of existing things, there was, strictly speaking, no point in conducting religious rites or in believing that the Gods interfere in human life and punish wrongdoing.

There was, then, a deep division between Xenophanes' two lines of attack on theology, a division which was logically insuperable. But it is probably wrong to explain this discord in his thought by saying that he did not intend to put forward serious opinions of his own but was content to assail this and that view with whatever weapon came to his hand. His

[32] Fr. 20.

fragments show an intense seriousness which makes
any such judgment untenable. He seems, indeed, to
have felt the difficulty and to have seen that on such
matters certainty was impossible, for he said:

καὶ τὸ μὲν οὖν σαφὲς οὔ τις ἀνὴρ ἴδεν οὐδέ τις ἔσται
εἰδὼς ἀμφὶ θεῶν τε καὶ ἄσσα λέγω περὶ πάντων·
εἰ γὰρ καὶ τὰ μάλιστα τύχοι τετελεσμένον εἰπών,
αὐτὸς ὅμως οὐκ οἶδε· δόκος δ᾽ ἐπὶ πᾶσι τέτυκται.[33]

There never was, nor will be, any man
With knowledge of the Gods and what I speak of.
For though he chance to speak the perfect truth,
He cannot know it. Fancy lies on all things.

In fact Xenophanes accepted the discord in his
thoughts, and combined a philosophy which practi-
cally excluded the Gods from life with a deep religious
respect for them and a high opinion of their importance. Nor need such a combination surprise us. It
was almost inevitable in his time, when a ruthless
spirit of enquiry existed in a society whose standards
and habits were deeply rooted in a conception of
man's dependence on the Gods. A similar discord
may be seen in the next century in Empedocles. In
his poem *On Nature* he put forward a purely naturalistic explanation of the universe which excluded the
Gods from any necessary participation, but in his
Purifications he advanced a view of life which was entirely theological and concerned with man's salvation
through the observance of certain rules. A similar

[33] Fr. 30.

discord may even be observed in Parmenides, who proclaimed on grounds of irrefragable logic that the universe was one and unchanging, but used for his description phrases and imagery borrowed from the language of mystical vision, which also knows, though in a very different way, of a timeless, unchanging One.

Xenophanes' personal and social feelings about the Gods are revealed in his longest elegiac fragment,[34] an almost complete poem, in which he shows how he put his opinions to his friends and how deeply he felt on the whole question. The lines were written for a festal occasion in a rich house, and like other elegiac pieces were sung at a feast when the tables had been taken away and the drinking was about to begin. The poem, true to earlier models, falls into two halves, of which the first gives a picture of the setting and the second issues instructions. Xenophanes is the "leader of the feast," and speaks with authority on how the other members of the company are to behave. The poem recalls a piece by Ion of Chios [35] which also gives instructions about libations to be made, drinks to be drunk, and songs to be sung. It was evidently a common form for a drinking party in good society, and the obvious richness of the surroundings which Xenophanes describes contradicts any view that his life was passed in poverty. He mentions all the circumstances of the feast, the wreaths and the ointments, the apparatus for mixing wine and water, the

[34] Fr. 1.   [35] Fr. 2 Diehl.

frankincense burning on the altar, the bread and
cheese and honey. In outward show the occasion
might be one for which Alcaeus composed a drinking
song, but in it Xenophanes sees a significance which
Alcaeus never saw, and from this he draws a moral
for the company.

Xenophanes emphasizes the purity and holiness of
the occasion. He points out that the floor is "pure,"
καθαρόν, and a little later he uses the same adjective
of the water. He calls the scent of the frankincense
"holy," ἀγνήν. This might not surprise us if he did
not pick up the same idea of purity in the second half
and apply it to the subjects of songs to the Gods,
καθαροῖσι λόγοις. He plainly saw a connection between the outward circumstances and the spirit
which was to pervade the occasion; he may even have
felt that this outward purity imposed an obligation of
inward purity on the guests.   In this he recalls a passage in Euripides' *Ion*, in which Ion tells the Delphian
servants of Apollo to wash themselves before going
into the temple and to speak only pure words:

> ἀλλ᾽, ὦ Φοίβου Δελφοὶ θέραπες,
> τὰς Κασταλίας ἀργυροειδεῖς
> βαίνετε δίνας, καθαραῖς δὲ δρόσοις
> ἀφυδρανάμενοι στείχετε ναούς·
> στόμα τ᾽ εὔφημον φρουρεῖν ἀγαθόν,
> φήμας τ᾽ ἀγαθὰς
> τοῖς ἐθέλουσιν μαντεύεσθαι
>   γλώσσης ἰδίας ἀποφαίνειν.[36]

[36] *Ion* 94–101.

Come, Apollo's Delphian servants,
Come to Castalia's whirling waters,
Silver-shining. Wash yourselves
In the pure spring and come to the shrine.
Seal your lips in reverent silence;
To all who would question the Oracle
Nothing unseal
But holy words from your lips.

The underlying idea in both passages is that physical
cleanliness is a preparation for moral cleanliness. It is
true that the Greeks did not make so exact a distinction as we might, and that all purity and purification
were for them ultimately a physical matter. But
Xenophanes and Euripides resemble each other in
connecting this cleanliness with words about to be
spoken. Both of them felt that words could defile as
much as actions and that there was a close connection
between physical purity and purity of speech.

The instructions which Xenophanes gives are exact
and follow the usual sequence of proceedings. First
the whole company sang a Paean. On this Xenophanes is explicit:

χρὴ δὲ πρῶτον μὲν θεὸν ὑμνεῖν εὔφρονας ἄνδρας
εὐφήμοις μύθοις καὶ καθαροῖσι λόγοις.[37]

First sing of God in joyfulness with modest
Stories and with tales of purity.

Though he uses two words, μύθοις and λόγοις, there
is probably not much essential difference between

[37] Fr. 1, 13–14.

them. The first are probably the actual tales told, the second the subjects or themes treated. But the distinction is fine and unimportant for the general meaning. In any case Xenophanes' μῦθοι are not like Plato's — untrue stories. They are simply stories, and in itself the word has no hint whether they are true or false. What is important is the choice of adjectives. The songs must be εὔφημοι and καθαροί. The first can be illustrated from a passage in the *Theognidea*, where the base are said to have learned worse from the low company they keep:

ἔργα τε δειλ᾽ ἔμαθον καὶ ἔπη δύσφημα καὶ ὕβριν[38]

Base deeds they learned and pride and words of evil.

This shows that ἔπη δύσφημα are connected with ὕβρις, insolence, and the usual qualities of the base. It follows that Xenophanes recommends the opposite, humble and reverent words to the Gods. And this interpretation is supported by Pindar's account of Apollo among the Hyperboreans, in whose εὐφαμίαι, reverent hymns, he delights.[39] The second adjective makes rather a different point. It must refer to moral cleanliness, and can best be illustrated by Xenophanes' own statement that Homer and Hesiod had attributed all "unrighteous doings," ἀθεμίστια ἔργα, to the Gods. He wishes the Paean to conform to his own high standards. There must presumably be no theft or adultery or deceit in it. Unfortunately we

[38] Theogn. 307.
[39] *Pyth.* x. 35. Cf. Aesch. *Supp.* 694–695.

know very little about such Paeans, but we can see
what Xenophanes means from hymns sung in company. Alcaeus, for instance, had told of Apollo's
cattle being stolen by Hermes, and the song of Demodocus at the court of Alcinous told of the loves of
Ares and Aphrodite. The first sang of theft, the
second of adultery, and in both there was a considerable element of deceit.

The libation was accompanied by a prayer, and
this is simply τὰ δίκαια δύνασθαι πρήσσειν, to be
able to do right things. Here again Xenophanes
assumes that he will easily be understood. His language recalls that of Theognis, who similarly lays
stress on being δίκαιος and makes it the opposite of
being proud. So in the prayer Xenophanes repeats
the thought of the Paean; it is to be for modesty and
right doing in the traditional sense of his time. But
this is only a prelude to the next stage, the singing of
songs by individuals, of σκόλια like those of Alcaeus,
Anacreon, and the Athenian nobles of Peisistratean
and Marathonian times. The character of such songs
was often festive, but that is not what Xenophanes
wants. His instructions are detailed and clear:

> ἀνδρῶν δ' αἰνεῖν τοῦτον, ὃς ἐσθλὰ πιὼν ἀναφαίνηι
>   ὥς οἱ μνημοσύνη, καὶ τὸν ὃς ἀμφ' ἀρετῆς.
> οὔ τι μάχας διέπειν Τιτήνων οὐδὲ Γιγάντων
>   οὐδέ ⟨κε⟩ Κενταύρων, πλάσμα⟨τα⟩ τῶν προτέρων,
> ἢ στάσιας σφεδανάς — τοῖσ' οὐδὲν χρηστὸν ἔνεστι —,
>   θεῶν ⟨δὲ⟩ προμηθείην αἰὲν ἔχειν ἀγαθόν.[40]

[40] Fr. 1, 19–24.

Praise him who drinks and gives a noble lesson
  From his memory, or of virtue speaks.
'Tis wrong to speak of Titans' wars or Giants',
  Or of Centaurs' — fancies of old time —,
Of bitter quarrels in which lies no profit;
  Honour to the Gods is ever good.

It is quite clear from this that Xenophanes was perfectly serious in proscribing certain subjects for
drinking songs. We know from the στασιωτικά of
Alcaeus, and from Athenian songs like that on the
fallen of Leipsydrion or the Harmodius Song, how
popular themes of political strife were. Of all such
Xenophanes disapproved, and he carried his disapproval to similar songs of strife among the Gods.
All the examples he gives are of intestine quarrels and
struggles, whether the war between Zeus and the
Titans, or the revolt of the Giants, or the many
bloody outbreaks attributed to the Centaurs. So in
his instructions here he forbids any reference to such
strife, whether in heaven or on earth.

The point is of some importance, and Xenophanes
has two arguments against such songs. The first is
that these stories are not true but the inventions of
earlier generations, and in this he recalls Pindar who
similarly denies early stories of strife, whether between Aias and Odysseus or between Heracles and the
Gods. For Xenophanes this was part of his case
against Homer and Hesiod, the sources of all such
stories. Secondly, he says that there is no profit,
οὐδὲν χρηστόν, in them, and here his choice of a word

"the inevitable collision between the old Hellenic aristocratic upbringing and the new philosophic man," [68] he belonged to an aristocratic society whose moral standards he shared and whose language he used. He had certainly little in common with Tyrtaeus, but he shared with Solon a conviction that the good life was a social thing to be lived in relation to one's city, that the Gods were an inherent power for good in public as in private life, that the greatest danger for a man was to be the victim of ὕβρις, and that it was best to live in the life to which one was born. He does not state these principles explicitly, but they underlie his exposition of particular points and give force to his arguments. As a thinker he was, of course, far more revolutionary than Solon, but he seems to have kept his speculations in a separate compartment or at least to have adapted them to the common moral standards of his day. He too was concerned with ἀρετή, and he found his own in the practice of a special kind of poetry. But there is no reason to believe that he rejected all other kinds of ἀρετή or dismissed any which was of use to the community.

[68] W. Jaeger, *Paideia*, p. 234.

V
THEOGNIS

his prayer was granted. If it was not, his position was quite clear. He was in favor of tyrannicide by any means and claimed that the Gods would not be angry at it.[14]

Theognis did not accept these political changes with a good grace. He did not even acquiesce in them, but continued to declaim against them. His poetry is largely concerned with the political philosophy which he offered in defense of his own class and views, and this was the product of the class war, in which he stood without reservations for the landowning point of view. Political experience had strengthened in Theognis a deep conviction that mankind was sharply divided into two classes. On the one side was that to which he himself belonged and which he calls ἀγαθοί and ἐσθλοί, good and noble: on the other were its opponents whom he calls κακοί and δειλοί, base and low. This is not actually a distinction between rich and poor, since, as Theognis says, now the low have money; but it is based on such a distinction as it existed before the changes began. It has become for Theognis a matter of birth and breeding. He views the matter as a stock-breeder might and applies the theory of raising animals to raising men. His complaint against the present is that the rules of breeding are not observed and that mixed marriages of good and bad are made for money:

> Κριοὺς μὲν καὶ ὄνους διζήμεθα, Κύρνε, καὶ ἵππους
> εὐγενέας, καί τις βούλεται ἐξ ἀγαθῶν

[14] 1179–1182.

βήσεσθαι· γῆμαι δὲ κακὴν κακοῦ οὐ μελεδαίνει
ἐσθλὸς ἀνήρ, ἤν οἱ χρήματα πολλὰ διδῶι,
οὐδὲ γυνὴ κακοῦ ἀνδρὸς ἀναίνεται εἶναι ἄκοιτις
πλουσίου, ἀλλ᾿ ἀφνεὸν βούλεται ἀντ᾿ ἀγαθοῦ.
χρήματα γὰρ τιμῶσι· καὶ ἐκ κακοῦ ἐσθλὸς ἔγημε
καὶ κακὸς ἐξ ἀγαθοῦ· πλοῦτος ἔμειξε γένος.
οὕτω μὴ θαύμαζε γένος, Πολυπαΐδη, ἀστῶν
μαυροῦσθαι· σὺν γὰρ μίσγεται ἐσθλὰ κακοῖς.[15]

Ram, ass and horse, my Cyrnus, we look over
With care, and seek good stock for good to cover;
And yet the best men make no argument,
But wed, for money, runts of poor descent.
So too a woman will demean her state
And spurn the better for the richer mate.
Money's the cry. Good stock to bad is wed
And bad to good, till all the world's cross-bred.
No wonder if the country's breed declines —
Mixed metal, Cyrnus, that but dimly shines.[16]

No other Greek aristocrat has so clear an idea of the
distinction between ἀγαθοί and κακοί. Pindar almost
ignores the existence of anyone outside his own privi-
leged circle, and though he called the people the "tur-
bulent crowd" [17] and believed as much as Theognis in
the power of birth, his belief was derived not from the
stud farm but from a deep conviction that the noble
of this world had still in them traces of divine blood
inherited from Olympian ancestors. For earlier generations like that of Tyrtaeus the question did not
arise. The only men who were thought to exist were
noble in Theognis' sense: the rest did not count.
Alcaeus, it is true, felt as strongly against the advo-

[15] 183-192.   [16] T. F. Higham.   [17] Pyth. ii. 87.

cates of political change as Theognis did, but he does not seem to have evolved any coherent theory of aristocracy or to have done more than compose some fine passages of abuse for his opponents' bad manners.

The trouble was that the basely born had come into prominence and even into power, and Theognis was sadly worried. The old test of wealth or poverty could no longer be applied, and he stated the change in a paradox that the serfs had become "noble" and that those who were noble before had become "base." [18] He did not mean this literally, but spoke with harsh irony in complaint of what he thought an intolerable state of affairs. The difficulty was indeed not his own. Alcaeus had felt it before him when he said that a poor man was neither noble nor honored.[19] But the lesson did not affect Theognis' belief in the natural superiority of the well-born man even if he had lost his money. Instead of changing his standards he looked for reasons to explain the revolution, and found them easily enough in the greed and insolence of the popular leaders. He tried to believe that the citizens were still sound,[20] but his attempt was half-hearted and he did not persevere with it. He saw them as the victims of deceit, especially of unjust decisions at law,[21] but when they got power, his hatred for them was only less than that for their leaders.

This simple philosophy of politics was expressed by Theognis through certain key words, which belonged to traditional Greek thought but acquired with him a

[18] 57–58. [19] Fr. 12 Lobel. [20] 41. [21] 45–46.

more specialized meaning. Of these the most fundamental is δίκη. We usually translate this "justice,"
but that does not cover the whole of its meaning.
"Right" is better, but even that is inadequate. For
the archaic Greeks δίκη was the principle of things
which made them what they were. So Homer uses it
for the "way" of slaves [22] or of gods [23] or of men,[24]
to describe something which is natural and characteristic of such types. And this use, with no ethical
connotation, survived into the fifth century, when
natural death was δίκαιος θάνατος and a healthy habit
of body δικαία φύσις. So it was assumed that every
city and society had its δίκη or natural state, and its
normal citizens called δίκαιοι. But of course an idea
like this must soon collect ethical associations when it
is applied to behavior, and with the Greeks such an
association of ideas came all the more easily because
the word was naturally used for judgments in the law
courts which decided the proper relations between
man and man. So as early as Hesiod δίκη has its
ethical coloring and is the child of Themis. So for
Theognis the δίκαιος was the man who does the
right thing, and it was such that he wanted Cyrnus
to be. And by it he meant something which he saw
quite clearly because it got its meaning from the life
to which he belonged. The "right-doing" man for
him was simply the true and typical aristocrat, the
man who accepted the traditional way of life and did
nothing to change it.

[22] *Od.* xiv. 59.   [23] *Od.* xix. 43.   [24] *Od.* xi. 218.

The importance which Theognis attached to this belief may be seen in a quatrain where, like Tyrtaeus before him, he defines the meaning of ἀρετή and of ἀνὴρ ἀγαθός. But unlike Tyrtaeus he does not find his definition through military prowess. He says:

> Βούλεο δ' εὐσεβέων ὀλίγοις σὺν χρήμασιν οἰκεῖν
>   ἢ πλουτεῖν ἀδίκως χρήματα πασάμενος.
> ἐν δὲ δικαιοσύνηι συλλήβδην πᾶσ' ἀρετή ἐστιν,
>   πᾶς δέ τ' ἀνὴρ ἀγαθός, Κύρνε, δίκαιος ἐών.[25]

> Choose, honouring the Gods, to live in dearth,
>   Not to be rich with wealth unfairly won.
> For in right doing lies all good men's worth:
>   That man is good by whom the right is done.

Theognis here uses, for the second time in Greek, the abstract word δικαιοσύνη for the quality of the δίκαιος. The line which contains it is a quotation from Phocylides,[26] and the words belong to traditional wisdom. But they are appropriated to Theognis' own kind of right doing. On this he was so clear himself that he did not often trouble to explain himself. He was more interested in general principles of δικαιοσύνη than in its details, but once or twice he makes some specific recommendation. Thus he says that there is nothing better in the world than a father and a mother who "care for holy Right," [27] and in so saying he praises the virtues of a good old-fashioned upbringing. He is a little more specific about the negative side of the question, on what is ἄδικον. Thus

[25] 145–148.   [26] Fr. 10 Diehl.   [27] 131–132.

he tells Cyrnus that he must not seek for wealth or honors by "base and wrong deeds," [28] and he recalls Solon's conception of unjust gain. He even says that it is wrong to feel anger, and his comment is instructive:

Οὐδέν, Κύρν', ὀργῆς ἀδικώτερον, ἢ τὸν ἔχοντα
πημαίνει θυμῶι δειλὰ χαριζομένη.[29]

Nothing is worse than wrath, which makes you smart
With grief, tho' bringing base joy to the heart.

Here the word ἀδικώτερον is applied to a frame of mind which is wrong for the ἀγαθός because it makes him like the δειλός. So it looks as if Theognis thought that anything was ἄδικον which might be condemned in a well-born man, that is, anything unbecoming to the ἐσθλός. And this included an emotion like anger which made a man lose his proper self-control.

In the main Theognis uses δίκαιος and ἄδικος as synonyms for ἀγαθός and κακός. The words are part of his partisan view of life. But there is a difference which is worth noticing. When he speaks of a δίκαιος, Theognis sees man as doing what the Gods want. That is why in his praise of just poverty he adds the important word εὐσεβέων "in reverence." His δίκαιος respects the will of the Gods. That is why his good parents have a care for "holy right": their interest in it is part of their sound religious outlook. Theognis felt in fact that the old order of society was based on divine laws which could only be broken at

[28] 29–30.   [29] 1223–1224.

the risk of divine vengeance. He did not see this vengeance as a natural process as Solon saw it. But his
belief was deeply rooted and he felt that δίκη pleased
the Gods. That is why he prayed:

> Εὐδαίμων εἴην καὶ θεοῖς φίλος ἀθανάτοισιν,
> Κύρν'· ἀρετῆς δ' ἄλλης οὐδεμιῆς ἔραμαι.[30]

Good luck be mine, and heaven may I please:
I ask no other excellence than these.

And this feeling underlay his dislike of tyrants and
conviction that they were rightly killed. They were
examples of that unrighteous doing which the Gods
disliked. So he said:

> Κύρνε, θεοὺς αἰδοῦ καὶ δείδιθι· τοῦτο γὰρ ἄνδρα
> εἴργει μήθ' ἔρδειν μήτε λέγειν ἀσεβῆ.
> δημοφάγον δὲ τύραννον ὅπως ἐθέλεις κατακλῖναι,
> οὐ νέμεσις πρὸς θεῶν γίνεται οὐδεμία.[31]

Honour the Gods, and fear them; that will stay
    Impiety in all you speak or do.
Strike down the ravenous despot in what way
    You will, the Gods will not be wroth with you.

There was certainly a theological background to
Theognis' political views, even if he did not often
refer to it.

For Theognis, the right-minded man observes the
Mean. Here too he took a traditional notion. The
Greeks had always believed in moderation, in not
going too far. The precise interpretation of the word

[30] 653-654.   [31] 1179-1182.

varied of course with what extremes the Mean was thought to lie between, but so long as life was fairly stable and ideas remained fixed, the idea was useful as an encouragment to self-control. So the quality which embodied the Mean was σωφροσύνη. It meant that a man must be content with his own station and not ask for too much. Alcman had made the doctrine of it the lesson of his Myth of Heracles and the Sons of Hippocoon and drawn the moral: "Let no man soar into the sky or try to wed Aphrodite," [32] and Pindar clinched it in the phrase: "Seek not to be a god." [33] Theognis saw it more plainly, and said:

Μηδὲν ἄγαν σπεύδειν· πάντων μέσ' ἄριστα· καὶ οὕτως,
Κύρν', ἕξεις ἀρετήν, ἥν τε λαβεῖν χαλεπόν.[34]

Seek not too much. The Mean is best. And then
Shall you have virtue, hard to find for men.

If a man seeks the Mean, he will have ἀρετή. The Mean is part of the good man's life. In detail Theognis gives two injunctions which show how the rule is to be applied. In both he takes the old figure of the road which was common both to popular and to philosophical language. In the first he tells Cyrnus to go on the middle of the road and not to give one man's property to another.[35] This simple rule covers a wide range of political activity and is specially directed against those who wished to redistribute the land of the rich to the poor. In the other Cyrnus is

[32] Fr. 1, 16–17.
[33] *Isthm.* v. 14.
[34] 335–336.
[35] 331–332.

told not to be too much vexed when his fellow townsmen are troubled, but to keep in the middle of the
road,[36] that is to keep his head in times of civil strife.
The Mean, then, could be applied both to public
issues and to private. It was connected with a frame
of mind which kept its self-control under any kind
of provocation.

The significance of the Mean can be seen more
clearly in contrast with its opposite, ὕβρις. To
Theognis the curse of the base man is that he is the
victim of ὕβρις, and will therefore be destroyed. He
sees the evil of insolence falling on his city as it fell on
the Centaurs, and he is afraid that destruction will
follow.[37] In another couplet he quotes the famous
cases of the past — Magnesia, Colophon, and Smyrna
— to warn Cyrnus of the danger which may fall to
him.[38] In the triumph of the base, it is their insolence,
combined with violence and love of gain, which has
thrown the city into an evil state.[39] Against this evil
he had a small remedy to offer — good judgment or
intelligence. He says that there is no better companion for a man than judgment,[40] γνώμη, that the
man whose heart is stronger than his head is always
in trouble,[41] that there is nothing better than judgment or more painful than the lack of it.[42] In one
place he gives a full account of it and its place in his
scheme, showing what importance he attached to it:

[36] 219–220.
[37] 541–542.
[38] 1103–1104.
[39] 43 ff.

[40] 411–414.
[41] 631–632.
[42] 895–896.

Γνώμην, Κύρνε, θεοὶ θνητοῖσι διδοῦσιν ἄριστον
  ἀνθρώποις· γνώμη πείρατα παντὸς ἔχει.
ὦ μάκαρ, ὅστις δή μιν ἔχει φρεσίν· ἦ πολὺ κρείσσων
  ὕβριος οὐλομένης λευγαλέου τε κόρου
ἔστι· κακὸν δὲ βροτοῖσι κόρος . . . τῶν οὔτι κάκιον·
  πᾶσα γὰρ ἐκ τούτων, Κύρνε, πέλει κακότης.[43]

Judgment is best of all the gifts Gods bring,
Cyrnus: it holds the ends of everything.
Happy the man who has it: stronger he
Than baleful pride or sad satiety.
Satiety's a curse. No greater woe
Is there than these: from them all evils grow.

Against the forces of pride and gain, right judgment
was the only defense that Theognis could offer, and
he does not seem to have been optimistic about it.

The virtue which Theognis admired above all
others was loyalty, and especially loyalty to friends.
He saw the matter both from a personal and from a
social standpoint. Cyrnus is in the first place ex-
horted to consort with the noble, to eat and drink
and sit with those who have power: for so he will
learn noble lessons from the noble.[44] If he wishes to
take counsel, he must not consult one of the base, but
find out one of the noble even if it involves a long
journey.[45] He must never make friends with a base
man: for such will not save him from trouble or share
any good thing with him.[46] This type of counsel
makes for an aristocratic solidarity and was no doubt
a product of the struggle between rich and poor. But

[43] 1171–1176.
[44] 32–38.
[45] 69–72.
[46] 101–104.

tor, unlike him in many ways but like him in this —
Heraclitus, who said "Character is man's destiny."

Theognis, however, was not always so cosmic as
this. In his lessons to Cyrnus he had time for quite
small matters of behavior, as befitted the instructor
of the young; and his advice on such subjects takes
us to the very heart of their relationship. Manners
rather than morals are his concern in these stray
couplets. Sometimes they are on how to behave in
company, as

> Μήποτε, Κύρν', ἀγοράσθαι ἔπος μέγα· οἶδε γὰρ οὐδεὶς
> ἀνθρώπων ὅ τι νὺξ χἠμέρη ἀνδρὶ τελεῖ[60]

> Boast not in company: for none can say,
> Cyrnus, what comes to him by night or day.

or

> Μήποτε πὰρ κλαίοντα καθεζόμενοι γελάσωμεν
> τοῖσ' αὐτῶν ἀγαθοῖς, Κύρν', ἐπιτερπόμενοι.[61]

> When others weep, we should not sit and smile,
> Rejoicing in our happiness the while.

He gives excellent advice on not believing slander
about friends or being intolerant of their faults,[62]
on hiding grief in misfortune [63] and on honoring
parents,[64] on not making friends with exiles in the
hope of a good turn when they are restored,[65] and on
not praying to have success and wealth.[66] From this
little collection of maxims we get a definite picture

[60] 159–160.
[61] 1217–1218.   [63] 355–360.   [65] 333–334.
[62] 325–328.   [64] 821–822.   [66] 129–130.

of the sort of man that Theognis wanted Cyrnus to be
— modest, careful, considerate, polite, and canny.
Lessons like these are far removed from the heroic
gospel of Tyrtaeus or Pindar's bright vision of the
noble man, but they show that Theognis, in spite of
his violence and bitterness, had a positive side to his
beliefs and really stood for an ideal of manhood which
was conceived in some detail and was not without
its elements of chivalry and courtesy.

The qualities which Tyrtaeus inculcated into
Cyrnus seem to have been put to the test by hard
events and notably by war. What the war was or who
the enemy was we cannot say, but some lines definitely refer to it. A beacon has proclaimed that the
enemy is near:

> Ἄγγελος ἄφθογγος πόλεμον πολύδακρυν ἐγείρει,
>   Κύρν', ἀπὸ τηλαυγέος φαινόμενος σκοπιῆς.
> ἀλλ' ἵπποισ' ἔμβαλλε ταχυπτέρνοισι χαλινούς·
>   δῄων γάρ σφ' ἀνδρῶν ἀντιάσειν δοκέω.
> οὐ πολλὸν τὸ μεσηγύ· διαπρήξουσι κέλευθον,
>   εἰ μὴ ἐμὴν γνώμην ἐξαπατῶσι θεοί.[67]

The voiceless herald at his post afar,
Cyrnus, arouses lamentable war.
Bridle the horses: let their swift feet go;
They will not fear, I think, to meet the foe.
He is not far, and they will find a way,
If the Gods have not sent my wits astray.

What the result of the fighting was, we do not know,
though in another place Theognis speaks of his city as

[67] 549–554.

about to be captured,[68] and in a third he tells Cyrnus
that they have fallen into a mischief from which he
hopes that death will take them.[69] But apart from
these stray hints Theognis says little about the events
of his life. He does, however, tell us something about
his feelings. In his more intimate poems to Cyrnus he
reveals the emotions and especially the doubts which
sometimes swept over him. His experiences had
soured him, and he expected little from life. Above all
he felt that his friends betrayed him, and this gave
him a low view of mankind. He says plaintively that
there are few who will share both good and evil fortune with a man or are worthy to be trusted in time
of trouble.[70] He seems, too, to have felt that his
efforts to pursue a honorable course in life had met
only with scorn, and there is a note of personal resent-
ment in the couplet:

'Ακρόπολις καὶ πύργος ἐὼν κενεόφρονι δήμωι,
  Κύρν', ὀλίγης τιμῆς ἔμμορεν ἐσθλὸς ἀνήρ.[71]

A man may like a tower or castle stand,
But gets small honour from his half-wit land.

To the faithlessness of his friends he added the unre-
lenting hate of his enemies, and though he prays to
get his own back on them, he knows that they rejoice
over his misfortunes.[72] So he gets the worst of both
worlds: his enemies triumph over him and his friends
find him a nuisance in his troubles. Theognis, in fact,

[68] 235–236.
[69] 819–820.
[70] 79–82.
[71] 233–234.
[72] 337–340.

is the first poet of persecution mania. His experience
had taught him to expect nothing and to trust
nobody.

This is perhaps not entirely true of his relations
with Cyrnus. For him he certainly felt a deep affection, and it looks as if Cyrnus shared the sorrows of
war and exile with him. But he was not always sure
of Cyrnus. Not only does he tell him to avoid all
double dealing, but even in the splendid poem in
which he proclaims Cyrnus' immortality through his
song he ends on a bitter note of complaint. The poem
shows Theognis at his best, and, famous though it is,
it can bear quotation:

Σοὶ μὲν ἐγὼ πτέρ' ἔδωκα, σὺν οἶσ' ἐπ' ἀπείρονα πόντον
    πωτήσηι καὶ γῆν πᾶσαν ἀειρόμενος
ῥηϊδίως· θοίνηις δὲ καὶ εἰλαπίνηισι παρέσσηι
    ἐν πάσαις πολλῶν κείμενος ἐν στόμασιν,
καί σε σὺν αὐλίσκοισι λιγυφθόγγοις νέοι ἄνδρες
    εὐκόσμως ἐρατοὶ καλά τε καὶ λιγέα
ἄισωνται. καὶ ὅταν δνοφερῆς ὑπὸ κεύθεσι γαίης
    βῆις πολυκωκύτους εἰς 'Αίδαο δόμους,
οὐδέποτ' οὐδὲ θανὼν ἀπολεῖς κλέος, ἀλλὰ μελήσεις
    ἄφθιτον ἀνθρώποισ' αἰὲν ἔχων ὄνομα,
Κύρνε, καθ' 'Ελλάδα γῆν στρωφώμενος ἠδ' ἀνὰ νήσους
    ἰχθυόεντα περῶν πόντον ἐπ' ἀτρύγετον,
οὐχ ἵππων νώτοισιν ἐφήμενος· ἀλλά σε πέμψει
    ἀγλαὰ Μουσάων δῶρα ἰοστεφάνων.
πᾶσι δ', ὅσοισι μέμηλε, καὶ ἐσσομένοισιν ἀοιδὴ
    ἔσσηι ὁμῶς, ὄφρ' ἂν γῆ τε καὶ ἥλιος.
αὐτὰρ ἐγὼν ὀλίγης παρὰ σεῦ οὐ τυγχάνω αἰδοῦς,
    ἀλλ' ὥσπερ μικρὸν παῖδα λόγοις μ' ἀπατᾶις.[73]

[73] 237-254.

I've given thee wings shall waft thee forth with ease
High o'er the land, high o'er the boundless seas;
No feast shall ever be but thou'lt be there
Couch'd on men's lips, for oft the young and fair
With ordered sweetness clear shall sing thy praise
To the clear flute; and when in after-days
To the dark and dolorous land thou com'st below,
Ne'er even in death shalt thou thy fame forgo,
But men will keep in memory unchanging
The name of Cyrnus, who shalt, all Greece ranging,
Mainland and island, pass the unharvested
Home of the fish, not Pegasus-wise, but sped
By the grand gifts of Them of the Violet Crown,
To all that ope their doors, and up and down
While earth and sun endure, world without end,
Shalt live a song to men; — yet I, sweet friend,
I have no honour small or great with thee,
But, like a child, with words thou cheatest me.[74]

This is the longest poem which is unquestionably by
Theognis, and though it is more elaborate and more
lyrical than most of his work, it is in its way characteristic. The root of it is his belief in the immortality
which song confers on those of whom it sings. This
belief finds here its first full expression. Homer perhaps had some small inkling of it when he made Helen
say that Zeus had sent an evil doom to her that in
time to come she and Paris might be remembered in
song.[75] But this fame is not for her a prolongation of
life after death; it is no more than fame. The idea was
taken a step further by Sappho, when she told an ill-

[74] Tr. J. M. Edmonds.
[75] *Il.* vi. 357–358.

educated woman that after death she would flit dimly among the unsubstantial dead because in life she never plucked the roses of Pieria.[76] In this there is certainly a trace of the belief that song somehow confers life after death on those whom it honors. But Theognis is more precise and more emphatic than Sappho. The fame which his song brings to Cyrnus is a real form of life. To us the immortality promised by song is a *cliché*. We accept it; we may even believe in it; but it does not touch us very deeply. It cannot compete with the promises of a Christian afterworld, and it means nothing to the agnostic. But the Greeks saw it differently. They felt no certainty of life after death. There might be something in a paradise below the earth or beyond the Western Sea, though of such beliefs Theognis shows no trace. More often they felt that the end was nothing, that it was better not to be born, that at the last a man's only possession was his cloak of clay. Against these recurring doubts, these moments of blackness, they armed themselves with a consolation. They believed that the best or the luckiest of them would have their lives prolonged by song. Nor was this a mere form of words. It was based on the belief that song and memory literally give life to the dead. Through song and the glory which it confers a man may to some extent partake of the glory of the Gods. Cyrnus will keep company with the Muses, who are not abstractions but real powers who give life and glory. He himself may go down to the House of

[76] γ 3 Lobel.

Death, but he will have another life on the lips of men.

Theognis closes this splendid rhapsody with a couplet of complaint about Cyrnus' treatment of him, and to some this may seem an anticlimax, while others have wished to excise it as an interpolation or part of another poem. But there is little doubt that it is genuine. Theognis felt that he had done much for Cyrnus, and got nothing in return for it. It is characteristic of his distrustful nature to speak like this. From such suspicions it was, apparently, impossible for him to escape. Something had embittered him and shaken his confidence in life and men. It may well be that the collapse of the society into which he was born and whose standards he accepted as beyond question was too much for him, that he was never again self-confident or confident of others. It is this fundamental weakness which makes him take a low view of mankind and apply suspicions even to Cyrnus.

For the historian Theognis is a valuable witness for Greek aristocracy at a time when it was challenged and threatened and forced to make its position clear. When Pindar wrote in the next century, it was far surer of itself than it was in Theognis' time, and he was able to put up a splendid case for it. Theognis belongs to a period of threats and doubt, and he tells us what no one else can. But for the student of poetry he has a different claim. His poetry has a special quality because it is the reflection of a singularly

candid and concentrated mind. It does not cover a
large range of experience, but what it touches, it
treats with a condensed power, seeing very clearly
what it sees and stating facts with perfect honesty.
It is of course incurably didactic, and modern taste
may turn from it as alien to the pure spirit of song.
But this is to apply to Theognis a standard which
neither he nor any other Greek would have recognized. He certainly regarded his work as song in the
most literal sense, as something which men could not
help singing. But he also felt that through song he
must convey lessons about life. It would be easy to
dismiss these lessons as fundamentally unpoetical in
character because of their instructional nature. But
that would be wrong. Theognis imparts to his maxims
and advice the dignity and grace which come from his
melodious handling of the elegiac couplet, but he in-
fuses into them his own special kind of emotion — a
tense feeling for the importance of what he says —
and he makes us feel that he was forced to say what
he did by the pressure which events put on him and
by the states of anxiety, sadness, or joy to which they
drove him. His maxims are not merely honest; they
are deeply felt, and that lifts them through his art to
poetry. Whatever we may think of his views, we have
to admit that they meant a great deal to him.

Theognis is, too, in his own way a considerable
craftsman. Through him the maxim gained a dignity
and power which was rare before him. There is wit in
the sharp couplets of Demodocus, and there is a

homely wisdom in the stray lines of Phocylides. But Theognis is a far more accomplished poet than either of these. He has an admirable eye for an image, and in many of his poems there is some picture, vividly seen and briefly presented, which enlivens the whole, like the color-changing cuttlefish, or the "voiceless messenger," or the fever which is better than poverty. He says without effort that a man is beating out fetters for himself, or tells Cyrnus not to goad him too much under the yoke, or sees the city in the pangs of childbirth, or compares the serfs on the fields to pasturing deer. And when he speaks directly without metaphor or simile he makes his points quickly and with force. He clinches a poem with a phrase that is almost an epigram or places his bitter truth, like a challenging paradox, at the opening. He finds no difficulty in saying tersely and vigorously what he means, and though his themes may have a certain monotony in them, he varies their presentation with considerable skill. His genuine poems have usually more power than those of his imitators, and when we compare any lines of his with, for example, Euenus' lines to Simonides, we can see how far more accomplished, tense, and personal Theognis is.

In the end we come to like Theognis for his own sake. In spite of his opinions which we may not share, he appeals by his frankness and strong feelings. Born into a Dorian world which expected a man to be self-controlled and self-sufficient, he was passive and tender. His violence was the other side of his softness, the eruption of a character which is appalled by insecurity. Unable to adapt himself to new circumstances, he fell back partly on abuse, partly on self-pity. The abuse was the natural reflection of his anxieties, the self-pity of his inability to stand alone. But he rose above his faults and his miseries by song, to which he gave both shapeliness of form and a liveliness which came from looking at himself with knowledge and even with courage. He did not attempt to believe that facts were better than he knew them to be or to deceive himself about the inherent blight of living. And why should he? He felt that he knew what was good, but that others, deluded by their own folly or the malice of the Gods, were wrecking what he honored and loved.

VI

SIMONIDES AND THE
SEPULCHRAL EPIGRAM

GREEK elegy found its most characteristic use as a flute-song in company. As such it grew in size and widened its scope until it treated of subjects far more various than its first military and convivial themes, and came little short of preaching the whole duty of man. But while it grew in this way to grandeur and to fame, a less prominent but hardly less distinguished connection was also finding a career. At the very beginning of its history the elegiac was also used in inscriptions to record some dedication to a god or to commemorate someone dead through lines written on his tomb. The earliest case of such a dedication seems to be on a stone from Perachora, where, though the inscription is too fragmentary to be elucidated, the surviving letters point to a date at the end of the eighth century. But we need not look only to evidence so broken as this. In the remains of Archilochus are two inscriptional epigrams, the one for the dedication of a lock of hair by a girl at wedlock,[1] the other for the tomb of two dead men.[2] It is with the second, and with its successors, that I wish to deal. So let us look closely at it:

Ὑψηλοὺς Μεγάτιμον Ἀριστοφόωντά τε Νάξου
κίονας, ὦ μεγάλη γᾶι᾽, ὑπένερθεν ἔχεις.

Great earth, beneath you hold Naxos' tall pillars,
    Megatimus and Aristophon.

[1] Fr. 16 Diehl.   [2] Fr. 17.

That is all, and there can never have been any more. There seems no reason to doubt its genuineness.[3] Naxos is the next island to Archilochus' home in Paros, and when so distinguished a poet wrote an epitaph for Naxian dead, the Naxians would be likely to remember it. Moreover, the crisp and powerful style proclaims that this is the work of no imitator. All is done by the simplest means — the resounding proper names, the single metaphor of the pillars, the epithet μεγάλη given to the earth which covers the dead, the contrast between ὑψήλους at the beginning and ὑπένερθεν at the end. The terse fullness, the finality of the whole, the inevitably right order of the words, proclaim the master's hand. But why did Archilochus write a sepulchral inscription in a meter that belonged to flute-song?

The elegiac was not the only measure used in archaic Greece for epitaphs. It had an early, if not an earlier, competitor in the hexameter, and inscriptions from Rhodes,[4] and Thera,[5] show that this use was well distributed before 600 B.C. The classic example of such an inscription was that written by Cleobulus of Lindus on the tomb of Midas. It is more literary and polished than those preserved on monuments, but it belongs to the same class:

> Χαλκῆ παρθένος εἰμί, Μίδεω δ' ἐπὶ σήματι κεῖμαι·
> ἔστ' ἂν ὕδωρ τε νάηι καὶ δένδρεα μακρὰ τεθήληι
> ἠέλιός τ' ἀνιὼν λάμπηι, λαμπρά τε σελήνη,

---

[3] But cf. R. Reitzenstein, *Epigramm und Skolion*, p. 107.
[4] Geffcken, *Griechische Epigramme* No. 17.   [5] *Ibid.* No. 18.

καὶ ποταμοί γε ῥέωσιν ἀνακλύζηι δὲ θάλασσα,
αὐτοῦ τηιδε μένουσα πολυκλαύτου ἐπὶ τύμβου
ἀγγελέω παριοῦσι Μίδης ὅτι τῆιδε τέθαπται.[6]

On Midas' grave, a maid of bronze, I lie.
While water flows and while the tall trees bloom,
And sun and radiant moon arise and shine,
And rivers run and ocean breaks in brine,
Abiding on this mournful mound shall I
Tell passers-by that this is Midas' tomb.[7]

When we add this to other early epitaphs in hexameters, a fact of some interest emerges. These inscriptions are more concerned with the monument itself and with the man who made it than with the dead man who lies in it. Two lines of the seventh century from Rhodes do not mention the dead man's name, but say simply:

σᾶμα τόδ' Ἰδαμενεὺς ποίησα, hίνα κλέος εἴη
Ζεὺ(δ) δέ νιν ὅστις πημαίνοι, λειόλη θείη.[8]

I, Idameneus, made this monument, that it
    might be a glory.
May Zeus utterly destroy whoso harms it.

A single line from Thera says:

Εὐμάστας μ' ἄηρεν ἀπὸ χθονὸς ho Κριτοβούλου [9]

Eumastas, son of Critobulus, raised me from the earth

and adds no word of explanation. In both these, as in Cleobulus' lines, the monument seems to be more important than what it contains.

---

[6] Diog. Laert. i. 6.
[7] Tr. Sir William Marris.

[8] Geffcken No. 17.
[9] Id. No. 18.

This silence of early hexametric epitaphs about the dead and this emphasis on the monument's permanence are due to the Greek desire to keep something of a man surviving after death. The dead man's name is not given in case it might bring bad luck to his corpse or spirit; the silence is a way of averting the jealousy of the Gods. The maker's name, however, is mentioned because through him and in his memory the dead man still lives, and of this memory the monument is a solid and visible sign. What matters is this remembrance and the tomb which embodies and preserves it. It was all very well for Simonides to deride Cleobulus for setting a gravestone against the everlasting powers of nature,[10] but Cleobulus was really concerned with the survival of Midas through the remembrance of him and the monument which expressed that remembrance. This type of epitaph survived and had some history. It sometimes gave the names of the dead in later centuries, sometimes not; it usually gave the name of the maker or dedicator. Good examples from the seventh and sixth centuries come from Methana,[11] Troezen,[12] and Corcyra.[13] At Corcyra, indeed, the tomb of Arniadas, who fell in war, does not say who erected it, but we may assume that it was his grateful countrymen who did not feel it was necessary to state a fact so obvious. Like

[10] Fr. 48. Cf. *Greek Lyric Poetry*, pp. 399–400.
[11] Geffcken No. 56.
[12] Id. Nos. 57–58.
[13] Id. Nos. 53–55. Cf. D. L. Page in *Greek Poetry and Life*, pp. 211–214.

Tyrtaeus' warrior, Arniadas survived in the memory
of his fellow citizens.

When we compare the earliest elegiac epitaphs with
the hexametric we find on the whole some differences.
First, the names of those who had the monuments
made are much less common. They can be found, as
on the tomb which Diodorus of Athens put up for his
son Stesias [14] or that which Philtiades put up for
Lampito.[15] But they are not usual, while the dead
person is almost invariably named. Secondly, the
elegiacs often take a special form. In them the dead
are imagined to be speaking. The epitaphs, so to
speak, are their last words to the world. Sepolia gives
a good example from the sixth century:

εἴτ' ἀστό]s τις ἀνὴρ εἴτε ξένος ἄλλοθεν ἐλθών,
   Τέττιχον οἰκτίρας ἄνδρ' ἀγαθὸν παρίτω,
ἐν πολέμωι φθίμενον, νεαρὰν ἥβην ὀλέσαντα·
   ταῦτ' ἀποδυράμενοι νεῖσθ' ἐπὶ πρᾶγμ' ἀγαθόν.[16]

Townsman, or stranger come from foreign ways,
  Pity brave Tettichus, and then pass by;
He died in war and lost young manhood's days.
  Weep, and go on to where your good deeds lie.

Thirdly, when the dead man speaks, he commonly
addresses the passer-by, as he does here, asking him to
stop and show pity. So another Attic tomb-stone of
the sixth century says quite simply:

ἄνθρωφ', ὅς στείχεις καθ' ὁδὸν φρασὶν ἄλλα μενοινῶν,
  στῆθι καὶ οἴκτιρον σῆμα Θράσωνος ἰδών.[17]

[14] Geffcken No. 42.
[15] Id. No. 46.
[16] Id. No. 47.
[17] Id. No. 41.

> Man, passing by with other thoughts maybe,
> Stop and have pity. Thrason's grave you see.

The dead man wishes to be remembered even by those who do not know him and whom he does not himself know.

These elegiac epitaphs differ in their art from the hexametric because they represent rather a different view of the dead man's place and relations with the living. First, they are much more personal. It is still the memory of the dead man that matters, but more than memory is asked for, notably pity, a human feeling, a stirring of the heart, which inevitably demands his name, that the feeling may be for a real individual. And as all memories of the dead demand some renewal of intercourse with them, so by a very human fancy the dead are actually made to speak, even if their words are short and unchangeable. Secondly, the relation of the dead to the living is no longer confined to one or to a few. The society of living men is now his only connection with earth, and he may address a stranger as well as a friend. So these elegiacs reveal a more vivid feeling for the dead and their state than the hexameters with their emphasis on the monument and their fear of giving the dead man's name. But though there is much pathos in these simple lines and this pathos is inspired by real affection, there is no word of lament. These are not ἔλεγοι in the Peloponnesian or Euripidean sense. They rise out of a view of man's life which gives dignity to the dead by making him keep to some extent the qualities which he had when alive. But even so this does not explain their artistic form, the use of the elegiac for them.

There is, however, an explanation. The elegiac, as we have seen, was often concerned with the nature of the good man and of his ἀρετή, and in many places a man became "good" by dying for his country. As such he was a model to later generations, and it was right to remember him as an example. A simple but instructive instance comes from Athens in the sixth century. There in Alcmeonid circles a couplet used to be sung which recalled the memory of one who had lost his life in an attempt to overthrow the tyranny of Peisistratus' sons:

> ἔγχει καὶ Κήδωνι, διάκονε, μὴ δ' ἐπιλήθου,
> εἰ χρή τοῖς ἀγαθοῖς ἀνδράσιν οἰνοχοεῖν.[18]

Pour wine for Cedon, servant, nor forget him:
    It is right to drink to gallant men.

Cedon by dying in a good cause had become an ἀνὴρ ἀγαθός, and it was right to remember him when his fellows met and drank together. The ceremony of pouring the wine is almost a libation, as when in the annual service of remembrance to the dead at Plataea the archon pledged the souls of the heroes and said: "I drink to the men who died for the liberty of Greece."[19] So the elegiac in this form, though still a

[18] No. 23 Diehl.   [19] Plut. *Arist.* 21.

flute-song, was associated with the memory of the dead. It was but a small step from this to inscribing elegiac verses as an epitaph on a tomb. The assumption then made was that the dead man, speaking in the first person, was present through remembrance and could ask others to have pity on him.

The elegiac epitaph found in the sixth century both a wide popularity and a considerable distinction of form. It usually consisted of two or four lines, and it could do little more than give the dead man's name and add some salient fact about him. This could be simple enough, like that of Lampito who "died away from her own land," [20] or Phrasiclea, who would always be called a maiden, "having got this name from the Gods instead of marriage," [21] or Xenophantus, to whom his father built a tomb "because of his virtue and his modesty." [22] Such epitaphs are anonymous. The poets who composed them did not put their names to them. But sometimes famous poets showed their skill at this delicate art. There survive under the name of Anacreon three charming epitaphs which may well be his. They are all in memory of men who are otherwise unknown and all show a high level of craftsmanship. One of them is for a man who died fighting for Abdera, and in Abdera Anacreon spent his early manhood. Moreover, Anacreon seems to have collected his epigraphic verses and included them in his collected works. For two dedicatory couplets certainly belong to the time when he was a

[20] Geffcken No. 46.   [21] Id. No. 49.   [22] Id. No. 43.

royal guest in Thessaly.[23] The force and skill of his epitaphs may be seen from that on Timocritus:

Καρτερὸς ἐν πολέμοις Τιμόκριτος, οὗ τόδε σᾶμα·
Ἄρης δ' οὐκ ἀγαθῶν φείδεται, ἀλλὰ κακῶν.[24]

Of brave Timocritus this is the grave:
The War-God spares the coward, not the brave.

There in his own way Anacreon proclaims that the dead man was an ἀνὴρ ἀγαθός and deserved remembrance. In another he takes four lines with the same implicit moral:

Ἀβδήρων προθανόντα τὸν αἰνοβίην Ἀγάθωνα
πᾶσ' ἐπὶ πυρκαϊῆς ἥδ' ἐβόησε πόλις·
οὔ τινα γὰρ τοιόνδε νέων ὁ φιλαίματος Ἄρης
ἠνάρισεν στυγερῆς ἐν στροφάλιγγι μάχης.[25]

Strong Agathon, who for Abdera fell,
    Was wept, when he was burned, by all the town.
For never in the battle's bloody swell
    Has Ares struck so fine a young man down.

There the remembrance belongs to the whole city which mourns at the funeral pyre.

The highest point of the elegiac epitaph was reached with the Persian Wars, when the liberties of Greece were threatened and men died for them. In later ages many epitaphs were quoted as coming from this time, and among them were a number attributed to Simonides of Ceos. When Meleager made his Anthology, he says that he included among its flowers καὶ νέον οἰνάνθης κλῆμα Σιμωνίδεω·[26]

the young vine-twig of Simonides,

and today the Palatine Anthology, itself based on Meleager's, contains many inscriptional and other epigrams under the name of Simonides. If all of these were genuine, we should have a rich collection of poems coming from a crucial period in Greek history. But the problem of their authenticity is one of the most vexed and complicated in Greek poetry. Certainly not all are genuine, but so far it has been hard to find any means of saying which are genuine and which not. The most diverse opinions have been held, and any solution is far from final.[27]

Simonides wrote other elegiac verse than for inscriptions. Such verses he probably collected into a book, and this book reached Alexandria. So if an elegiac poem of his is demonstrably not epigraphic, there is a reasonable chance that it is genuine. The collection included poems of different kinds, some of which look like epitaphs but are not. Among these is the biting couplet on Timocreon of Rhodes,[28] which must have been written before Timocreon died, since he outlived Simonides. In it Simonides adopts the sepulchral form to mock Timocreon for some mischance, and the point of the lines is in the ambiguous

[26] *Anth. Pal.* iv. 1, 8.

[27] Cf. especially Wilamowitz, *Sappho und Simonides*, pp. 192–232; A. Hauvette, *De l'Authenticité des Epigrammes de Simonide;* M. Boas, *De Epigrammatis Simonideis.*

[28] Fr. 99 Diehl. Cf. *Greek Lyric Poetry*, p. 380.

word κεῖται which means both "is dead" and "is down." To the same collection belong certain verses written in memory of dead men but meant to be sung over the wine, as the verses to Cedon were, not to be inscribed on tombs. To this class belong some lines written in memory of a countryman of the poet, Cleisthenes of Ceos. His body was lost at sea, and Simonides commemorated him:

Σῶμα μὲν ἀλλοδαπὴ κεύθει κόνις, ἐν δέ σε πόντῳ,
  Κλείσθενες, Εὐξείνῳ μοῖρ' ἔκιχεν θανάτου
πλαζόμενον· γλυκεροῦ δὲ μελίφρονος οἴκαδε νόστου
  ἤμπλακες, οὐδ' ἵκευ Κέων πάλιν ἀμφιρύτην.[29]

A strange land holds thy bones; the Euxine Sea
  Has brought thee, roving Cleisthenes, thy doom.
No honey-sweet returning was for thee,
  Nor sight of thy sea-girdled Cean home.[30]

There the essentials are mentioned, the dead man's name and life and home, the place and the manner of his death. Simonides does not explicitly say that he is remembered because the poem is in itself proof of such remembrance. But these essential facts are presented with great art and considerable appeal to the emotions. There is pathos in the contrast made between the foreign land where Cleisthenes is buried and the charm of his own sea girt land. There is tender irony in the account of the wanderer who has failed to return. The poem is much more than a statement of fact. It is a statement of regret and of pity.

[29] Fr. 135.   [30] Tr. Walter Leaf.

So Simonides remembers another dead man, this time in a couplet:

Σῆμα καταφθιμένοιο Μεγακλέος εὖτ' ἂν ἴδωμαι,
οἰκτίρω σε, τάλαν Καλλία, οἷ' ἔπαθες.[31]

Whenever, Callias, I see the tomb
Of Megacles, I pity your sad doom.

This is in the first place a poem of consolation to Callias for the loss of his friend, Megacles. But in its essentials it is commemorative of the dead man. For the grief which his death has caused is evidence for his excellence when he was alive.

Other poems, which have been taken for actual epitaphs, belong to this same class. They have the conciseness and tenderness of epitaphs, but since in them the dead man does not speak and there is no mention of his grave, they cannot be real epitaphs. But their language and thoughts are akin to the style of epitaphs, and they are really commemorative. Such is the quatrain on Timomachus, son of Timenor:

Φῆ τότε Τιμόμαχος, πατρὸς περὶ χεῖρας ἔχοντος,
ἡνίκ' ἀφ' ἱμερτὴν ἔπνεεν ἡλικίην·
"ὦ Τιμηνορίδη, παιδὸς φίλου οὔποτε λήξεις
οὔτ' ἀρετὴν ποθέων, οὔτε σαοφροσύνην."[32]

When in his father's arms he lay
And breathed the joy of youth away,
    Timomachus for good-bye said, —
"Son of Timenor, mourn your son,
Look not for such another one,
    A heart so brave, so cool a head." [33]

[31] Fr. 84.   [32] Fr. 128.   [33] Tr. T. F. Higham.

always to the taste of later ages, which demanded
something more colored and more emphatic. This
may be illustrated by a simple case. Plutarch quotes
four lines as having been written by Simonides for the
Aeginetans who fell at Salamis:

> Ὦ ξεῖν', εὔυδρόν ποτ' ἐναίομεν ἄστυ Κορίνθου,
>   νῦν δ' ἄμ' Αἴαντος νᾶσος ἔχει Σαλαμίς·
> ἐνθάδε Φοινίσσας νῆας καὶ Πέρσας ἑλόντες
>   καὶ Μήδους ἱερὰν Ἑλλάδα ῥυσάμεθα.[43]

> Friend, once we lived by Corinth's lovely water:
>   Now Aias' island, Salamis, holds our grave.
> Phoenician ships, and Medes, we gave to slaughter,
>   And Persians, that fair Hellas we might save.

The quatrain has excited suspicions. The short final
syllable of Πέρσας in the third line is a Dorian trait
which comes strangely from the Ionian Simonides;
the distinction between Medes and Persians is hardly
one made by the Greeks of this time; the second
couplet has been thought redundant and rhetorical.
But such arguments weighed little against the
authority of Plutarch until an inscription was found
at Salamis which contained the first couplet and can
never have contained the second. The first is certainly ancient, though it is not certainly the work of
Simonides; the second is nothing but a forgery. This
discovery opens up some ugly doubts. There are
other quatrains attributed to Simonides, which may
have been swelled out in the interests of rhetoric and

[43] Fr. 90 c.

pathos, and the better the addition is, the harder it is
to detect. What for instance are we to say of four
famous lines, written, it has been thought, for the
victory of the Athenians over the Chalcidians and
Boeotians in 506 B.C.?

> Δίρφυος ἐδμήθημεν ὑπὸ πτυχί, σῆμα δ' ἐφ' ἡμῖν
>   ἐγγύθεν Εὐρίπου δημοσίαι κέχυται,
> οὐκ ἀδίκως· ἐρατὴν γὰρ ἀπωλέσαμεν νεότητα
>   τρηχεῖαν πολέμου δεξάμενοι νεφέλην.[44]

> On Dirphys' wrinkled side we fell;
>   And where the Narrow Waters drift
> Our countrymen, to mark us well,
>   Raised up this cairn, their gift.

> A gift deserved: for youth is sweet,
>   And youth we gave, nor turned away,
> Though sharp the storm of battle beat
>   That darkened all our day.[45]

The second half is undeniably effective, but some
critics have felt doubts about it. In any case it is un-
necessary, and we cannot deny that it may be a later
addition, especially as the continuation through the
words οὐκ ἀδίκως is actually to be found in an epitaph
of the fourth century.[46]

To these two doubts we must add a third. Some
later writers liked to write epitaphs in the manner of
Simonides, and their imitations were passed off as his.
In the third century Mnasalcas was accused by

[44] Fr. 87.   [46] Kaibel, *Epigrammata Graeca* No. 38.
[45] Tr. T. F. Higham.

Theodoridas of such imitations,[47] and there must have been others beside him. We cannot say how seriously they intended to deceive, but they certainly succeeded, and there are Simonidean epitaphs which were written centuries after Simonides' death. Sometimes they can be detected. For instance, there are two epitaphs, attributed to Simonides, on men who fell in defense of Tegea.[48] That he should have written at least one of them is by no means improbable. His support of Tegea may well have been inspired by the anti-Spartan policy of Themistocles after the Persian Wars; in this the revolt of Tegea from Sparta was an event of some importance. Of these two epitaphs the first is impeccable in form and content. But the second betrays the forger:

Εὐθυμάχων ἀνδρῶν μνησώμεθα, τῶν ὅδε τύμβος,
    οἳ θάνον εὔμηλον ῥυόμενοι Τεγέαν,
αἰχμηταὶ πρὸ πόληος, ἵνα σφίσι μὴ καθέληται
    Ἑλλὰς ἀποφθιμένη κρατὸς ἐλευθερίαν.

Here let them lie, remembered well,
    Who died for Tegea, spear in hand,
The guardians of her citadel
    And flocks that graze her land.

With Hellas' freedom for their crown
    In battle onward still they thrust,
That she might live, nor tumble down
    Her garland in the dust.[49]

Despite his gift for genuine pathos, the poet gives himself away by confusing two types of epigram in a

[47] *Anth. Pal.* xiii. 21.   [48] Frs. 122 and 123.   [49] Tr. T. F. Higham.

way impossible for Simonides. When he refers to the tomb of the dead, τῶν ὅδε τύμβος, he implies that this is a real epitaph, but when he uses the word μνησώμεθα, he follows a different and incompatible model, the commemorative elegy like that to Cedon. In this case there is no doubt about imitation. But it is at least possible that other imitators were more successful and that among the pieces attributed to Simonides are other copies of his manner.

So much for the doubts. They are far-reaching and difficult to answer. But some sort of answer, incomplete though it is, can be found which at least suggests that some of the Simonidean poems are genuine. There are a few tests which may be applied, and though they are not decisive, they are evidence for at least probable authenticity. First, some epitaphs are attributed to Simonides on authority so good that it cannot be denied. Foremost among these are the lines on the seer Megistias,[50] whose genuineness rests on the direct statement of Herodotus; those on Archedice,[51] affirmed by Aristotle; those on the fallen of Marathon found in the Agora: to these we may add the two epitaphs on the fallen of Thermopylae,[52] which Herodotus does not state to be the work of Simonides but quotes in the same context as the lines of Megistias as if they were. Secondly, there are some which agree so well with the circumstances of Simonides' life that they may with some probability be regarded as genuine. The real epitaph on the

[50] Fr. 83.   [51] Fr. 85.   [52] Frs. 91 and 92.

fallen of Tegea [53] suits his Themistoclean politics.
The lines on the hound Lycas [54] recall his sojourn in
Thessaly. The collection of Corinthian epigrams gets
some support from stories which connect him with
Corinth. The famous two epitaphs on the fallen of
Plataea [55] may well have been written by the laureate
of Marathon. Lastly, there are some which may be
attributed to Simonides on stylistic grounds in that
they show certain traits in construction and language
which recall his genuine work, such as that on the
Tyrrhenians who were lost at sea when bringing
offerings to Delphi.[56] Of course few of these are indis-
putably genuine, and there are others which may be.
More than that we cannot say.

Even so, from this small residue we may form some
idea of a Simonidean style and see how he managed
this remarkable form with its strict traditions and
limited space. It is well to start with this art at its
finest and see what Simonides could do. His most
famous epitaph was inscribed on the tomb of the
Spartans who fell at Thermopylae:

> Ὦ ξεῖν' ἀγγέλλειν Λακεδαιμονίοις, ὅτι τῃδε
> κείμεθα, τοῖς κείνων ῥήμασι πειθόμενοι.[57]

Tell them in Lacedaemon, passer-by,
That here obedient to their words we lie.

To understand these eleven words we must look at the
circumstances in which they were composed. The

[53] Fr. 122.　　[55] Frs. 121 and 118.
[54] Fr. 142.　　[56] Fr. 97.　　　　[57] Fr. 92.

Spartans who fell at Thermopylae became heroes
after their death. In Sparta there was a cult of their
memory, and they became for all time the pattern
of Spartan manhood which found its highest realiza-
tion in a noble death for its country. For them
Simonides wrote a noble ode in which he stressed
their achievement and their glory.[58] But here his art
is quite different. He says nothing about glory; there
is no word about heroization, no word even about
saving Sparta or Greece from the Persians. There are
only these quiet, unassuming words. Their meaning is
singularly exact, although it has often been misunder-
stood. All depends on ῥήμασι, and it means simply
"words." So Simonides uses it in his lines on Danae,[59]
and so he uses it here. Later ages had a different
meaning for the word and thought that here it meant
"laws" or "commandments." But it is simpler than
that, and refers to those Laconic sayings by which
the ideals of manhood were instilled into Spartan
youth.[60] The dead men are true to their upbringing.
So even Cicero was wrong when he translated:

> Dic, hospes, Spartae, nos te hic vidisse iacentes
> Dum sanctis patriae legibus obsequimur.

Still more wrong were the later Greeks who altered
ῥήμασι πειθόμενοι to πειθόμενοι νομίμοις.

The meaning then is clear and simple. But its
presentation is the work of consummate craftsman-

[58] Fr. 5.   [59] Fr. 13, 17.
[60] Cf. W. Rhys Roberts, *Eleven Words of Simonides*, pp. 7–11.

ship.[61] First, there is the order of the words, where all
lead up to the final πειθόμενοι to show that this
heroic death is an example to all men of obedience.
Next, there is the use of the infinitive for the imperative in ἀγγέλλειν. This was a military use, and is
therefore peculiarly appropriate here. But it was also
a Spartan use; for the only time when it occurs in
Thucydides is when he makes Brasidas, also a Spartan, say to Clearidas σὺ δὲ Κλεαρίδα . . . . αἰφνιδίως
τὰς πύλας ἀνοίξας ἐπεκθεῖν καὶ ἐπείγεσθαι ὡς τάχιστα
ξυμμεῖξαι,[62] "and you, Clearidas, open the gates
suddenly, dash out, and press home the attacks with
all speed." Next, there is the great resounding word
Λακεδαιμονίοις holding pride of place in the first line.
The dead men are not named, but they were Lacedaemonians, and it is by other Lacedaemonians that they
wish to be remembered. Lastly, there is the simple
euphony of the words which arises partly from such
devices as the repetition of the letter κ in κείμεθα
and κείνων, and the five times in which the diphthong
ει is used. The result is as simple as can be asked, but
it is based on a technique which overcomes all its
difficulties with effortless power.

Simonides did not write the same type of epitaph
for everyone. He appreciated the individual charac-
ters of Greek cities and the differences between the
ideals which they honored, and with a quiet tact he
observed these differences when he celebrated the
dead. This may be seen in two epitaphs which he

[61] Cf. Rhys Roberts, *op. cit.* pp. 12–14.   [62] Thuc. v. 9.

wrote for men who fell at Plataea, the one for Spartans, the other for Athenians. In the first he wrote:

"Ασβεστον κλέος οἵδε φίληι περὶ πατρίδι θέντες
κυάνεον θανάτου ἀμφεβάλοντο νέφος·
οὐδὲ τεθνᾶσι θανόντες, ἐπεί σφ' ἀρετὴ καθύπερθεν
κυδαίνουσ' ἀνάγει δώματος ἐξ Ἀΐδεω.[63]

Into the dark death cloud they passed, to set
  Fame on their own dear land for fadeless wreath,
And dying died not. Valour lifts them yet
  Into the splendour from the night beneath.[64]

In these lines Simonides shows that he has absorbed the ideals of Tyrtaeus. The men who died, died not for their own glory but for their country's, and in this they live on, as Tyrtaeus' brave man lives on under the earth. Their glory is immortal just as he is, and they have found, as he has, the only true ἀρετή, which comes by dying for Sparta. There is nothing here that a Spartan would not accept as traditional and right. The language, with its single metaphor of the cloud of death is also traditional, though the cloud is more usually of battle. What is new is the concentration of the whole, the reduction of an old idea to the fewest possible words. With this we may contrast the lines for the Athenians:

Εἰ τὸ καλῶς θνήσκειν ἀρετῆς μέρος ἐστὶ μέγιστον,
  ἡμῖν ἐκ πάντων τοῦτ' ἀπένειμε τύχη·
Ἑλλάδι γὰρ σπεύδοντες ἐλευθερίην περιθεῖναι
  κείμεθ' ἀγηράντωι χρώμενοι εὐλογίηι.[65]

[63] Fr. 121.   [64] Tr. H. Macnaghten.   [65] Fr. 118.

If Valour's best be gallantly to die,
   Fortune to us of all men grants it now.
We to set Freedom's crown on Hellas' brow
Laboured, and here in ageless honour lie.[66]

Here there is no word of immortality, no word even of
Athens. To die in battle is, of course, a noble end, but
Simonides gives it a purpose quite different from the
defense of home. It is to give freedom to Greece, and
here surely he catches the true spirit of the Athenians
who fought against Persia. He recalls the great cry
which Aeschylus says went up at Salamis:

ὦ παῖδες Ἑλλήνων, ἴτε,
ἐλευθεροῦτε πατρίδ᾽, ἐλευθεροῦτε δὲ
παῖδας, γυναῖκας, θεῶν τε πατρώιων ἕδη,
θήκας τε προγόνων. νῦν ὑπὲρ πάντων ἀγών.[67]

   Sons of Hellas, on!
Set free your fatherland, set free your sons,
Your wives, the seats of your ancestral gods,
Your fathers' graves; now we must fight for all.

For this death the Athenians are rewarded with glory
in words which recall the passage in his Funeral
Speech where Pericles says that those who have
died for the city have won ἀγήρων ἔπαινον, "unaging
praise." [68] Both epitaphs are of universal appeal, but
each was written with a full appreciation of the kind
of men whom it commemorated.

In the remains of his lyrical poetry Simonides
shows a visual imagination in his choice of colors and

---

[66] Tr. W. C. Lawton.
[67] *Persae.* 402–405.
[68] Thuc. ii. 43, 2.

visible details which gives a remarkable vividness to
his work. In the short space of the epigram there
was not much room for such an art, but we can sometimes see how Simonides gives life to a scene by a hint
of its setting. So in his lines on the fallen of Tegea, he
says:

> Τῶνδε δι᾽ ἀνθρώπων ἀρετὰν οὐχ ἵκετο καπνὸς
> αἰθέρα δαιομένης εὐροχόρου Τεγέας·
> οἳ βούλοντο πόλιν μὲν ἐλευθερίαι τεθαλυῖαν
> παισὶ λιπεῖν, αὐτοὶ δ᾽ ἐν προμαχοῖσι θανεῖν.[69]

No cloud of smoke, from Tegea thrown
In blaze of ruin, smote the sky;
Such men were these, she holds her own,
    And wide her acres lie.

As counting freedom hard to lose,
To sons they left her prime unspent;
Themselves the battle's front they chose,
    And went to death content.[70]

Here of course the essential thought is contained in
the second half, but the glorious death there celebrated is given a setting. Simonides draws a short but
vivid picture of the burning town, as it might have
been if the Spartans had captured it. In the few
words about the rising smoke he hints at this, and
then passes on to his main purpose. Nor is his adjective εὐρυχόρου simply decorative. It is true of Tegea,
which lies in a level rich ground south of the moun-
tains of Arcadia. It was this land with its open places

[69] Fr. 122.   [70] Tr. T. F. Higham.

that the Tegeatans died to save. So in his epitaph on the hound Lycas he mentions the places where she used to hunt:

Ἦ σεῦ καὶ φθιμένας λεύκ' ὀστέα τῶιδ' ἐνὶ τύμβωι
ἴσκω ἔτι τρομέειν θῆρας, ἄγρωσσα Λυκάς·
τὰν δ' ἀρετὰν οἶδεν μέγα Πήλιον ἅ τ' ἀρίδηλος
Ὄσσα Κιθαιρῶνός τ' οἰονόμοι σκοπιαί.[71]

Although beneath this grave-mound thy white bones now
    are lying,
    Surely, my huntress Lycas, the wild things dread
    thee still.
The memory of thy worth tall Pelion keeps undying,
    And the looming peak of Ossa, and Cithaeron's lonely
    hill.[72]

Here too the scenery is entirely appropriate. For it was in this mountain landscape that the hound ran when alive, and it is different now that she is dead.

The ideas that underlie these epitaphs are, of course, conventional. The men who ordered them expected the right thing to be said, and Simonides said it. There is not the slightest reason to doubt his sincerity or to think that he adapted his opinions to the many different circumstances in which he found himself. Like most intelligent men of his time and class, he combined a deep belief in some traditional ideas with a certain skepticism about current theology. But his doubts only made him regard the Gods as more powerful than most men regarded them, and his reverence for them was in no way impaired. His

[71] Fr. 142.   [72] Tr. F. L. Lucas.

fundamental opinions were such as Pindar and Aeschylus also held, and they may be seen in his lines on Archedice:

> Ἀνδρὸς, ἀριστεύσαντος ἐν Ἑλλάδι τῶν ἐφ᾽ ἑαυτοῦ
> Ἱππίου Ἀρχεδίκην ἥδε κέκευθε κόνις·
> ἣ πατρός τε καὶ ἀνδρὸς ἀδελφῶν τ᾽ οὖσα τυράννων
> παίδων τ᾽ οὐκ ἤρθη νοῦν ἐς ἀτασθαλίην.[73]

> The child of Hippias, foremost captain once
>   In Hellas' land, lies here, Archedice.
> With lords for father, husband, brethren, sons,
>   She lifted not her heart to vanity.[74]

Archedice, the daughter of Hippias and grand-daughter of Peisistratus, was married to the tyrant of Lampsacus. Her family had come in Athens to be regarded as the real type of tyranny and all its vices. But when Archedice died, Simonides wrote these lines on her tomb. In them he accepted, as most Greeks would have accepted, the view that pride was a great sin. But though it would be easy to accuse Archedice of it, Simonides went out of his way not to. He proclaims that in spite of temptations of birth and position, she kept her modesty, her σωφροσύνη. His judgment is interesting because he had in his time been a friend of her father and found patronage at his court. In spite of this he had been accepted as its chief poet by the Athenian democracy and quite lived down any connections he once had with tyrants. For this he has been suspected of too much worldly

[73] Fr. 85.   [74] Tr. Walter Leaf.

wisdom, of disloyalty and trimming. The case seemed
strong against him because of a couplet in which he
says that "a great light came to Athens when Harmodius and Aristogeiton slew Hipparchus." [75] It
would certainly be disloyal to praise the murderers
of an old friend, even if they had become national
heroes. And this he seemed to have done, for the lines
looked like a convivial couplet and so were thought to
be genuine.[76] But now it looks as if they were not.
They seem to have been inscribed on the statues of
Harmodius and Aristogeiton which were erected in
the Agora in 476 B.C., and since they are after all epigraphic, their authenticity is at once a matter of
doubt. Simonides seems indeed to have kept his
loyalty to the house of Peisistratus, though he did not
allow it to blind him to the sinfulness of pride.

In another epigram he shows his religious feelings.
It was written for his friend, the Spartan Megistias,
who fell at Thermopylae.

> Μνῆμα τόδε κλείνοιο Μεγιστία, ὅν ποτε Μῆδοι
>   Σπερχειὸν ποταμὸν κτεῖναν ἀμειψάμενοι,
> μάντιος, ὃς τότε κῆρας ἐπερχομένας σάφα εἰδὼς
>   οὐκ ἔτλη Σπάρτης ἡγεμόνας προλιπεῖν.[77]

This is the grave of famed Megistias, whom
  Beside Spercheius' stream the Persian slew:
A seer he, who dared to share the doom
  Of Sparta's leaders, though that doom he knew.[78]

[75] Fr. 76.
[76] Cf. Wilamowitz, *Sappho und Simonides*, p. 211.
[77] Fr. 83.
[78] Tr. G. B. Grundy.

Behind this lay a famous story. Leonidas wished Megistias, who had foretold that death awaited the Spartan defenders of Thermopylae, to go away "that he might not perish with them." Megistias sent his son away, but stayed himself and was killed.[79] There was no question about his prophetic gift, and Simonides did not doubt anything so amply justified by the event. But though he accepted this, he did not see that it made a man fatalistic. He believed that Megistias died of his own accord because he had not the heart, οὐκ ἔτλη, like the true Spartan that he was, to desert his leaders. So the lines show how Simonides combined an old religious belief in the power of prophecy with a simple and natural conception of man's capacity to act freely and to do his duty. Simonides wrote the lines for Megistias, as Herodotus says, "out of the love he bore him," and they are a tribute both to the dead man's wisdom and to his courage.

These few examples show some of the salient qualities of Simonides' epitaphs. They show how he took the old form and instead of altering and enlarging it kept its traditional features while he gave it additional strength and greater fullness. His work was greatly admired. His lines on the fallen of Marathon were preferred to those of Aeschylus, and the Spartans asked him, an Ionian, to write the epitaph for the fallen of Thermopylae. As a writer of epitaphs he had a truly Panhellenic renown and position,

[79] Hdt. vii. 221.

which he justified by his sympathy with the tastes and ideals of the different Greek cities and by the high conception which he had of the issue for which the Greeks fought in the Persian Wars. For he certainly saw the struggle as one for the liberty of all Greece, even at a time when hardly anyone but the Athenians had taken the field. He showed this in his epitaph for the Marathonian dead, in which he said that they died

'Ελλάδα μὴ πᾶσαν δούλιον ἦμαρ ἰδεῖν.

that all Hellas might not see the day of slavery.

He raised the epitaph from being the concern of a few friends or of a town to something which spoke to all Greece and made men remember that heroic qualities such as he celebrated in it were the concern of everyone and called to be honored and imitated.

INDEX

INDEX